The Home Child

Richard P. Tanos

Cover Illustration: Cindy Tallman

Cover Design: Amy Young

Printed in Victoria, Canada

National Library of Canada Cataloguing in Publication

Tanos, Richard P. (Richard Paul), 1951-
      The home child / Richard P. Tanos.
ISBN 1-4120-0544-2
      1. Home children (Canadian immigrants)—Fiction.
I. Title.
PS8589.A7938H64 2003   C813'.6   C2003-903934-X

TRAFFORD

This book was published *on-demand* **in cooperation with Trafford Publishing.**
On-demand publishing is a unique process and service of making a book available for retail sale to the public taking advantage of on-demand manufacturing and Internet marketing. **On-demand publishing** includes promotions, retail sales, manufacturing, order fulfilment, accounting and collecting royalties on behalf of the author.

Suite 6E, 2333 Government St., Victoria, B.C. V8T 4P4, CANADA

Phone	250-383-6864	Toll-free	1-888-232-4444 (Canada & US)
Fax	250-383-6804	E-mail	sales@trafford.com
Web site	www.trafford.com	TRAFFORD PUBLISHING IS A DIVISION OF TRAFFORD HOLDINGS LTD.
Trafford Catalogue #03-0913		www.trafford.com/robots/03-0913.html

10   9   8   7   6   5   4   3   2

The Home Child

Dedication

This novel is dedicated to Henry and Elizabeth Dewberry for demonstrating to all of us that integrity, honesty, and commitment are the three most important character traits for a successful life journey. The pain, humiliation, and intolerance that Henry and Elizabeth suffered must have been a great burden to conceal for all those decades. For this, I admire their humility and self-respect. I consider myself a product of Henry and Elizabeth's environment, and I truly thank them.

Richard P. Tanos

The Home Child

Foreword

My family trips to Waterford, Ontario, Canada, started when I was around four or five years old. Throughout the years, my family made this trip (they were actually few in number). Yet, every time we went, it seemed that it was so far away and that these trips (especially true of a youngster) took a long time. I do recall that it was a much simpler life in Waterford than it was in my hometown of Niagara Falls. To this day still, that difference still intrigues and mystifies me.

My mother's brother and his wife always greeted us with affectionate hugs. I eventually became accustomed to these as I grew. However, the very first hug that I received from my aunt Judy left me with a frightened image that took years to overcome.

Like most children, I was very impressionable, and I can still close my eyes and visualize my mother's mother, her dark dresses, her dark hair, her black boots, and that white apron. Somehow, the apron made her darkness seem all right. Yet, for some unexplained reason, I was frightened whenever I was around her.

Later in life, when I occasionally visited my sister's farm in Dunnville (a town fairly close to Waterford), the stored mental images of farm life from my childhood would return. And now, my oldest sister was actually living that lifestyle—raising seven children, dealing with a dairy farmer for a husband, and coping with life in the best way that she knew how!

After reading Richard P. Tanos' The Home Child, I returned to the time when I was a child, visiting relatives in Waterford. I also remembered the times I was frightened. I realized that I had suddenly found answers to why my father was the way he was. I had had no idea that my dad experienced these disturbing events at such an early age. He was really not much older than I was when I shared similar fears. I count my blessings that my mother was there and had met my father. I'm sure that she gave my dad the hope and the drive to handle his environment.

While reading The Home Child, I was tossed around by my emotions. Then, after I finished reading this story, I felt a renewed sense of pride to be the youngest daughter of Henry and Elizabeth Dewberry.

Shirley Laslo

The Home Child

Chapter 1

The Day It All Started - Waterford, Ontario, Canada, 1907

Lizzie turned her head on the pillow and slowly opened her eyes. The morning view out her window was a misty blanket that covered the tops of the gently rolling fields. She had seen this view several times during past late-summer months; it reminded her of the off-white canopy of her friend Clara's four-poster bed. Lizzie had known Clara since time began it seemed, and because they were close in age, they had become best friends. Both girls were fortunate to come from loving homes and, although separated by class—Clara's family was considered upper class because they owned one of the biggest tobacco farms in Canada West, and Lizzie's family was middle class—they maintained a strong friendship.

"Lizzie!" called a voice from the room across the hall, "Lizzie, are you up?"

Lizzie usually hated to hear Mary's soprano tone so early in the morning. On this morning, however, she detected a faint hint of anticipation in Mary's voice. The two had a normal relationship: sometimes laughing; sometimes fighting; and on certain occasions, sharing thoughts and dreams. Although Mary, Lizzie was sure, wished that her little sister was older, Lizzie often managed to bridge that four-year gap.

Lizzie rolled, yawned, stretched, and spoke softly as to not awaken her brothers. "Yes, Mary; I'm up."

Mary, now on her tiptoes and swinging her arms, entered Lizzie's room as if she had a secret about something; but then, she usually moved and spoke quietly. "Lizzie, do you remember what day this is?"

Lizzie tried to gather her thoughts but was still groggy. "No," she said, quietly wiping the sleep from her eyes. Mary sat on the edge of the bed, glanced out Lizzie's window, and then leaned close to Lizzie. "It's Saturday. The passenger train is arriving today. Three o'clock, I think."

Lizzie's eyes opened wide. How could she have forgotten! Today, she would go to the station to see the passenger train arrive! Mary had told her on several occasions about this day, promising her little sister that when Lizzie turned twelve, she would go with Mary to participate in the ritual of greeting the train. To Mary, who turned sixteen in January, it was important to meet her friends and study the passengers arriving from Toronto. Lizzie's big sister was interested in boys, and it was funny to hear her go on about this new boy she saw, or that new boy she had spoken with, or even boys she had dreamed up. Lizzie listened intently when Mary shared stories of kissing and touching, and she often encouraged Mary to talk more about it. Mary couldn't help` herself; it was her nature to tell Lizzie and probably anyone else who would listen.

Except for the rain, Lizzie's twelfth birthday came and went like all the previous ones. The silver necklace a gift from her Mom and Dad, which was lightly decorated with blue stones, hung on the dresser corner, reflecting the early-morning tangerine light. Her open window usually allowed a late summer breeze to enter, but on this day, the air carried the clean-smelling dampness of morning dew.

"I can wear my new necklace today," Lizzie decided, now feeling important and far older than her twelve years. She thought of the dress she would wear and then remembered that Mary would probably pick it out for her anyway.

"Wear the dress that matches your necklace," suggested Mary.

The girls came downstairs to breakfast this beautiful late summer Saturday morning, Lizzie following Mary like a baby duck following her mother, and both of them took their place at the big table in the dining room. To Lizzie, her dining room table was the biggest that she had ever seen, even bigger than Clara's. Lizzie gazed around the table at her family, who gathered for the morning meal.

Across the table sat Fred, her oldest brother. At fifteen, Fred's only ambition was to be exactly like his Father. Fred was a short boy of medium stock with dark brown hair that had a wave in the front. He didn't have a girlfriend yet—well, as far as Lizzie knew he didn't—and he was never home. Fred was acting important this morning because he would go with father to work on the new town hall.

Sitting next to Fred was Arthur, who was ten. Arthur was the quiet one; the one who never got into trouble and never left the house, except for school. Arthur seemed a little tired and sleepy on this morning; Lizzie felt that he liked his bed way too much.

Next to Arthur was Cecil, the baby. Cecil was a happy five-year-old who was always smiling and always trying to amuse others. This wasn't too hard because his large, protruding ears demanded attention wherever he went.

William, Lizzie's dad, sat at the head of the big table, already looking tired and weather-beaten as he read the newspaper. William—most people called him Will—was a small man with dark brown eyes, a big black prickly mustache, short hair that was beginning to thin, and (what Lizzie hated the most) his large, rough hands. She hated it when he would grab her cheeks, as if he were holding a ball, and proceeded to kiss her. This happened only on those mornings he was still at home and hadn't yet left for work. Today, of course, was one of those days, and Lizzie knew of no way to avoid it. Lizzie wondered why everyone seemed quiet this morning. Did they know about her first trip with her sister and her sister's friends to the Waterford Station? She had been to the town square several times, but not directly to the station. Had Mary told everyone? Lizzie, thinking about her sister's plans for her on this day, suddenly felt upset.

From the kitchen, Nellie, their mother, shouted, "Mary, come here now!" Mary sprang from her chair and bolted to the kitchen. Nellie was one to be respected, especially when preparing meals. As Mary disappeared, the whole table fell silent, and they all cocked their heads to hear what Nellie would say. "Mary, you know you're..." In a flash, Lizzie silently had completed her mother's sentence; "You know you're not taking Lizzie to the train station today." As quickly as Lizzie's mind completed this sentence, she heard something different, something she had never before heard from her mother.

"You're going to be leaving this house for good pretty soon." Then, in an imperious adult voice, her mother added, "But until that time, you will help with the meals. Do you understand, young lady?"

"Yes, Mother," faintly echoed through the room.

Over the years, Lizzie had heard several child-rearing lectures from her mother and, although she was very good at delivering them, they all sounded the same. The knot in Lizzie's stomach disappeared when her mother didn't say anything about the station.

Mary carried in two giant serving plates piled high with hotcakes and sausage, and then she placed them in the center of the table. Mother followed with a plate of toast and a plate of scrambled eggs. Everybody remained quiet until Nellie sat down. Lizzie's mother was a large woman with light-brown hair pulled back into a neat bun, small brown eyes, and a pink skin that turned bright red when she was angry. Lizzie glanced at her; the red slowly faded back to pink.

They all bowed their heads and held hands as Will said the Morning Prayer. It was usually short, and Lizzie figured that this was because of hunger and not because of his religious beliefs. He did not tolerate small talk when food was on the table. Rather, the family usually ate their meals quickly and quietly. However, after the meal, and when he sat back in his chair and picked up a toothpick, talking was allowed.

Mary complained about unimportant things such as lipsticks, clothes, and shoes looking for and not receiving attention from her mom and dad. Lizzie couldn't understand why her sister never talked about her great job at the bakery, which gave her the money to buy those fancy clothes and stylish shoes.

Fred, trying to be like father, asked boring questions about laying bricks, mixing mortar, using trowels, and cutting stones. Arthur complained about his chores until Will gave him "the glare," and he knew then to grow quiet.

Cecil, with his funny ears, just smiled at anyone who would look at him. Once in a while, Cecil would manage to say something, only to be immediately followed by Fred or Arthur, who advised him, "Cecil, be quiet."

Lizzie wanted to talk about the station, but decided it was best not to draw attention to her and Mary's plans. After a few seconds of silence, which meant conversation time at the table was over, Arthur immediately excused himself to start his chores. This was one point of etiquette that the family always followed. Before you could leave the table, you asked permission to leave, and Will or Nellie would grant it or if they felt you needed to eat more, they would simply say 'no.' On this day, Will instructed Fred to pack up the work wagon. Nellie, on the other hand, gave Mary "the look," and they proceeded to carry dishes to the kitchen.

Will pushed back from the table, stood, stretched a little, and then walked directly to Lizzie. Here it comes, she thought, and she was right. Those hard hands came up from his sides and cupped her cheeks as he gave her lips a soft kiss, and then he started to walk toward the back door. Suddenly, Will stopped, turned, and stared into Lizzie's eyes for what seemed an eternity and pulled something from his trousers. He held it in a clenched fist as he walked back to Lizzie.

"Here's something. Use it at the town square today."

He bent over and quietly whispered into her ear, "Have fun darling." Lizzie was amazed; her father had never given her money to have fun with. It had always been her mom who handed out the money, and at that, only to buy things at the town square. This time, the money was for fun!

She counted twelve cents and thought about all the candies—especially her favorite, red licorice—and other things that she could buy. Suddenly, it hit her; how did her father know about today? Did her mom know too? Did her brothers know? Did Mary tell the whole world? Was it all a joke?

The special day that Mary had planned for Lizzie no longer seemed special. Lizzie returned to her room, confused and feeling betrayed by her big sister. She stared out the window, hypnotized by rolling hills, lush green fields, tall poplars, and mist as it quickly lifted in the bright warm sunshine. Although they actually lived in town, this side of the house faced farmland. Lizzie was grateful for this because Fred's view was of neighbors' houses and one lonely elm. Late summer was Lizzie's favorite time; it offered cool evenings and warm, dry days.

The sound of the closing door pulled Lizzie back to her room. Mary entered.

"How could you?" blurted Lizzie sounding distressed.

"How could I what?" Mary snapped back, surprised.

Lizzie spoke quietly. "The train station. You told Dad!"

Mary seemed confused. "No I didn't!"

Lizzie's felt her face redden. She grew angrier, and now she looked directly at Mary. "Did you tell Dad?"

"No," said Mary. "I wouldn't tell him...that's between us." Lizzie felt a little relieved. She leaned forward and whispered. "How come he gave me money this morning and said it was for me to use today and have fun with? He never did that before."

"Oh," said Mary, beginning to grin. "He did the same thing when I we nt on my first visit, and I got ten cents. Dad knows these things. He's not stupid, you know."

Lizzie rose from the bed, looked in the mirror, and began playing with her hair, stroking it from side to side, front to back. She turned and looked directly at Mary, blinked twice with those large brown eyes, and grinned. "I got twelve cents."

They began planning the rest of their day. Lizzie still had a little trouble accepting that this day, of all days, would be special. She had been to the town square several times and saw the station, and it really wasn't a big event. On the other hand, Mary had never let her down before.

Chapter 2

The Deusling Girls

Lizzie Deusling and her family lived on the corner of Cottage and Main Streets in Waterford, Ontario, a small farming town in southwestern Ontario, Canada. Their house was small, a light-gray modest two-story square, trimmed in white. It looked like the other houses in the neighborhood and stood close to the town square. It held five bedrooms upstairs, one for each of the children, which on Lizzie's account, made the living arrangements tolerable. Downstairs, the house had a huge kitchen, a spacious living room and a large dining room. Will and Nellie's bedroom was also located downstairs, next to the back door.

The front of the house faced east, and here, Nellie kept her manicured flowerbeds, one on each side of the front porch. These flowerbeds were kept routinely neat and provided beautiful colors from tulips, marigolds, daises, roses, and fire bushes. During the spring and summer, the flowers strutted colors of yellow, red, blue, and white. The bathroom was outside, ten feet behind the house, in a little one-door outbuilding that always emitted foul odors through two vents. The back door led directly to the smelly-house, as Lizzie called it. She hated this building and felt sorry for Fred, who had to clean it every other day.

About ten or twelve feet or so from the outdoor bathroom stood the stable house, which housed two buggies, father's mason tools, supplies, and Big George, their means of transportation. Big George, as the kids affectionately called him, was a huge old brown-and-white horse with a bad smell, huge feet, and a tremendous appetite. This was Fred and Arthur's area; the girls were not allowed any where near the shed. Lizzie's dad insisted that Mary and Lizzie not play around this area because he did not want them to spook Big George. Besides, he also kept his mason tools there, and these tools could be dangerous.

The water pump, which was surrounded by a wooden platform, stood in front of the shed and had several buckets. Lizzie's main household chore was washing, rinsing and then filling all of the seven water pitchers. This chore took about an hour—half that if she worked quickly. She would first scrub the inside of the buckets and then once she felt they were clean enough, she would rinse the buckets and then line them up to indicate that they were ready to use.

In the spring, when the snow melted, Lizzie knew it was time for her to start her bucket routine; besides, Lizzie also knew that her mother would certainly let her know. During the winter, the buckets were piled up in the house, next to the back door, and Lizzie had to draw water in the frigid cold air. She didn't look forward to this; she simply didn't like winter.

Lizzie's house didn't stand out from the others; it blended in with all the other middle-class houses. The town square was eight minutes by foot, and Lizzie had walked this distance several times to run errands for her mother.

Clara Culmer's farm was about thirty minutes by foot in the opposite direction from the town square. Lizzie had walked this distance a couple of times and knew this to be laboring. Both Clara and Lizzie were the same age, but only for six months, and then Clara would advance a year. Lizzie enjoyed Clara's birthday parties because it provided another sleepover, great food, and lots of nice gifts.

Martha, Clara's older sister, was a year older than Mary. She seemed very mature at seventeen. Martha was somewhat homely, and she looked exactly like her mother. She acted like her, too.

Lizzie sometimes thought that, instead of thirty minutes away, it would be nice if Clara lived on the farm that stretched out before her bedroom window. This window provided countless hours of ever-changing vistas to go with Lizzie's thoughts and dreams. The view from this window eased her sorrows and brought her peace. Every day, the view was a little different, especially as the seasons changed.

Lizzie wasn't sure who owned the "window" farm. To her knowledge, neither her father nor her Uncle John ever talked about it. She liked Uncle John, a small man several years older than her dad, rounded at the corners, and highly respected in the community. He wore a bushy full-length beard of graying hair and was always pleasant to talk to. He was a permanent fixture in Lizzie's house; he would always show up early in the morning and right after dinner in the evening. However, Uncle John had one uncomfortable flaw: He loved to talk, he loved to eat, and he loved to drink. The flaw was that, when eating and speaking—and always after a few drinks—he would spit bits of food, uncontrollably, toward the person he was talking to.

Lizzie felt that her Uncle John should just move in. He lived thirteen houses down Cottage Street, in an immaculate green-and-white house, with two work sheds, two horses, and even two outhouses. She never understood why people needed two of those disgusting huts, especially when Uncle John and Aunt Mabel had no children. One day Mom had told Lizzie and Mary why Aunt Mabel couldn't have children, but today that reason evaded Lizzie.

"Mary!" yelled her mom from downstairs.

"Yes, Mom?"

"Can you come down?" Lizzie knew that Mary was still thinking about the scolding that she'd received earlier, and Lizzie watched with a little smile as her big sister quickly started her descent of the stairs. "Coming!" she yelled.

Nellie handed Mary the piece of paper. "Here's a list of things I need from the square. Can you pick them up for me?"

"Sure, Mom," replied Mary, perhaps thinking that if she did this, she might be off the hook for being a little lazy earlier. Lizzie knew that Mary liked to pick up things for her mother at the town square on Saturday's because Tom, a school friend who she kind of liked, worked at the general store.

On the bed upstairs in Mary's room lay the list. Lizzie read: three colors of yarn, two needles, salt, and two rolls of linen. "Lizzie, you can meet Tom today," said Mary.

Lizzie was busy thinking about her upcoming afternoon today, and wasn't really listening to her sister. She caught the last couple of words and countered with, "Your boyfriend from church?"

"Be quiet! He's not...my boyfriend." Mary turned and blushed a little. She then faced her closet with her hands on her hips. Lizzie, now lying on the bed, chuckled quietly. She really didn't want to make Mary angry, and she knew that if Mary heard her, it would upset her. Lizzie's mind again wandered, and the questions started surfacing again. Why is today special at the train station? Why is Mary acting funny?

Lizzie blinked twice hard, shook her head. "What time are Martha and Clara coming by?"

"Around one," replied Mary.

Finally, Mary pulled a bright baby-blue dress from her closet. It still had store tags. "This will do nicely,"

She pulled out two pair of black shoes, one shiny and the other having a dull matte finish. With the dress draped over her arm and a pair of shoes in each hand, she dropped them on the bed beside Lizzie. Mary backed up to have a better look. "Which pair do you prefer?"

Quickly, Lizzie answered, "I like the shiny ones." She didn't really care which shoes her sister picked. As far as Lizzie was concerned, shoes were not to be studied—like getting ready for a school test or something—they were for wearing.

"I think, the new ones today," said Mary, as though she long deliberated over this decision. This trait of Mary's bothered Lizzie; she knew that her older sister would pick those shoes, no matter what.

"You have so many clothes." Sitting on the edge of the bed watching Mary, Lizzie had mixed feelings. On one hand, Lizzie admired Mary for her clothes and style. However, she didn't like it much when Mary acted as though she was better than everyone else.

Mary smirked at Lizzie with a half-loaded smile, hinting to Lizzie to back off, and then said, "I'll help you pick something nice."

Lizzie appreciated it when Mary picked clothes for her; now, Lizzie wouldn't have to waste time deciding. She also knew what she would look like because she had inherited Mary's clothes as she outgrew or simply grew tired of them. Because their mother Nellie was a great seamstress, it took Lizzie only a couple of pleadings to have her alter clothes. Mary worked at the Owen Bakery in the town square. She worked three evenings a week during school and three days a week in the summer.

Mr. Owen, a short, round man with thinning hair, seemed nice to work for, and he treated Mary like one of his own children. He had lost his daughter three years ago to a mysterious disease that, to this day, stumped Doc Hunter. Mr. Owen always wore a white apron and a smile that showed his two missing bottom front teeth. Mary would always spend her ten-cent-an-hour pay on clothes. Mr. Owen always paid her just before she left for the day. Mary liked this.

Mary pointed at the shiny pair of black shoes on the bed. "Lizzie, you can wear these shoes."

"Oh, can I? Can I?" Lizzie was a little smug because she would probably soon get those shoes anyway.

"Go downstairs and get newspaper to fill the toes," Mary said as she sat on the bed holding the shoes. Lizzie got up, thinking about all the other times Mary had sent her for things. She remembered when Mary would yell her name and say, "Go for this, Go for that," or simply just plain "Go." Lizzie resented this, but because of her upbringing, she would never confront her bigger sister with it.

She shuffled her feet to demonstrate her displeasure, knowing that Mary would never pick up on it, and she slowly climbed down the stairs. She crossed the dining room to the living room and retrieved the newspaper from the coffee table—she had to make sure. She'd better be sure. There it was: the Waterford Star, the local newspaper, dated "Friday, Aug 9, 1907." The headline read, "Bell Unveils Plans to Build Airplane in Brantford." She quickly thought, Nope can't use this one; Dad and Uncle John would thrash me.

"There it is," she muttered. Lizzie picked up the newspaper lying on the floor next to the coffee table. "Wednesday Aug 7—this one's old enough." Lizzie knew the routine. Uncle John would drop off the paper early every morning, except Saturday and Sunday. The paper didn't publish on weekends.

Her uncle would pour a cup of coffee—he claimed that Nellie made the best coffee in the world—and usually Lizzie's father would join him. Only a couple of times did Lizzie see her Uncle John place the newspaper on the coffee table—he came very early in the morning! Both father and Uncle John always enjoyed reading about the rich farm owners. The local newspaper would print where the farmers and their families would take vacations, spend money, receive visitors, or simply spend time. It seemed that each farmer tried to outdo the other, and the newspaper reporter took the bait, hook, line, and sinker. Whenever the name "Culmer" was printed, Uncle John would tease Lizzie, and Lizzie would study the story to see if it was the correct Culmer. Clara's Uncle Todd also owned a farm about fifteen miles from Clara's. Nevertheless, Lizzie didn't pay much attention to the teasing.

Lizzie always thought it strange the she never saw Aunt Mabel during the week; only at church on Sundays. Maybe Aunt Mabel doesn't know how to make coffee, thought Lizzie with a crooked smile. Lizzie rolled up the old newspaper, tucked it under her arm, and then scampered upstairs.

"Did you—?" began Mary. Lizzie, knowing exactly where she was going with this, cut her off, "Yes, I checked the date. I'm not stupid."

"Ok," said Mary. Then she added, "Just put a little in."

Lizzie tore and waded up a half-page and slid half of it into each of the toes. She prodded it, as if poking bread to see if it was fresh.

"There," exclaimed Lizzie as she left Mary's room for her own.

Lizzie washed her hands in the big porcelain bowl with milky water that sat on the dresser and dried with a small white towel. She opened the closet, pulled out an off-white dress that was trimmed in cream lace, and draped it on the bed. Looking at it, she mumbled to herself, "I'm acting just like Mary!"

"Is it going to move by itself?" She always wondered why Mary would stand in front of the closet and ponder the hanging clothes for so long, even the same clothes that she had already pondered in the store before buying, and even the same ones she would ponder again after she'd put them on. Just pick one and wear it, Mary! What does she think? What's the big deal? They're only clothes.

Lizzie quickly dressed. She put on her new necklace, and then twisted the waist of the dress to line up the seam. Lizzie walked into Mary's room and saw what she always saw on Sunday mornings: Mary in front of her mirror, her light brown shoulder-length hair perfectly combed, her dress a perfect fit, and her trim waistline accented with a bow. Her stockings were flawless, and the new-style shoes looked funny, but Lizzie had to admit they worked well with everything else Mary had picked out. Lizzie noticed that Mary's light makeup gave her face a pale, smooth appearance.

During the past few months, Mary had worked with Lizzie and educated her in the art of makeup and application technique. Lizzie liked learning, and she got good at putting on Mary's makeup, but only when Mary allowed it. During these times, Mary told stories about boys, the kissing and the other things that Lizzie should know. Mary's face today was a pleasing mix of crèmes and pinks, and Lizzie knew that this surely was a special day. Lizzie, catching a scent of something, stuck her nose in the air and sniffed, like a rabbit. "What's that?"

"It's new toilet water from France," said Mary. "That's what they told me at the store in Simcoe."

Lizzie laughed. "Toilet water!"

"Don't be childish. Look here." Mary showed Lizzie the writing on a small green bottle. "See, Eau de Toilette."

The liquid had a pleasing, almost sweet scent. It filled the room with the smell of fresh-cut flowers. Mary twirled, raised her arms, and asked, "How do I look?"

Lizzie, quickly studying Mary from head to toe, replied, "You look really nice."

Suddenly, Mary moved toward Lizzie with her hand straight out, aiming her finger at Lizzie's head. Lizzie knew her big sister was weird at times, and she also knew that Mary would never hurt her, but, suddenly frightened, Lizzie froze. Mary stopped in front of her and gently dabbed the right side of Lizzie's neck, then the left, and finally fixed the bow that was tied in the front of the dress. The toilet water, Lizzie realized.

Mary retreated a few steps and grinned. "Lizzie, you look like a little girl playing dress up." The dress was a little big, the shoes were almost clownish, and the skinny legs were covered in white stockings. She stood awkwardly, with her knees almost touching. They took a final look at each other, smoothed out a couple of fabric wrinkles, picked some lint, and carefully walked down the stairs. Mary went first, and then Lizzie, who clumped after her in oversized shoes. They finally made it outside, into the bright mid-day sun, and stood on the front porch.

"Hello," shouted Mrs. Glimsky from across the street. Mrs. Glimsky was a big plump woman, and she always wore the same old blue duster, with a white apron that stretched nearly to the ground. Her black hair was poker straight and glistened in the sunshine. "You girls look nice today."

"Thanks," replied Mary, and Lizzie smiled.

As they waited for Martha and Clara Culmer to arrive, Mary looked at Lizzie, noticing again that her little sister was beautiful, especially with those large brown eyes. She was growing up so fast, and soon, she would be the only girl in the house. As she gazed at Lizzie, her little sister returned a warm smile, neither of them realizing that today would change their lives forever.

Chapter 3

The Town Square

Lizzie and Mary strolled a few blocks up Cottage Street until they arrived at the corner where they agreed to meet Clara and Martha. The wind blew from the east, which meant the horse smell from the square would blow the other way. Horses frightened Lizzie, and she did all she could to avoid them. They intimidated her—probably because of their size and possibly because several years earlier, Big George had stepped on her foot.

On Saturdays, the farmers and townspeople gathered at the square and parked the horses and buggies behind the row of shops. Depending on the wind's direction, the smell was foul or pleasant. On this Saturday, the air was pleasant. Lizzie gazed down Main Street: A buggy was approaching. It was Mr. Jones, the funeral director, and Mrs. Jones and their three children. They waved and said hello as they passed, and so did all the others, including Mr. Bennett, the town lawyer, who was Jake's dad. Mary had had a crush on Jake for several months.

Lizzie looked down the empty street and, with anticipation in check, asked, "What time is it?"

Mary nodded toward the square and the big black clock that stood at its entrance. "It's one-fifteen."

Just then Lizzie started waving excitedly.

Mary rolled her eyes and in a stern voice said, "Stop that; you're embarrassing." Lizzie looked up at Mary, grinned, and then stopped.

Lizzie recognized the Culmer buggy immediately because of it large size, the deep blue color, and Mr. Nate's tall black hat. Mr. Nate was a big man, always sweating and smiling. He had one lazy eye that always seemed to be a few seconds behind the other and a big scar on the side of his face that was mostly covered by large wide sideburns. Clara had mentioned that a farm accident with a sickle distorted his face.

All in all, he was a good polite man who drove the Culmer children almost anywhere, and Mr. Nate was fond of Lizzie.

"Lizzie, Lizzie!" Clara shouted from the buggy.

"Hi, Clara," answered Lizzie, trying to stop herself from waving but slipping in a few small waves when Mary wasn't looking.

Mr. Nate guided the horse slightly to one side and then stopped the big buggy directly in front of Mary. Lizzie quickly moved behind Mary whenever a buggy approached; to others, it must have seemed as though she was possibly slow. Lizzie anxiously jumped into the buggy and sat next to Clara since it was the safest spot—away from the back or side of the horse.

Clara looked at Lizzie carefully and noticed the hint of makeup on her cheeks. "You look nice."

"Thanks," said Lizzie. "You do too." Lizzie thought to herself that, just once, she wanted to say something like "Clara, you look awful." Instead, she smiled at her best friend. Only one person was worse than Mary was when it came to clothes—yes, that was Clara, who never wore hand-me-downs.

"Good afternoon," said Mr. Nate, tipping his hat. Mary and Lizzie both smiled and answered respectively. Mary climbed up and sat next to Martha while they exchanged pleasantries—the newest fashions and the current hairstyles. Mary liked to tease Martha since Martha wore her hair like an old lady and, in complete contrast to her, Mary always wore the current style, which she would find in the magazines at the town square. Snap, Snap! —the reins sliced the air, and the buggy continued in a slow approach to the square. Lizzie thought, a buggy ride to the square...how slow, how ridiculous. She could have walked there by now and eating candies.

She wondered what might make this day special. So far, they crawled like snails. In the past, going to the square was usually considered a chore only to get things for her mother and then return home as quickly as possible. Today, Lizzie got to stay there with the girls, but for what?

As they approached the small bridge that arched over the Grand River and the train tracks, they were provided with a great view of the town square.

Actually, it was not really a square at all; rather, it was a giant backward L. All the stores were connected, and they formed a long row along the west side of Queen Street. The other side of the street offered a well-manicured, grassy, winding walkway from the clock to the Waterford Train Station. This walkway, about thirty yards wide, ran the entire length of Queen Street. Next to the walkway flowed the twenty-foot-wide Grand River, with its gray and green slow-moving water. The town had constructed eight new buildings at the north terminus of Queen Street. These buildings faced Main Street. At the southern end of the row of buildings lay a large cobblestone parking area, and beyond it hulked the station and its platform. Behind the row of stores lay a huge parking expanse for the buggies, drivers, and horses. Sometimes, Fred and Arthur would hang out there and act as though they were the drivers or groomers. On one occasion, Fred actually made ten cents for brushing a horse! Lizzie's father told them to take up brushing as weekend work. Today, he could have made a lot of money.

As the Culmer buggy made the right turn onto Queen Street, Lizzie looked at the big clock: one-thirty. Hundreds of people already bustled around the town square.

Because the town had built those eight new buildings at the north end, the buggies were forced down Queen Street, past the stores. Once at the end, the buggies could make the left turn to the parking area. The town had constructed those eight new buildings to block off the northern buggy access. Most of the members of the town committee owned shops on Queen Street. One night, Lizzie overheard Uncle John tell her father that the town committee wanted everyone to pass their store windows before parking.

As the Culmer buggy approached the first store window, they all heard someone shouting their names. "Lizzie! Mary! Lizzie!" The call came from across Main Street.

Lizzie stood in the buggy, turned, and looked back; her brother Fred waved his arms frantically. "Come here, come quick! We're going to be in a photograph!"

Everyone in the Culmer buggy—in fact, the entire buggy procession— stopped. To Lizzie's recollection, the people of Waterford never got an opportunity to witness a picture-taking event of this magnitude. The photographer, Hubrey Spence, had come south from Brantford, the second biggest city in Canada West. He was a tall, clean-shaven young man with glasses, a well-trimmed gray suit, polished shoes, short, and oily-black hair.

"You, I mean you..." Hubrey called to a man in the third-floor window, "turn sideways. Everyone, now; stay perfectly still!"

As Mary, Martha, Lizzie, Clara, and about fifty other people made their way across the street, it became clear now what was going on. The town committee had ordered a picture taken of the newly constructed town hall building. The structure, however, was still under construction and far behind schedule (according to Uncle John) because of poor weather. Expecting the building to be completed by this time, the town committee had hired the photographer to be in Waterford on this day. The building, which reached three floors tall, was the highest structure for miles, and the committee wanted a picture of the milestone.

"You, yes, you…trade places with him." Lizzie imagined a frame around what Hubrey was looking at and decided it would make a fine photograph. There was Father, Uncle John, Fred, and many others she had met at the house over the years. It looked like a proper portrait, the way they all stood, knelt, or leaned from glassless windows, especially the rail-thin woman on the third-floor window, who dangled her legs.

Hubrey stood directly in front of them with a large pole behind him that had a bar on top with a wire running down to Hubrey's hand. Lizzie thought that this was a lot of stuff just for a picture. Just then, Hubrey shouted, "Stay still!" He removed his jacket and hung it on the pole. Nobody even smiled. There was a soft explosion and an enormous light gray cloud of smoke rose above Hubrey's head. The picture was taken and everybody started mulling around shaking hands, like they accomplished something great. Everybody was smiling now. Lizzie thought it seemed odd. "Why didn't they smile for the picture?"

Mary watched Hubrey as he packed his camera equipment in a large black case. She liked his manner. He had an air about him that the local boys lacked, probably because Hubrey was a professional or maybe he came from good stock. Mary's father approached Hubrey with his hand out. They shook hands as Mary watched her dad whisper something in Hubrey's ear. Hubrey nodded a couple of times and laughed.

Mary knew she would have to act fast to be able to meet him.

Lizzie and Clara turned and walked back to the buggy. "Are you coming, Mary?"

"No, Lizzie; go ahead—I'll catch up later." Mary was still gazing at Hubrey. Lizzie had seen her sister swoon over boys before, but never like this. A small breeze could have knocked her over! Clara and Lizzie both laughed as Mary stood there statue-like, staring straight at Hubrey Spence.

Lizzie mumbled, "Look who is embarrassing who." Both she and Clara laughed again. The buggy moved forward toward the parking area. The first stop was always the general store because it had the best things— like candy and sodas. Lizzie and Clara made their way to the back door of the General store, now filled with people who were mulling around smiling and talking as they shopped. There it was, the long line that stretched almost to the front door, all waiting to use the telephony.

The general store was the closest place to use the talking device for those town people who did not have one in their homes. Lizzie and Clara selected and paid for their drinks and candies, and then they pushed through the front door. In the square, they sat on a bench and sipped their drinks.

"My dad is going to get one," Clara swallowed a candy.

"One what?" asked Lizzie, chewing on a licorice.

"One of those telephony's," said Clara. "You should get one too."

Clara leaned over close to Lizzie's ear and said, "Then we could talk to each other whenever we wanted."

"Maybe," answered Lizzie, leaning forward.

"Do you know what's going to happen at the train station today?" asked Lizzie, changing the subject because she knew her dad would never get one of those talking boxes.

"Dad told me the train's arriving around three," said Clara taking another sip. "I'm not allowed down at the train station," said Clara and then added, "My dad would kill me if went there." They looked south, toward the station's platform.

The towering poplar trees behind the station looked peaceful. Once, she saw them bend in a windstorm and was amazed that they didn't break. They also saw a few people gathering on the platform benches. This was so confusing to Lizzie, and she wondered why she was the only one feeling this way about the station today.

"Hi, Lizzie," said a voice to her right. Lizzie turned to see Greta, a German girl that Lizzie knew from school.

"Hi," answered Lizzie as she glanced at Clara with her eyes crossed.

"Are you ready for school yet? Only three weeks of summer vacation left," Greta spoke as if only she knew about this mystery.

"Not really," said Lizzie, trying to ignore Greta and hoping the girl would go away, since no one really liked her; she always smelled bad.

"Bye. See you later," said Greta as she walked away.

Clara, gulping her soda, looked at Lizzie. Her eyes widened with excitement and finally, she said, "We'll have to have another sleepover before school starts."

"That will be fun," said Lizzie. They sat back, eating candy and sipping sodas. Finally, Mary drifted up to them, dreamy-eyed and, Lizzie thought, acting a little strange.

"Did you see Hubrey?" asked Mary, trying to attract anyone who would listen. She often did this.

"Yes," said Clara.

"Yes," echoed Lizzie.

"He's coming to our house later."

"What for?" asked Lizzie, confused.

"Uncle John has to pay him for the picture," said Mary. "You know, he is the town treasurer."

"Clara, you don't mind if I walk home later?" asked Mary.

"No, I don't mind." Clara glanced at Lizzie, puzzled.

"If my friends ask after me, tell them I've gone to find Martha." With that, Mary strolled off, along the row of stores.

Lizzie and Clara watched as, about a block up the street, Mary met up with Martha. They exchanged words, chuckled a bit, and then entered the dry-goods store, probably to get the things that Lizzie's mother needed.

"It's almost three," said Lizzie.

Clara nodded,

After they finished their sodas and candy, they stopped at the bakery. They wanted some cakes; the ones that Mr. Owen baked were the best.

"Hi, Lizzie," said Mr. Owen, and then added, "Hi, Clara." They both answered at the same time "Hello, Mr. Owen."

"Where's Mary?" asked Mr. Owen. "I need to give her the schedule for the next two weeks."

"Chasing boys," Lizzie laughed. Clara also laughed, and Mr. Owen just tilted his head and smiled showing his missing teeth.

"Lizzie, how is your baking coming?"

"Just fine, Mr. Owen," said Lizzie.

"If your sister leaves me, just come around, and you can have her job." This was the second time today she heard something about Mary leaving.

Clara and Lizzie each picked out two cakes. "I'd like that, Mr. Owen. Thanks."

They left the bakery, crossed the street to where fewer people walked, and sat on a bench that faced the row of stores to eat their cakes. As three o'clock neared, the square grew congested with people, including the transients, who stood in tight circles near the train tracks. They all held duffel bags, with hats tilted down, as they looked for free passage to the next town.

More buggies than usual were in town, and they overflowed the parking area behind the town square. Lizzie had never seen so many buggies on a Saturday. The two constables strolled around, swinging their sticks, talking to the townspeople, and watching for pickpockets.

"Clara, do you know what is going on today?" Lizzie pleaded.

"I don't know," said Clara.

Mary quietly walked up behind them and asked, "Are you ready, girls?"

"Ready for what?" asked Lizzie, now a little angry.

"The train is coming," said Mary. "You watch."

Lizzie stood and looked Mary in the eyes and said, "Mary, the train comes through here all the time. We can hear it from our house."

"Those are regular trains." Mary cocked her head and smugly added, "Today's train has lots of boys."

Clara stood and then said quickly, "I have to go back to the buggy."

"Why?" asked Lizzie, trying to grab Clara's hand.

"There's my dad with the work wagon," said Clara. "I'm not supposed to be here when the passenger train arrives."

"Why not?" Lizzie asked, now getting frustrated.

"Please believe me," pleaded Clara. "I have to go! I have to go, right now!"

Lizzie considered leaving with Clara but something—curiosity, perhaps—stopped her. She grabbed Clara's arm. "Come with me." Clara began to cry.

"Stop that, stop it," said Lizzie. "Come on; I know a place closer to the station where we can watch and nobody can see us. Come on, let's hurry!" Lizzie dragged Clara toward the river and then led her south, along the riverbank, to a clearing right in front of the train station platform. They were now on the side of a grassy hill, close to the train tracks and closer to the riverbank. Lizzie had been right; the people on the other side could not see them if they lay down.

"How did you know about this place?" asked Clara, now on her stomach.

"I overheard Mary tell her friends that she used to come here and fool around with Tom."

"Nobody can see us here," said Lizzie. Now, all they had to do was wait for the train and not be seen by the hundreds of people gathered for the train's arrival.

Chapter 4

The Train Station

A tall thin man in a white shirt, dark trousers, wide suspenders, and a narrow-brimmed hat stood on the platform and yelled twice, "The train from Toronto will arrive at three-twenty."

Lizzie knew all about the Waterford Train Station; her father had built the stonework around the fireplace and the doors. It was only two years old, and she remembered how it caused a lot of friction with the town committee. Her Uncle John had once told her that the railway company was hard to work with, and it was the westernmost station on the Toronto–Hamilton–Buffalo–Railway—the THBR, the locals called it—a simple triangle of tracks that ran through the golden horseshoe from Toronto to Buffalo to Waterford. Also, The Michigan Central Railway, or MCR, ran its trains from Detroit to Buffalo and shared that part of the THBR tracks from Waterford to Buffalo. This made Waterford a busy station for both railroad companies.

Lizzie's Uncle Jim approached the station in his uniform. He was there to assist the other two men already inside. Lizzie saw her uncle only on special occasions and then only for a short time; she did not know him well and was sure he did not know her either. However, knowing her uncle was here gave her a sense of safety.

Usually, only cargo trains, sometimes two or three times a day, stopped and unloaded contents at Waterford. A passenger train was a rare thing, arriving about once a week and always on Saturday. Of course, this didn't include the nonpaying passengers who traveled with the cargo trains. Over the years, Lizzie had seen scary-looking men jump from a train, wait on the riverbed, and then jump back on the next train that came through. She remembered that this was one of the complaints by the town committee; they didn't want derelicts in town, but the tracks always brought these people. Usually, it didn't take long to unload a cargo train because the station workers helped stack feed, seed, and other things that the general store would use. During the winter, cordwood, which the farmers used, always came through the station. Today, however, it was definitely a passenger train.

Peering over the grassy ridge just a few feet from the station, Lizzie's mind started to wander. The train tracks lay only four feet before them. Across the tracks, farmers lined up with their work wagons ready to haul, but what would they be hauling today? Certainly not wood. Lizzie recognized only Clara's dad and uncle, Todd, who owned a livestock farm near Simcoe, a few miles south from Clara's. Lizzie knew that she and Clara weren't supposed to be there. If one of the railroad workers made them move, Clara would surely get caught; her dad and uncle were only fifty feet away. If a stray dog came by, it would surely draw attention and possibly give away the girls' position. So far, they were lucky—no dogs and no station workers.

A loud steam whistle blew once, twice, then three times. The last was a longer blast that echoed like a cannon shot through the town square. Lizzie and Clara rolled sideways. Big white plumes of smoke billowed in the air a quarter mile away. Lizzie rolled back onto her belly and spotted Mary across the street, in front of the department store. Mary held three large bags and was talking to some friends, occasionally stretching her neck trying to see something. She was sure that Mary was trying to locate her and Clara because Mary's eyes roamed the entire length of Queen Street, not once, but twice. Lizzie alternated her view between Mary and the train tracks. Finally, when Mary looked in her direction, Lizzie stood up quickly and then waved as a signal to Mary that everything was okay. Mary waived and smiled back; she knew that Clara and Lizzie were all right.

"Lay down!" cried Clara as the rumbling grew louder. The ground vibrated, and the train rounded the small bend just before the station platform.

"Magnificent!" thought Lizzie. She always liked trains; their size, their power. She especially liked the caboose, which reminded her of a small wooden house on wheels. She couldn't understand why she hated horses but loved trains. It had to be because horses are unpredictable and trains did the same thing all the time. As the train approached with wheels reversing, it seemed that it would never come to a complete stop.

Clara shook. Lizzie held her tightly as they lay face down on the grass, only four feet from the train, as it slowly rumbled past them. A loud blast of steam from the side of the locomotive startled them as the train finally stopped. Lizzie noticed that some of the train cars were different from the others; they were square boxes, painted in a dull green, with lots of blacked out windows.

The girls watched; so far, everything seemed peaceful as several people left the train. Uncle Jim and the other two men assisted people by carrying bags and boxes to the platform. Because the train had stopped on the curve, they couldn't see the caboose. They watched people, luggage, children, and sometimes pets, but no boys. Possibly, there were none today, or maybe they had all gotten off in Toronto. Lizzie didn't feel right about this, as she glanced at the seven farmers who were standing in front of their respective wagons across the parking lot area, off to one side of the station. They were standing and waiting. Lizzie suddenly knew the boys were on this train.

"Lizzie!" whispered Clara, as she tugged hard on Lizzie's dress, "Look!"

Just like a dream, walking next to the train toward the station platform, were two rows of boys, all dressed the same, passing through the steam where each train car was joined. They were walking in military-like fashion, swinging their arms and in unison.

Wide eyed, Lizzie and Clara stared. These boys were all different heights and, as they approached, Lizzie noticed that they all wore wooden rectangular plates on their chests, which were supported by brown yarn. Numbers were written on the front of the plates. Two elderly people, one a sweaty man with a clipboard and the other a big woman, marched the boys up to the platform. These were all young boys. One short boy seemed little more than a baby.

"Halt!" shouted the man with the clipboard. The boys stopped, rigid and expressionless. It looked to Lizzie as if this exercise had been staged several times before. They all looked tired and scared. All were thin and hollow-faced. They wore gray caps with small brims, dark blue jackets, dirty white shirts, blue pants, and scuffed shoes. Halfway down the line, Lizzie noticed one taller boy, who wore a black cap and light blue pants. She could barely make it out, but he had the number 30 tagged on his chest plate. Lizzie also noticed that these boys had no luggage.

This is what Mary is doing for me on my birthday, thought Lizzie.

It was odd for both Lizzie and Clara, not being able to move. They could only watch. They were so close, they could hear them breathe, see fear in their faces, and see their tears. The locals started to move back toward the town square, leaving the farmers still standing there. The first farmer approached the platform, positioning his wagon in front of it. He walked up the platform and stood directly in front of the big woman. "Mr. Smitts," he blurted out his own name, and the big woman called, "Numbers thirteen, twenty-eight, thirty-one, and fifteen, come here!" As the sweaty man wrote on his clipboard, four boys ran to the front of the line and then removed the numbered wooden plates, which they laid at the big woman's feet. Mr. Smitts handed something to the big woman and then marched the boys down the platform, toward the wagon. The boys jumped in, the farmer mumbled something to them, and away they went.

"Mr. Ross!"

"Numbers two, five, nineteen, thirty-six, and twenty-nine, come forward!"

The same thing happened again, but this time, Lizzie saw what Mr. Ross gave to the big woman. A bag of money fell on the floor, and several silver coins rolled out. Money.

"Why were the farmers buying these boys?" whispered Lizzie. "Clara, do you know about this?"

"No!" exclaimed Clara, who squinted and then quickly blinked hard. "Wait. I heard my dad say that it was a good idea and the middle of August was great and it would help the harvest, and the price was right. I didn't know he was talking about buying boys."

Lizzie looked up and saw a tall boy with wide shoulders, a jacket that was a little too small, blonde wavy hair, blue eyes, and a black "8" on his chest plate. He looked scared.

"Tawny," called a voice from the back of the line. Lizzie not only heard it, she saw who yelled. It was that different boy, the one in black, number 30, who was yelling.

"Yeah," said the boy wearing number 8.

Lizzie's mind worked overtime, trying to piece together this puzzle. Tawny.

"How are we going to stay in touch?" said number 30.

"I don't know," replied number 8.

"Be quiet!" belted the sweating man, who now walked up and down the rows of boys, smacking the clipboard in his hands. The boys returned to their original position.

Tawny, Tawny, Lizzie thought. What kind of name is that? She found herself looking at him so intensely.

"Numbers one, three, sixteen, twenty, thirty-three, and nine please come forward."

Another farmer took these boys away after paying the woman. Then Mr. Culmer approached and spoke his name. Clara hid even closer to Lizzie. Numbers 34, 14, 21, 25, and 30 were all taken away to Clara's farm.

"Where are they all going to sleep? I don't need six more brothers!" exclaimed Clara, now deeply concerned.

"I don't know Clara; you'll find out when you get home. Tell me at church tomorrow?"

Just as Mr. Culmer pulled his wagon away, one the boys sitting in the wagon waved back at the boy named Tawny. Tawny returned the friendly gesture suddenly feeling exhausted and somewhat sad. Still feeling a little frightened, he then looked around at the remaining boys noticing that they too all had a scared look, even the younger boys, who's lips' were noticeably quivering.

Mr. Williams, next in line, received five boys. He too paid with a sack of money. How much are they paying the lady? Lizzie wondered. Her mind filled with questions, and she grew confused. She knew her father would help her figure this one out later, after dinner.

Mr. Lathrope approached the woman and paid for six boys, including number 8, Tawny. Lizzie, now concentrating solely on this boy, was disappointed that Clara's uncle didn't take him. As the boys walked down the platform to the wagon, the smaller boy behind Tawny clumsily stumbled forward into the taller boy's back and legs. Tawny fell onto the gravel, face first. Tawny lifted his head—bleeding above his right eye from his fall on the gravel—as the farmer roared, "Get up boy; get in the wagon!"

Of all the boys, only Tawny fell, and he was the one Lizzie liked the most. He was clumsy, she thought and then, like a bolt of lightning, Tawny lifted his head and in a push-up position stared directly into Lizzie's eyes. He smiled at Lizzie. The stare and smile only lasted a few seconds, but to Lizzie it lasted a lot longer; for her, it was an eternity.

Who is he? Where is he going? Who is Mr. Lathrope? These questions cycled through Lizzie as she watched Tawny brush himself off and climb into the wagon. He looked at her at least four more times, or maybe it was five. This number would grow to more than twenty after Lizzie told the story a few times.

"Give me your shoes," growled Mr. Lathrope, holding a canvas sack. The boys looked at each other, confused.

"I said, give me your shoes!" Lizzie watched as all the boys removed their shoes and handed them to Mr. Lathrope. The shoes were put into the bag. Finally, the wagon left the station.

Clara's uncle received the last five boys. He paid the woman, but he also argued about a sixth boy whom he was promised. The big woman politely said, "We had a problem. No concern of yours, Mr. Culmer." The platform now stood empty. The hands on the town square clock pointed to four-fifteen. Lizzie and Clara were free to leave their hiding spot.

"Let's go," said Clara as she stood and brushed grass and dirt from her dress. She then noticed that Lizzie was laying on her back, staring into the sky. Lizzie looked a lot like Mary often did when she was thinking about boys.

Tawny and the other five boys, now shoeless, sprawled in the wagon as it rattled down Main Street. Tawny stretched and put his hands behind his head. He was somewhat grinning and definitely thinking of the cute brown-eyed girl he had seen.

Tawny started to unwind as the late afternoon sun beat down on his gravel-dusted face. Finally, the grin slowly disappeared and he was verging on a nap, thinking of how long it took him to get here, wondering whether he would like Canada, and if he would ever see the brown-eyed cutie again.

Chapter 5

The Orphanage – London, England, 1907

On the south side of London squatted the Bagan Christian Orphanage, a five-story square of a building with a church on one side and a dark alley on the other. This building was home to Henry Dewberry. It was, in fact, the only home Henry had known. He had no memory of his parents, siblings, or even pets. Henry knew he'd always lived in this orphanage, and he knew the building well—every nook and cranny. He also knew that, when he turned eighteen, he could leave. Over the years, Henry had seen hundreds of children, both boys and girls, come and go. It was however, odd that most of them had left within the past two years, and most of them were far younger than eighteen.

Orphanage life was routine. To Henry, this meant boring and disciplined. Life included two meals a day, a weekly bath, classroom instruction, and all the books you could read. Henry sat on his cot, wiped his tired blue eyes, tucked himself into bed, and then started squirming and kicking until he finally got his legs to fit the undersized cot. He had grown eight inches within the past six months, and now he no longer fit the bed. He looked at the empty bed to his right, where Brian had slept the night before, the cot that was now empty. Brian was just one of many who had suddenly disappeared. This bothered Henry, who avoided making friends because he knew they would eventually leave, and he felt terrible about losing friends. His first best friend, Richard, had suddenly left after three years. Keeping track of time in this place was difficult because each day was a monotonous twin of the previous day. On the left side of Henry's cot was a boy named Colin. He was about a year or two younger than Henry, and recently, Colin was always coughing.

"Lights out," called Mel, the portly second-floor monitor.

Mel's bed guarded the door to the dormitory. Over the years, Henry and Mel became the kind of friends who helped each other tolerate their surroundings. The only three floors in the orphanage that had permanent monitors were the first floor (for the entrance and infant center), the second floor (which housed the boys), and the third floor (which housed the girls). The third-floor monitor also slept near the door opening. The fourth floor contained offices and sleeping areas for the staff. The recreation room occupied the entire fifth floor. Here, all the books were kept in three large racks that stretched from floor to ceiling.

The basement (Henry's favorite floor) contained the kitchen, dining hall, the furnace room, and storage rooms. Usually, he had trouble falling asleep, but on this night, he was tired—probably because he had spent the entire afternoon cleaning the kitchen floor with vinegar and water. Henry fell asleep quickly.

Henry awoke and looked out the window that broke the wall between his bed and the now-empty bed. He saw a dull gray morning sky; it would rain. Henry felt that it rained most of the time, and he grew to accept it. However, he hated that the roof leaked and that the fifth floor required special maintenance. Henry often had to mop puddles on the orphanage's fifth floor, so he sometimes hid in the furnace room, where no one could find him on rainy days. He had a blanket and a pillow stashed down there. Mel didn't even know about this escape place.

"Twenty minutes to breakfast!" shouted Mel. He stood next to his bed, at the entrance of the second-floor room.

The room filled with noise as seventy boys rose and readied for breakfast. It usually took about ten minutes for everyone to drift into the dining hall in the damp basement. The boys sat on one side of the room, and the girls sat on the other side. The head table was elevated and ran along the top of the room. The floor monitors all took their places, followed by the staff, and then, Dr. Charles Heddon, the headmaster, who occupied the middle seat and who had the biggest chair. Mr. Heddon stood and said a quick prayer and then sat back down. The doors on one side of the Dining Hall opened, and servers brought trays of food to the tables. Starting with the head table, of course, thought Henry.

The morning meal consisted of bowls of porridge and plates of toast. Henry didn't know what day it was. Most of the breakfast meals were the same, unless it was a special day for some reason, and then sausages were added to the menu.

The staff, having completed their meal, grabbed their yardsticks and patrolled the rest of the dining hall, looking for unruly children. Elbows had to be off the table, feet squarely on the floor, no bending over, and hats off! Smacking on the head, ankles, and hands was common. One forgot only once.

After breakfast, Headmaster Heddon returned to the head table, stood, and mumbled a few words (which he did each morning). Some speeches were short and others were long. This morning, Heddon announced that

Mel, the second-floor monitor, had been promoted to travel advisor. He also heard that his replacement would arrive later that day. Mr. Heddon sat back down, sipped some tea, and then stood again, and called out, "Henry Dewberry, after meal, come to my office."

Henry left the dining room and started up the stairs, past the first-floor reception and the infant area. He heard the babies crying through the blue doors and waved to the monitor at the entrance. After reaching the fourth floor, he strolled down the long corridor and approached the door at the end of the hall. He knocked.

"Come in," answered Heddon.

Henry opened the door and, like always, he was amazed at the size of the bookshelves, the desk, the couches, the tables, and the old rugs. "Yes, Headmaster?"

"Got a new one for you, Henry," said Heddon, now sitting at a small table smoking a cigar and sipping tea. "Ten o'clock—sharp. Be extra nice; he's special."

Henry knew that a rich kid was coming, and Heddon wanted no problems. Once, Henry had greeted a boy from a rich family and within two minutes, a full-scale battle erupted that included Mel, Henry, and Heddon. They finally had to give the boy back to the parents.

"Ok, governor," said Henry. Then he added, "Don't want no p roblems, now, do we?" Henry looked around slowly. His gaze paused at the world globe. He liked this large mounted globe, and he tried to read it whenever he had a chance. "What's the name?"

"Burke, James Burke," replied Heddon. With a wave of his hand, he added, "That will be all."

Henry left the office and made his way back to the reception entrance on the first floor. He stood next to the entrance monitor, a sour old man who controlled who entered and left the building. He was so fat and Henry knew the old man couldn't stop anyone. Finally, a carriage pulled up; a small boy got out, hugged a woman (Henry decided this was his mother), and with tears in his eyes, walked to the front door.

The carriage left as quickly as it arrived; its driver was bent on getting away from the orphanage. Henry knew that rich people often did this because they were embarrassed to be seen dropping off a child.

"James Burke?" asked Henry.

"Yes. Jimmy." The little boy's lower lip was quivering.

"Come on now, Jimmy. I'll show you around," said Henry as he patted the smaller boy's shoulder.

"What's your name?" asked Jimmy.

"Henry. Friends call me Tawny... after the owl, you know."

They went to the first-floor reception office and then up to the boy's second-floor bedroom.

"This is your bed," said Henry, pointing to the empty bed next to his.

Jimmy, still intermittently weeping, sat on his bed and began saying, "Father's moving to South Africa. I will only be here a little while. Mummy is coming back for me soon."

Henry asked, "How old are you?"

"Nine," said Jimmy. "Just had my birthday two weeks ago. Mum gave me a big party with cake, candies, and presents." After a long pause, Jimmy muttered, "Mum will come for me soon. You see, Mother and Father are divorcing, and Mum said she'll get me as soon as she can."

Henry had heard this story before, but he kept quiet. Once, he was punished for telling a boy that his parents would never come back. Henry had been forced to spend two days up on the fourth-floor, in the detention room—the one room in the entire orphanage that had a one-way lock on the outside of the door. He knew better now.

"Birthday," Henry said to himself. I don't even know my birth date. How old am I? He guessed his age to be somewhere around thirteen; he was one of the tallest boys in the orphanage and was mature enough to be used by the Head Master to greet the new boys. Both Jimmy and Henry spent the rest of the afternoon walking the halls.

Finally, the dinner bell rang, and the boys made their way to the basement. The dining hall quickly filled with hungry children, and dinner was served in the same fashion as breakfast. Henry noticed a new face at the head table. "Who's he?" Henry thought out loud.

Jimmy, who sat beside him, looked up at Henry. An elderly frail-framed man, with a gray beard, thinning hair, and big eyebrows that resembled wings, sat peering out over his round glasses at the crowd, as though looking for someone.

Again, after dinner, Headmaster Heddon stood and spoke. Mr. Geoffrey Tanner, the new second-floor monitor, was introduced. Mr. Tanner stood, said a few words, thanked Heddon, and then sat back down quickly.

Jimmy and Henry left the basement and walked past the closed front doors. These doors were permanently locked for the night during dinner and would not be reopened until early the next morning. They walked to the fifth-floor Recreation Room. This room was very large and broken by pillars every so often, with rags sometimes lying on the floor, sucking up ever-present pools of rainwater. Chairs and tables were scattered about.

Henry took a seat in the corner and returned to an earlier thought: When is my birthday? This tortured him; he had no idea! "I'll find out," he muttered as he stared past the barred window into the darkness.

Henry paid no attention to Colin, who came in still coughing and who took the seat between Henry and Jimmy. Henry didn't even hear Jimmy mumbling or sobbing about having his mom come for him.

One of the floor monitors entered the room. "Bed time!"

The girls quickly retreated to the third floor and some of the boys, who were talking about the new floor monitor, retreated to the second floor. There was no way Henry would sleep tonight. He was planning a raid on the headmaster's office. One problem: the new floor monitor, Mr. Tanner.

Henry knew that after Mel was asleep, you could ride a horse past and not wake him. Mr. Tanner, however, presented a new obstacle, but Henry couldn't put off his plan. It had to be done tonight. Jimmy tried to fall asleep, but because of the newness, or perhaps fear, he could not, and every once in awhile he would look over and see Henry staring at the ceiling, eyes wide open. A few hours passed, and Henry sat up and put socks on his feet. He knew this would remove sounds, especially on the creaky old stairs.

This wasn't the first time Henry went for a late-night stroll through the building. In fact, Mel had given Henry his "Tawny" nickname after catching him wandering around late in the night, for the fourth or fifth time.

Henry crept toward the door, approaching Mr. Tanner. The old man moved a little as he slept against the wall outside the door. Henry stood silent for a couple of seconds and watched him sleep. Then up the stairs Henry went, walking as close to the rail as possible, to avoid creaky stair steps.

The third floor was in sight, and Henry knew that somewhere here, a bad floorboard lay between the entrance to the third-floor girls' bedroom and the stairs to the fourth floor. He had heard that the board was there on purpose to protect the girls' floor from intruders. He didn't know whether this was a true story, but he did know that the board, if stepped on wrong, squeaked. To bypass the bad board, Henry edged past the third-floor monitor's bed.

This was the worst part of the trip up to the fourth floor. He slipped sideways past the bed on tiptoes. The third-floor monitor was a large lady. She too slept well. She suddenly rolled over, and Henry's heart went into his throat. In a jerking motion, with his arms swinging, he leaped past her and scurried up the steps to the fourth-floor hall. Only now did he consider himself safe.

Once on the fourth floor, Henry padded down the corridor to the headmaster's office door. He passed the sleeping rooms of the staff and the headmaster himself. He noticed flickering candlelight coming from frosted windows of certain doors. Although scared, he continued, ducking as he passed doors. Finally, he was at the main door. He took out a special comb that he had made just for this kind of occasion. The teeth were broken away, and the end of the comb looked like a skeleton key. He inserted the smartly crafted false key, and with a little jiggling the door popped open. He entered and quietly closed the door behind him.

He moved to the large filing cabinet to the left of the desk. Henry knew where to go because he had been in this office several times and so far, he had never been caught. Once, he had accepted a dare from another boy to steal Heddon's umbrella. Henry couldn't pass up this challenge. The umbrella found itself in Heddon's chair in the dining hall.

He sat on the floor in front of the cabinet drawer and opened it slowly, straining to see names on the file folders. Then he saw it: Dewberry, Henry 1899. He hastily pulled the file and laid it between his outstretched legs. The darkness prevented him from reading the writing. He stood, took a candle from the shelf, and dug in the desk for matches. Finally, he lit the candle under the table. His eyes grew large.

"September 26, 1895," he said under his breath. He quickly did the math on his fingers. "It's 1907." Henry paused, "I'm twelve."

Then he noticed other things in the file. He craned his neck and looked up over the desk toward the door. Should he continue, or should he leave now? His curiosity proved overpowering. He looked back down toward the file and started to read: "Admitted to the orphanage, 1899."

"I was four," he mouthed quietly. He had been here for eight years. Then he saw it, shook his head twice, and said, "Father committed suicide. That's why I'm here."

Henry, now in a daze, folded the file and returned it to where he thought was the original place. He couldn't help but notice that his mother's name was Sarah and his father's name was William. Henry quickly rose, pushed the drawer back in, tapped the candlewick with his fingers, and put the candle back on the shelf. Henry left the same way he came in and returned to his second-floor bed.

Very early that morning, Henry awoke to see Headmaster Heddon bending over his bed, his face red with anger. "Wake up, you bloody bastard." Henry had never heard that much anger in his voice. "Come with me now."

Heddon jerked Henry out of bed, grabbed his left ear, and dragged him up two flights of stairs to his office. As they entered the room, Henry saw smoke all over the interior and thought, Where did the fire come from? I tapped out the candle. I know I did!

"What in God's name were you doing in here last night?" yelled Heddon, glaring at Henry. The boy looked down and saw the file on the desk. He knew he had been caught red-handed.

"I only wanted to know my birthday," Henry said, feeling shame on one hand, but because of his age, a bit rebellious.

"You almost burnt down the building, you stupid fool!" cried Heddon. His teeth were clinched inches from Henry's face. "The wicks on the candles were smoldering. This happens when you do not put them out properly."

"How did you know it was me?" asked Henry.

Heddon shook his head. "Your file had been placed backward in the drawer." He wiped sweat from his forehead and spoke softly, but harshly, as he looked out the window. "It's time for you to go." Heddon drew a breath and then said, "Go to your bed. I'll deal with you later."

Henry slightly bowed his head, left the office, returned to the second floor, and sat on his bed, pondering what his punishment was going to be. Over the years, Henry had experienced food deprivation, many yardstick beatings, tongue-lashings, and the odd practice of isolation therapy. Which is it this time? He wondered.

After several hours of rest, Henry remembered the last thing Headmaster Heddon had said. He was going somewhere. He was going to be like all the others who left the orphanage. Where? He could not imagine in his wildest dreams what lay ahead.

Chapter 6

The Boys

Tired from his escapade and embarrassed, Henry finally fell asleep. Everyone else had left for breakfast. About and hour later, the boys returned and strolled noisily around the second floor. Henry awoke and looked at Jimmy, who sat on his bed and stared back at him.

"What do you want?" said Henry angrily, trying to get up.

"You missed breakfast, so I brought you back some toast." Jimmy pulled mangled pieces of toast from his pockets and handed them to Henry.

"You fool," said Henry. "You'll get smacked if you get caught, smacked hard."

Jimmy's eyes got big. He cocked his head and asked, "What should I do?"

Henry told him to go to the third floor and throw the toast in the trash barrel next to the stairs. Jimmy quickly grabbed the pieces back from Henry. Crumbs flew everywhere. He stuffed what was left of the toast back into his pockets and followed Henry's instructions. The boys were preparing to go to the classrooms, which were located on the first floor behind the infant room.

Classes were not well structured but were fun. Besides, the boys learned new and interesting things. Henry's favorite class was music and he loved playing the trumpet and any horn instrument. Over the years, Henry had grown to be a fair horn player, and sometimes Heddon would even ask Henry to play a song.

"Henry, Henry Dewberry," Mel said as he approached the bed with a wicked smile. "What did you do? Heddon is in an uproar." He wiped his brow with a white hankie and stuffed it into his jacket pocket.

"I just wanted to know when me birthday is," Henry said softly.

As soon as the last word was spoken, Heddon appeared at the door and shouted, "Henry, Jimmy, Colin, William, George, Walter, Thomas. Come to my office right now."

"Mel, what is this all about?" Henry whispered.

Henry, frightened, stood, stretched, and looked around the room for the other boys who were also called by Heddon. They too were looking around at each other, trying to figure out what was going on. Henry took a couple of steps when Mel stepped close and said, "Bring your stuff."

Henry was puzzled. "What do you mean?"

"Henry, you aren't coming back. So, pack your stuff."

Henry's stomach ached, and his fear was changing to outright fright. He swallowed hard. Henry donned his jacket, stuffed his pockets with his key comb and a few pieces of crumpled paper, laced his shoes, and then put his hat on. As Henry looked around the room, he saw that the other named boys were all doing likewise, as if they were following Henry's lead.

"Hurry, boys!" shouted Mel. Finally, all the marked boys slowly followed Henry, walking up the stairs toward the fourth-floor office.

"Don't worry, lads," said Mel as he followed behind them. "It's a much better place than this." Henry, who seemed to be leading the pack, looked back at Mel. "Keep moving, lads."

Soon, they all stood together in the middle of Heddon's office. Henry, the tallest and probably the oldest, could still smell a hint of smoke. In the corner of the room, Henry noticed a chair and, in front of it, a large box with a brass tube, which sat on a three-legged stand. A black cloth draped one side of the device. He almost didn't see the two men who were standing next to it.

"It's time for you boys to start your new life," said Heddon, standing and smoking a cigar. "Ok, one at a time...we need a photograph." Heddon pointed at Henry. "You go first."

Mel grasped Henry's shirtsleeve, led him to the chair, and pushed him into it.

"Just sit still," said the man as he disappeared under the cloth. After a moment and some activity under the cloth, he reappeared and pulled a cap off the end of a tube on the box. There was a bright flash and a rising cloud of smoke that drifted toward the open window. The man then threw up the cloth and said, "That's all. You can go. Next."

Henry stood slowly, walked past the device, and then returned to the pack. The others took their turns. The picture-taking exercise, required for the orphanage's records, was something to see as the two men scrambled in preparation and then stood still. They repeated their routine and, for the moment, seemed to comically remove some of the tension the boys felt. Thomas, who went last, even smiled, showing his stained and crooked bottom teeth. On his way back to the circle, he made the kind of face that only Thomas could make, which made the rest of the lad's chuckle.

The boys huddled in the middle of the room and chatted to each other as Heddon and Mel bent over the big desk, looking at a piece of paper and talking; they weren't speaking loud enough for Henry to hear. Heddon gave a yellow envelope to Mel, who stuffed it in his inside jacket pocket.

Henry left the pack and approached one of the men, the taller one who took the pictures, who was placing the device into a box, and asked, "What is that?"

"A camera. A new one too—great photographs; uses film rather than plates. You'll see." Henry looked at the camera a little more and then returned to the circle of boys.

"'A camera,'" he said quietly as he leaned into the center of the pack. "You know—it's used to take a photograph."

Just then, Mel cleared his throat. "Come, lads; we've a long trip ahead of us." Colin coughed a few times and before any of the boys could say anything else, Mel herded them out the door. The tension returned quickly.

"Henry," commanded Heddon.

Henry stopped and looked back at Heddon, who was standing with his arms crossed in front of the window looking like a shadow. "Take care," he said.

Henry, still a little scared, replied, "Ok, governor. You, too."

The boys, still in a huddled pack, whispered to one another as they walked through the long hallways and made their way down four floors and out to the main entrance. Henry's mind was busy with the words he had just heard. He was pondering these words such as trip, better place, not coming back, and finally, where are we all going?

Mel lined up the boys along the main entrance hallway, just behind the old grumpy monitor. "Wait here."

"What's going on?" cried Jimmy, his eyes swimming in tears.

"I don't know," said Henry. Suddenly, two brown, covered work wagons stopped in front of the main door. Atop each wagon sat two men, with one holding reins to two black draft horses.

Mel pushed the boys out the door and down the stairs to the street. "Come on, lads, get in. We'll take the last wagon."

The boys climbed into the back of the second wagon and sat cross-legged on the hay. Mel climbed in too, tossed his travel bag in a corner, and sat on a small wooden box. Holding his clipboard tightly against his chest, he shouted, "Be off!"

The drivers snapped the reins, and the wagons lurched forward. The view from the back of the wagon seemed strange, as if everything was going away from Henry.

"Where are we going?" asked Jimmy, wiping his cheeks every two seconds. Henry looked at Mel. "A fair question, Mel. Where are we going?"

Mel glared at them. "We have two more stops to make, so sit back and be quiet. First stop is South Hampton. Ask no more questions. You will find out later."

The wagons kept a slow roll through the streets, swaying from side to side, and then suddenly stopped.

"Stay seated." Mel got out and stood behind the wagon.

A large lady arrived, holding a clipboard similar to Mel's. They engaged in quiet conversation. Then Mel returned.

"Move over," said Mel to the boys in the wagon, and suddenly, from around the side of the wagon, a line of different boys started to climb in and take their places along the other side of the wagon. These boys also looked scared and, for the most part, were about the same age. Now this wagon was full. Mel shouted, "Ok, let's load the next one!"

Mel and the woman disappeared for a few minutes, and the boys just sat and gazed at each other or stared down at the straw. Mel returned, and they started moving through the streets.

Henry and Jimmy counted the boys who were just picked up; eleven sat on one side and seven on the other.

After an hour or so, the wagons stopped again. Henry peeked through the canvas and saw sixteen more boys climb into the first wagon. Another, smaller man handed Mel some papers, shook his hand, and then left. Mel got back into the wagon and, still clutching his clipboard, yelled, "Carry on!"

By Henry's calculation, they now numbered thirty-six. Mel leaned back and stared out the back, watching the scenery drift away. It had been hours in the wagon, and Henry noticed that the view had changed. Slowly, buildings were replaced with trees, and the roads were replaced with trails. It looked so beautiful and peaceful compared to what Henry was used to. No more clotheslines stretched from building to building. No more fire cans surrounded by people simply trying to keep warm. It was a pleasant view and all the boys stared in that direction.

Over the hours, the countryside again changed. The view reverted to buildings again, and the trails became roads. The aroma in the air had also changed. Henry could smell something new. What is it? he wondered, and then he heard loud chirping and squawking. The wagon suddenly turned and started down a small hill. The drivers shouted to the horses to slow.

The view suddenly changed to a blue-green hue. Henry thought to himself what a pretty blue-green color and quickly realized what he was seeing. "The ocean."

He knew this because of looking at the globe in Heddon's office, but he couldn't remember what it was called. The wagon came to a stop, and Mel jumped out.

"Where are we?" cried Jimmy.

"Hold on," replied Henry. He looked around intently. "Just stay at me side."

"All right," said Jimmy. The other boys all looked surprised as well.

Mel pushed his round face through the canvas curtains. "Get out. Line up in single file."

The boys jumped out of the wagon, brushed themselves off, and stood in a single-file line, looking at the ocean. The big woman counted the boys by walking down the line, tapping them on the head as she passed.

"Thirty-six," she called to Mel.

Mel gave something to the driver of the first wagon, and both wagons made a slow turn to creep up the hill. As the wagons rolled out of sight, the boys turned one at a time. They were amazed. It was the biggest thing they had ever seen.

"Wow!" cried Jimmy.

"Look at that!" exclaimed Thomas.

"What a site!" said Colin, who held back a cough.

It seemed that every boy took a turn saying something aloud.

On one side, in large white letters, read, "DOMINION." Henry noticed giant smokestacks painted with red and white stripes sticking straight up into the sky, shooting out wispy clouds of white smoke.

"Follow me!" bellowed Mel.

They walked with wide eyes toward the big ship. The immense object sat in front of them in the water beside the dock. It seemed to grow larger as they approached. Finally, they all stood directly beneath the ship on the huge wooden dock. Giant ropes dangled from the ship first into the water and then to immense posts built into the dock.

Two policemen approached the boys, dragging another young boy. The tall constables walked up to Mel. Tawny could see the fear in the boy's face.

"Here, you take him," said one of the officers to Mel.

"What's his name?" asked Mel.

The other constable rapped the boy. "Answer him."

"They call me Billy. Short for William." At one glance, Henry knew instinctively that Billy was going to be trouble.

"Get into line, Billy" growled Mel, as he gave something to one of the constables and thanked him.

Mel's voice was growing coarse. He wrote something on his clipboard, dragged Billy up to the line, and threw him directly in front of Henry and behind Colin. Billy seemed as though he had to keep moving, from something or somebody—the nervous type who always had something to hide. Henry wondered what Billy was hiding.

Henry looked down the line; the boys were all scared and chatting nervously. Henry also knew that they would get on this ship. All thirty-seven were silently asking one troubling question: Where are we going?

Chapter 7

The Dominion

Mel now looked and acted exhausted, angry, and miserable. "Sit down, over there; a single line."

The boys quickly sat down and leaned back against a wall that was actually a building opposite the huge steam ship. One of the boys said, "That bloody thing will never sink."

"Too damn big," said another.

"How does it stay up, being so heavy?" asked William.

"Look at all that brown stuff," said George as he pointed to a rusted section of the ship close to the waterline.

Henry smiled at Jimmy and asked, "Have you ever been on one of these?"

"No," answered Jimmy, and then added, "seen a picture once. I think me Dad was on one." Then Jimmy started to cry. Henry wondered if Jimmy had finally realized that his Mum and Dad were not coming back.

"Stop that," said Henry, as he nudged Jimmy's shoulder.

"Get hold of yourself," said Colin.

Suddenly, a loud blast came from the giant ship's steam whistle. The noise shook the wall of the building they were leaning against. Henry watched as Billy, who squirmed nervously, was alternating his stares between Mel and the end of the dock. "Should make me run now," muttered Billy as he stood up, crouched over, and then looked in Mel's direction.

"Sit back down and stay there," yelled the woman, moving close to Billy. She pushed him roughly to the ground. Henry, Colin, and Jimmy started laughing, and before long all the boys were giggling like little schoolchildren.

"Two of them, aye," said Billy, flushing with embarrassment.

"Yeah," said Henry. He'd been right about Billy.

The laughter quickly turned to silence as the boys sat along the wall and watched the activity on the ship. They watched white and gray seagulls hovering and squawking. The odor of dead fish filled the air, and the sky remained cloudy and gray. Afternoon slowly passed. It seemed that Mel and the big lady were getting anxious and a little irritated.

Mel scolded a boy for standing up and fixing his trousers. Henry thought that it wasn't a good sign. Mel was almost at his limit and should not be pushed further. Billy stood. Henry thought, This kid never gives up, and here comes the straw that breaks the camels' back.

Billy shouted, "Where are we going!"

Henry watched Mel, his round face angry, "Shut up. Sit down. I'll tell you later, after we board."

That's it, Henry thought. They were going on this huge ship. But the question was where?

A few more hours passed, and now it was almost completely dark. The only light came from the big ship itself.

Jimmy pointed to the ship. "Look!" A man walked down a covered tunnel ramp from the ship. The man was dressed in a dark blue suit, a white cap, and gleaming shoes. He stood at the entrance of the boarding tunnel and waved. Mel acknowledged the wave, turned to face the line, and shouted, "Ok, lads; let's go!" The boys marched in single file toward the well-dressed man.

"Thirty-seven, governor, and two travel advisors," said Mel, as he and the man swapped pieces of paper and exchanged smiles. The man handed Mel a ring of keys.

"Hurry now," said the man. "Get these kids down to F deck."

"You heard him," commanded Mel. "Move."

They zigzagged up the ramp, then found themselves under the covered portion of the ramp, and approached the hole, which led into the ship. As they neared it, Henry realized the hole was actually a large door. The big woman cupped her hand around her mouth and bellowed, "Follow me!" They trailed her through low-ceilinged hallways, down narrow stairs and past many oval-shaped doors. Finally, they stopped in a long narrow corridor.

Mel, at the back of the line, walked slowly, squeezed himself past the boys to the woman, and then whispered something. Mel then turned and walked back, but partway down the line, he stopped, yanked out a key, and then pushed open the door. It was marked with a brass-plate 17F. Mel peeked inside and then swung his arm between two boys.

"In here," said Mel. The last twelve boys in the line entered the room. "Wait here. I'll be back." He closed and then locked the door.

At the next door, Mel said, "You are in here: eighteen-F."

Mel unlocked the door, pushed them into the room, and locked it. The final group of thirteen boys was stuffed into room 19F. Now, for the first time in a long time, it was only Mel and the big lady.

"You are in here," said Mel as he opened door 20F. The big lady entered the room, placed her bags on the floor, and then looked at the surroundings, which would be her home for the next few days. Mel gave her the key and told her that he would be in the next room, 21F.

"When will you tell them?" asked the big lady.

"As soon as we're at sea, and they can't get off." Mel then added, "Heddon told me to do it this way. You know, this being me first trip an' all."

It was growing late, and Mel figured that if he was hungry, so was his traveling partner. On the ship's itinerary, Mel saw that dinner was in thirty minutes in room 1F. He washed his face, placed his toiletries on his night table, and returned to the big lady's room. He knocked three times and she let him in. He told her about dinner, which seemed to excite her, and then he watched her hang up a couple of dresses on a hook on the wall next to the door. The thirty minutes flew by as Mel thought about these boys and the long journey ahead of them.

"Come on," said the big lady. "Let's get these rascals fed and back to bed." Mel and the big lady left her room, unlocked the three other rooms, and lined up the boys against the corridor.

Mel and the woman pushed them down the narrow hallway toward the end. Finally, they reached room 1F, the general all-purpose room that would be their dining room. Room 1F was large, painted white, and contained wooden tables and stools. The room had no windows, just a lot of pipes that ran up the walls. The boys took their seats. A steward who was dressed in a dirty white shirt spoke with Mel. Mel nodded, stood, and cleared his throat. "Ok, boys, just like before. Get into line."

The boys stood and formed a line around the room, starting behind Mel and the big lady. The half-doors opened, and the boys could see a kitchen area and three people working.

"Right here," said one of the kitchen staff. He pointed to bowls and spoons at the end of the counter top.

The woman stood to one side, folded her arms, and watched every move that the boys made. Soon Henry, Colin, and Jimmy sat at the table; before them sat bowls of white rice, a piece of stale bread, and a glass of water. The boys looked disappointed at the fare.

"That's it," said Billy, as he stood up in disgust.

Henry poked Jimmy in the side. "Watch this."

Mel turned, saw Billy, and hunched down like a bull, snorting and ready to charge. He moved toward Billy and, with his arms bowed, stood in front of the boy. "Shut up, sit down, and eat!"

Mel then pushed Billy to his chair in one quick motion. "Don't get up until everyone is done!"

Henry hated rice but knew that breakfast was a long way off. He also knew that, just because they were on this immense ship, they had no right to act different and that things would be done in the same fashion as if they were still at the orphanage.

After dinner, Mel and the woman ushered the boys to their rooms and locked the doors. Henry had overheard part of a conversation between Mel and the big lady, where Mel described the dining room on the upper deck of this ship, where he and the lady would dine after the boys were packed back into their rooms.

Mel awoke first around 5:30 A.M. to the cries of gulls and fishing vessels leaving the port for the day's work. He noticed that the ship was still docked, and then suddenly, there came a knock on the door.

Mel rolled out of bed and opened the door to a steward, who said, "Good morning, sir," and handed him a piece of paper. Mel grunted and started to read the fine print: "Please keep the children on deck F until the ship leaves the port, approximately noon." The First Officer had signed it in such a rough scrawl that Mel couldn't read the signature. Mel started to close the door, suddenly stopped, rubbed his eyes, and then quickly took a few steps to door 20F only to place his ear up to the keyhole. He could faintly hear her snoring and grinding her teeth to an almost-musical beat. He laughed a little, knocked twice, and then scampered back to his own room.

Before long, Mel and the big lady had dressed and were ready for the day. They unlocked the boys' doors and took them for breakfast. Just like the night before, the boys were treated to a bowl of warm white rice, stale bread, and a glass of warm water.

"This, again?" asked Jimmy.

"Just eat it," said Mel. "We'll be leaving around noon today."

Henry finished his rice, disliking each bite, and made his way over to where Mel stood. "Colin's sick," said Henry, staring expectantly at Mel.

"Was he up all night coughing?"

Henry nodded.

"Ok, leave it to me." Mel looked at Colin, who was coughing, sitting hunched over, pale, and slowly eating his rice.

After breakfast, the boys were herded back to their rooms and locked in. "We're prisoners," said Thomas, as the door closed behind them.

"Where are we going?" whispered William.

"Quiet," said Henry. "We'll find out soon enough; just be patient."

The morning went by slowly, and then around noon, they all felt the engines begin to turn. The ship was moving. After a while, Mel unlocked the doors. "Ok, lads, we're on our way." He pointed and then told them the upper deck was that way.

The boys made a beeline up the stairs to the top level. Once outside, they hung on the rails at the back of the ship. They watched as other passengers waved to people on the dock. They watched the water froth as the propellers turned, even though they could not see the actual propellers. They watched the dockworkers handle the giant ropes. They watched everything, because it was the first time they'd ever seen something like this. It was sunny, with white clouds scudding against a deep blue sky, and the sun's heat warmed them.

Where are we going? thought Henry. The water rushed by, and the port grew smaller as it slowly faded away behind them. The ship held a lot of people; most were at the bow, sporting hats, canes, parasols, and colorful clothes. The men in the tower peered intently at the ocean. Henry decided that these men must be the drivers.

Mel and the woman finally appeared topside only to sit on a bench to soak in the sun and watch the ocean. Occasionally, Mel glanced in the boys' direction; they were scattered all over the rear of the ship. Mel knew it was "all clear" and actually felt a little relaxed because the only way the boys could get lost was if they jumped overboard, and by now, Mel didn't care one way or the other.

"Time to tell them," said the woman.

"Right," said Mel. "Henry, come here."

Henry made his way to Mel. "What do you want?"

"Round up the boys and bring them here," said Mel in his friendly voice, the one that Henry liked. It only took a few minutes before all the boys sat cross-legged before Mel's bench.

"You are all going to Canada," said Mel.

"Canada," echoed William in a surprised tone.

"Isn't that a colony?" asked George.

"It's pretty far away," said Jimmy.

"Yes, Canada," replied Mel.

The woman spoke up. "I hear it's beautiful and growing fast. You will all have much better lives there. Nothing left for you in England but despair and poverty."

"Canada," thought Henry. Then he understood. He looked at Jimmy and said, "I've seen the wagons. You know. Those dressed up wagons that you see around the streets in London. You know—the ones that advertise about Canada."

Henry felt a little relieved but still frightened. He was trying hard to accept the idea that he and the others were going to this new place called Canada.

"How long before we get there?" asked a voice from the back row.

Mel smiled. "Nine or ten days."

Henry thought that nine or ten days would be nothing. He had served longer isolation punishment back in the orphanage.

"Canada," said Jimmy, feeling a little better about this whole ordeal. Now knowing where he was going, his biggest fear was that he didn't know if his mother knew. He looked up at Henry. "I'm sure they will tell me mum where I'm going, won't they."

Henry didn't have the heart to tell Jimmy the truth, so he bit his tongue and said nothing. He just nodded and smiled at his little wide-eyed friend.

Chapter 8

The Ocean Voyage Begins

The boys split up into smaller groups and spent the afternoon discovering what the ship had to offer. Billy and Ian learned that another group of twelve children was also traveling to Canada. Meanwhile, William and George overheard two adults in the first-class section talking about Canada's riches, opportunities, and vast landscapes.

Mel and the woman strolled around the rear deck of the ship taking in the weather and enjoying calm seas. Suddenly, a loud bell rang twice, and Henry and Jimmy noticed the passengers starting to leave the decks.

"Time to round up the boys," said Mel, waving to every boy he could find. Eventually, the boys strayed back, like cattle returning to the barn. Mel led the pack down to the F deck and into room 1F. A small buzz grew around the tables as each boy shared what he had discovered. The boys were happier than yesterday and excited about crossing the ocean.

Dinner was served buffet style, of course. It consisted of chicken, potatoes, gravy, and bread. Could this day get any more perfect, thought Henry as he devoured his meal and then chased everything down with a glass of water.

"Did you see the engine room?" asked Thomas, looking at William.

"My god, you should have seen the bridge," blurted William.

"Did you look over the steering wheel?" said another boy.

"I saw the first-class dining room," laughed George. "Kicked me out fast, they did."

Henry sat back on his stool, looked at Colin, and asked, "How are you feeling tonight?"

"Not bad. Really enjoyed the food," said Colin, still looking pale and sickly. "I think I'll go to bed early; maybe I'll feel better tomorrow."

Billy jumped up, leaned over the table, and shouted, "Did you see that girl in the green dress?"

William smiled. "Wow, she was pretty, she was."

"I'll be going back there after dinner," said Billy. "Do you want to come along?"

"Sure," said William.

"Ok," said the little boy named Ian, who had been hanging around Billy like glue for the past day. Henry knew Ian from the orphanage, but felt strange to see Ian attached to somebody, since Henry always thought him a loner.

"Should be able to move around better at night," said Billy. "Can't see us from the bridge in the dark."

"The bridge," said Jimmy. "There's a bridge on this boat?"

"They call the tower the bridge, little fool," replied Billy.

Henry glared in Billy's direction, but it was ignored.

Dinner was over and Mel announced, "Remember boys, be back in your rooms before night falls."

The boys nodded and waved; some answered ok; others just smiled and quickly left the dining room, scattering all over the ship like ants searching for food.

Henry helped Colin down the hall to room 18F. Colin's coughing had become more severe and violent. Mel followed them, leaned over Colin's bed and said, "I'll get the ship's doctor tomorrow morning."

"Goodnight, Colin," said Henry.

Just then the door swung open, and Billy hastily entered the room. He took off his jacket and tried to freshen up by splashing a little water on his dirty face. Henry noticed that William was waiting in the corridor, sometimes peeking in to see what was going on. Mel had just left the room.

"Ok, where's my comb?" bellowed Billy, loud enough to wake the kids in the next room.

"Shut up," said Henry. "Can't you see that Colin's sick?"

Billy stopped, glanced around, walked a few steps, and then stared at Henry. "What did you say?"

Henry stared back with a clenched jaw and eyes narrowed. They both looked like two rams squaring off.

"I said shut up. Colin's sick and in bed."

William's eyes opened wide. He knew something was going to happen because he had seen Henry's angry look before. Henry also knew this was going to happen sooner or later, so he just accepted that this was the time, this was the place, and it would happen right now.

Billy smiled, rolled his head, and said, "Who's going to make me—you?"

Henry replied, "Do you see anybody else here...stupid?"

With that Billy leaped forward and jumped on Henry, throwing wild punches in all directions hoping one of them would reach his target. Henry knew the best way to survive this kind of attack was to get really close to

Billy's chest and wait for his own opportunity. They grabbed hold of each other. The wrestling continued. A couple more boys had joined William and were now watching through the door, mostly cheering for Henry. The two young fighters got close to Colin's cot and for some strange reason, Colin stood and tried to help, but Billy quickly pushed him back down. Henry continued staying close to Billy's chest and face to avoid being hit. Billy, who had tired of throwing punches, stumbled and fell backward right onto Colin's chest and Henry went along for the ride.

"Get the hell off," yelped Colin. He started to cough violently.

Henry wanted to help his friend, but knew if he turned his back or let go of Billy for a second Billy would get the best of him. It was time to end this fight, thought Henry. He wadded up his right fist and tried to position Billy's face within striking range. Suddenly, Billy turned to his left and dropped his right arm just enough, and then a loud smack was heard all the way down the corridor. Billy fell, with half of his body landing on a bed. His nose was bloodied; he had a huge welt forming on his right cheek. Henry went to Colin's bed and said, "It's all right, it's over. Try to rest."

Colin replied, "Thanks, Tawny."

A smaller boy who observed the altercation approached Colin. "Who was that boy?"

"His name is Henry," Colin replied, and coughed. We call him Tawny. You know, after the owl."

Mel bolted through the door, pushing it in with all his might, knocking Billy to the floor. "What the devil is going on in here?"

"It's over; no big deal," said Tawny, pointing at Billy.

Mel grabbed Billy by the shoulders and dragged him out to the corridor. He knew that for Tawny to fight, it had to be a serious problem. He remembered that, to his recollection, Tawny only scrapped twice before and on both occasions Tawny had stuck up for other smaller friends.

"Get out of here," yelled Mel. He pushed Billy so hard that Billy bounced off the wall and landed on the floor. Mel looked down at Billy's purple, swollen face and said with his teeth clenched, "If I hear of any more trouble from you, I'll personally throw you overboard myself."

Billy's eyes grew huge as he got up slowly, put his hat on, and climbed the stairs until he was out of sight. Tawny smiled at his friend William, who had witnessed the whole fight from the hallway, and the both of them went up to the outside deck and breathed in the early evening air.

"One punch," said William.

"Forget about it," said Tawny, his right hand shaking. "Bloody hurts bad."

The air was cooler and now all one could see was water in all directions. Tawny saw most of his friends running around the deck, looking at things and being pests, and for now, it didn't matter because they were happy. Two stewards approached the big woman, who was sitting on the bench enjoying the scenery.

"Is this one yours?" said one of the men, cuffing a youngster by the shirt.

"No, not mine but in our group," she said.

"Caught him in first class, near the dance room." He handed George over to the big lady.

Tawny and William started to laugh at George for being caught, and as Tawny recalled, if he had to name one boy who couldn't do anything right and would always get caught, he would name George.

"Thanks," she said. She looked at George. "We told you boys don't go where you're not allowed. Now get out of here."

Jimmy came up to the outside deck and asked Tawny about the fight. Tawny just brushed it off. William said two words to Jimmy, "One punch."

George, with a goofy expression, the kind only George could do, strolled over to Tawny and Jimmy and said, "They have a music band. They play music; sounds really good too."

Tawny's ears perked, as he strained to hear some music, but nothing was there.

Jimmy smiled up at Tawny and said, "Today was a good day."

Tawny answered him by nodding "yes," although his right hand was throbbing around the knuckles.

Night came quickly, and the boys retreated to their rooms. Tawny made his way back to 18F. Once in a while he looked over his shoulder for Billy. Tawny instinctively knew that this thing with Billy was not over yet.

To Tawny's relief, all the boys were accounted for, and he didn't have to worry about being hit with a foreign object or something. He wouldn't put it past Billy to do something rash, so he remained on guard. Tawny looked at Colin and heard his rhythmic breathing patterns, which seemed soothing at times, and helped Tawny to go to sleep on troublesome nights. He was almost asleep when Billy entered with little Ian following him.

"Eight more days to go," said Tawny to himself. It was his last thought before falling asleep.

Morning came quickly. Tawny joined the other boys as they got up and made their way down the corridor to the dining room. They had a breakfast of scrambled eggs, toast, and porridge. Tawny looked at Jimmy.

"Did you see Colin this morning?"

"No," replied Jimmy, taking another quick scan of the room.

Tawny knew Colin enjoyed breakfast the most and knew eggs were Colin's favorite.

"I'll go get him," said Tawny. He left the dining room rubbing his sore right hand.

In room 18F, Tawny shook Colin once, then twice, and then a third time, but got no response. "Get up Colin, they have eggs," said Tawny, still shaking his friend. Tawny rolled Colin over and saw a blank, white face with a crooked mouth looking back at him; Colin's eyes were fixed on an invisible object above. The boy's skin felt cool to the touch.

"He's dead," cried Tawny, starting to shake. Jimmy entered the room and Tawny repeated, "He's dead. Go get Mel."

Jimmy ran as fast as he could and fell a couple times on the slick floors. Back in the dining room, he got right in Mel's face. "Colin's dead."

Mel threw his stool aside, moved down the corridor like a bull, bolted into the room, and pushed Tawny away. He looked at Colin's lifeless face. "Yes, he's dead, all right. Poor boy; must have died in his sleep."

The big lady appeared behind Mel. "My God!"

"Tawny," said Mel, "go get the steward, quick." He covered Colin with the blanket.

The steward and Tawny returned to the room to find all the boys standing around, somber, trying to get a glimpse of the dead boy.

"You boys," said the steward, pushing and shoving his way to the cot, "nothing to see here. Go topside now."

Mel, the big lady, and the steward huddled in the corner of the room near Colin's bed, talking softly. Tawny saw this because he was last to leave the room. Feeling down, Tawny went topside, where yesterday's sun was replaced by gray skies. It was quite windy and much cooler.

"He was a good friend," said Tawny, looking at Jimmy's innocent face. "We had been through a lot over the years. Got into some good trouble. Too bad he got sick." Tawny stopped. He was rambling. "Sorry," Tawny said.

"It's ok," replied Jimmy, patting his friend on the back.

Tawny and Jimmy both watched as the steward carried a rolled blanket over his shoulder across the deck. They knew it was Colin and wondered where he was taking the body. Jimmy watched as the body disappeared into the big tower building—the bridge.

The rest of day two was miserable. It rained, and the boys had to retreat to their rooms for most of the day. The only bright spot was that dinner consisted of pork chops and mashed potatoes. After dinner, room 18F was quiet, and every boy stared at Colin's bare cot. It was eerie. A light reflected off of Colin's silver cot springs. It was the only cot reflecting light in the whole room. There was one small problem with this light, thought Tawny: There were no lamps and no windows.

Chapter 9

The Ocean Voyage Continues

It started around five in the morning, or maybe a little earlier, as Tawny figured it; it was hard to sleep on this strange night. Suddenly, the ship began to roll slowly from side to side. The ship's bow rose and fell rapidly. It felt like a long slow roll, then a jolt, followed by another long slow roll, the kind of roll that gives one enough time to ask oneself if the roll is ever going to stop. Tawny managed to get to his feet once and then was quickly thrown back into his cot.

"What is going on?" asked Jimmy, hanging on to the sides of his cot.

"Don't know," said Tawny. "Just stay in bed and hang on, damn it."

Tawny knew that if he could make it to the hallway, where there were handrails, it would be better, but then he asked himself better than what? Regardless, Tawny figured out a plan, and staying on his cot was not it.

"I'll be back, Jimmy." Tawny fell to the floor and then crawled on his belly, banging into and passing several cots to the door.

It took a lot longer than normal to reach the top deck, directly into a severe storm. The rain and wind viciously whipped the ship from the front. Tawny had never seen so much water flying (he had learned the names of ships parts yesterday). Tawny hung onto the wet handrails as the ship crashed into the black waves. He quickly figured out that it was much worse up topside.

"Get back to your room!" yelled a voice behind Tawny.

It was Mel. He was standing at the bottom of the stairs, soaking wet. "Come on! Bloody hell! Get back to your room!"

Tawny started back to his room, returning the same way he had come, very carefully. He informed the boys that it was just a bad storm.

William had just thrown up on his cot. George, who was watching him, couldn't hold back anymore and joined in on the festivities.

Tawny quickly realized that it might even be safer fighting the weather topside rather than fighting the smell that engulfed this room. Tawny opened the door and wedged another boy's shoe in it. William and George tried to retrieve water and rags from the steward to clean up the mess.

They struggled to stand on their feet. A big wave hit, jolting the ship, and William went for another turn. To everybody's delight, he hit the rag on the floor, and the boys cheered.

Most of the boys lay on their cots holding onto the side rails, sliding around, holding their breaths to avoid the stench, and bumping into each other. Finally, the rolling subsided, and the bed crashing almost ceased, but the smell was still prevalent. How could anybody think about breakfast now? Perhaps William and George could; their bellies were empty for sure. As Tawny's mind started to work, he knew he was hungry as well.

The dining room looked like an explosion hit it during the night. Chairs and tables were strewn everywhere. The stewards served toast and sausages in the boys' hands since plates would be useless and would end up all smashed anyway. The boys leaned against the walls and ate as quickly as they could.

"William. William!" called Billy as he walked back into 18F.

"What do you want?" replied William, who was still cleaning his mess.

"Want some day-old porridge? You know the kind that has skim stuff on top?"

"Stop it," said William. He jerked over, retching, but nothing came up.

The boys spent the rest of the morning in their rooms, laying around and making fun of William and George. Lying quietly on his cot, Tawny started to get sleepy as the ship rolled back and forth in a normal pattern of slow rolls, the jolts having disappeared completely. A sadness suddenly came over him. His eyes started to fill with tears. His best friend Colin was gone, and he remembered all the times they got into trouble at the orphanage. He recalled one time when Colin put crushed crackers in the third-floor monitor's bed then waited in the stairwell for her reaction. Once she hit the bed, she saw Colin. She chased him all over the orphanage, screaming at him and calling him all kind of names. Tawny finally fell asleep, still thinking of his best friend.

They spent the whole third day in that foul-smelling room, 18F, with the door wedged open. By mid afternoon, the ship had stopped the worst of its rocking, and the boys were finally allowed to go topside to breathe the fresh air. The rain had turned to drizzle, and the wind had calmed a bit. Tawny noticed that the ship had a clean fresh look. Everything was wet and shining. The air felt cold and crisp, and it didn't take long for Tawny's knees to start shaking.

"It's bloody freezing out here," said George, who wrapped himself in his cot blanket.

"Is Canada going to be this cold?" asked Thomas.

"I hope not," said Jimmy.

The rain finally stopped. The boys now roamed about the ship, each one of them covered by his cot blankets.

Mel and the woman came to the upper deck also tightly wrapped in their blankets, as Tawny thought, How did she get that blanket around her? Tawny watched them as they made their way to the bench seats, not saying much and looking tired and beat up. Toward the front of the ship, Tawny saw Billy talking to a first-class passenger: the cute little girl. How did he get up there? Tawny felt a little pain in his right hand.

A man dressed in white quickly approached Mel and handed him a piece of paper, which Mel read and acknowledged by shaking the man' s hand. Tawny suddenly found himself in a trance, the kind of trance that feels so peaceful you don't want to break it. He started to walk toward Mel for some unknown reason. He looked just like a zombie, covered in the blanket and all. Finally, Tawny stared into Mel's weather-beaten portly face.

"Are you ok?" asked Mel.

"Fine," said Tawny, breaking the spell.

"They are going to bury Colin early tomorrow, around five o'clock in the morning," said Mel.

"Bury him? Bloody where?"

"Sea burial, Tawny" replied Mel, holding the piece of paper that made it all legal and real.

"What's that all about?" asked Tawny.

"I'll come and get you in the morning, and you'll see," said Mel. "Be off, lad, and enjoy the ship."

Tawny spent the next couple of hours walking around the rear deck making small talk with Jimmy, George, Thomas, and William. By now, the boys knew all about the sea burial scheduled for tomorrow morning. They all wanted to witness Colin's burial, and they collectively decided that they wanted to pay their respects to Colin. A bell rang twice, and the boys quickly made their way down to the dining room. Tonight's special menu was chicken, rice, bread, gravy, and water. Tawny knew second helpings of his favorite part of the dinner, the bread and gravy, were going to happen.

Billy and his new little sidekick, Ian, entered, grabbed a tray of food, sat down, and started to eat. Tawny watched Billy, whose face was bruised, and Ian, who Tawny had known a little in the orphanage, throw food into their mouths. He came to a conclusion that these two boys were great entertainment during dinner: Billy, the large one, and Ian, the runt.

"Meet you topside," said George as he left the room.

"Ok," replied Tawny, still keeping Billy and Ian within eyesight.

The boys and their cot blankets spent the entire evening on the top deck huddled around each other. The main topic of discussion was Canada, and once in a while, Colin was brought up by his closest of friends. The skies cleared to reveal a fantastic site: The entire sky was filled with bright big stars, all flickering at different times. The boys stared into the heavens. The moon, big and bright, provided enough light to the great final spectacle of a very long and boring, not to mention smelly, day.

"Couple of more days left," said William, pondering the heavens.

"Can't wait to get my feet on land," said George, rubbing his belly.

"I heard that Canada is large," said Thomas, as he too gazed upward and then added, "Hundred times bigger than England."

Tawny noticed that several ship stewards were scrambling around on the bridge, all pointing at something on the right-hand side, possibly the port side or the other word that temporarily slipped Tawny's mind. Tawny walked toward the commotion and looked; there it was—a huge white mountain, sticking out of the water. As he looked harder at the object, he could see another one to the left. It was an unbelievable site. He yelled and waved to the other boys to come over.

"Iceberg," shouted a lady from first class who was leaning over the rail.

The boys watched this magnificent mountain of ice for hours, as the site gradually disappeared. It was late, and the boys were told by the stewards to return to their cabins.

Five o'clock in the morning came quickly. Mel pushed Tawny's shoulder a couple of times.

"Get up! Get up!" he demanded.

"All right, I'm up." Tawny rubbed the sleep from his eyes.

"A couple of others want to come too."

"Ok, get them up," said Mel.

William, George, Jimmy, Thomas, and Tawny followed Mel and the big lady up the stairs to the upper deck. A man dressed in white waited, and they all walked to the center of the ship, where another two men carrying rolled-up bedding met them.

"Let's make this quick," said the man in charge.

The man in white took a bible from his pocket, and after a few words were said, the bedding was thrown overboard into the icy water.

As the crew left, Tawny overheard one of them say, "Captain will be happy we used only six pieces of coal to weigh the bloke down."

Mel and the boys returned to their rooms, where it was warmer.

Breakfast on the fourth day was eggs, toast, porridge, and water. The boys ate and after an hour or two were topside again. The sky was a bright blue; the seas were much calmer; the temperature was rising; and by the afternoon, it was pleasant enough for the boys to remove their jackets. They enjoyed the afternoon by talking and exploring. The next few days mirrored each other with one exception; the temperatures got warmer each and every day.

Thomas, who slept next to Billy, came to Tawny somewhere on day eight or nine—it was hard for Thomas to keep time when every day blended into the next.

"Heard Billy telling Ian.... Something's up tonight. You know, I like Ian. Too bad he's fallen in with bad company."

Mel approached the boys quickly and, with a big smile, said, "Captain said we are going to dock tomorrow afternoon."

The dinner bell rang twice, as always, and the boys retreated to room 1F. After dinner, a huge plate of leftover chicken, chops, rice, gravies, and bread, Tawny and Thomas went back to the upper deck.

"We do nothing," said Tawny, after they discussed Billy and Ian for a couple of hours. By now it was dark, and Thomas agreed to the plan.

"Tomorrow is going to be a long day," said Tawny now feeling tired and full of bread and gravy—he had passed on the rice and had thirds of gravy and bread. "I'm going to bed." Tawny knew it was going to be tough getting sleep tonight, knowing they would dock in a few hours.

The boys were in their cots, most of them still awake and excited. Suddenly, Billy left the room and Ian scrambled after him. Tawny thought about following them and then remembered what he and Thomas had agreed to. About an hour later, Billy and Ian returned, clumsily got into their cots, and pretended to be sleeping. Tawny saw Ian put something between his thick bottom blanket and the cot frame.

Morning came and the boys were up early and excited about docking. George and William were excited just to get off the ship. Breakfast was the best yet. Everything left in the kitchen, even from the night before, was put in front of the boys. They had a feast.

Mel entered the dining room with instructions about docking and getting off the ship. Then, they went to the upper deck. The boys' mission was simple and easy: look for land.

Tawny noticed a strange thing: Ian and Billy were not together.

Ian, for the first time, was hanging around Jimmy, a boy of his same height, and Billy was hanging around another group of boys.

A passenger in first class shouted and pointed, "Land! There—land!" The boys looked at the horizon and saw a coastline similar to the one they left behind. The land got closer as the next hour passed. They could see the first-class passengers preparing for departure.

Suddenly, three agitated ship stewards approached Mel, they exchanged words, and now all four angry men approached the boys. "Come here. Quick, come here!" bellowed Mel.

The boys all gathered around him because they hadn't ventured far on this last day.

"Billy," asked Mel, "did you steal jewelry last night?"

"No," replied Billy. He turned his pockets inside out. "See, nothing."

"We were told it was the one with the bruise on his face," said a steward.

Tawny stepped forward and said, "Sorry gentlemen, Billy was with me last night. We talked almost all night, you know about docking and things." Billy looked without expression at Tawny.

Mel smiled with his lips closed, and the three ships officials left, perhaps to track down another group of boys. Suddenly, the woman tugged on Mel's jacket sleeve and pointed in a jerky motion. There it was—Canada, as big as life. The boys saw hills, rocks, and large pine trees. A steward approached slowly and handed Mel some papers. With a proud stance and a half-smile, he shouted, "Welcome to Halifax, boys; you are now in Canada."

Chapter 10

The Train from Halifax to Toronto

Leaving the ship was about as exciting for the boys as getting on. They lined up, single file, and then walked up the stairs, through the corridors, and eventually back through the door to the ramp. They walked down the wooden ramp toward a huge crowd of people who gathered to greet passengers, but not them. After they docked, Mel and the woman instructed the boys to walk to Terminal Building A. The building was relatively close, down the wooden pier to the first large building. Mel and the woman followed, toting their bags, taking in the sights and sounds, and perhaps trying to enjoy what little they could as it was their first visit to Canada.

"Should be thirty-six here," said Mel, as he motioned for the woman to count. The big lady counted heads, and, yes, thirty-six were present and accounted for.

"Well all right then," said Mel. "Wait right here; we shouldn't be too long."

Jimmy stood still and held his arms straight out from his sides, then closed his eyes, only to quickly open them, looked at Thomas, and said, "Can you feel the ground move?"

"Yes; close your eyes," answered Thomas, doing the same thing as Jimmy. Briefly, Tawny closed his eyes: It was strange, having his body sway with his feet securely planted on the ground. Before long, most of the boys were copying the stance and commenting on how it felt.

"Thanks," whispered Billy into Tawny's ear.

"I did it for Ian," replied Tawny. He quickly walked toward George and William.

The boys drifted toward the big sliding doors, the Terminal Building's doors. Standing inside, the boys turned one at a time to view the city of Halifax, Canada. The city was actually built on a hillside. All the buildings ran in a straight line, and from the boys' perspective, the buildings seemed to be piled on top of each another. It was late in the afternoon now, but the sun still felt warm and the wind was almost nonexistent. Just then, a man approached Mel. They spoke briefly. Then Mel stepped outside, looked up the giant hill, took a deep breath, and turned back to the boys. "Ok, up the hill."

Tawny knew that the boys would make it easily, but he wasn't so sure of the big lady or Mel. All thirty-six lads trekked up the hill, actually enjoying the scenery, especially the rows of buildings that cut into the side of the hill. The big lady had to stop several times to catch her breath, and Mel wasn't too far behind her, probably because he was overweight and just plain out of shape. Finally, there it stood—the Halifax Train Station. The station was a big building with a large wooden platform that gave everyone a spectacular view of the harbor. They could see ships lined up at their berths, and William spotted the Dominion, only now the ship looked smaller, and the words on the front were barely readable. A steam whistle blew, and a long train slowly approached the platform. Tawny noticed that several people waited along the entire length of the platform. The empty train stopped and people climbed aboard, dragging luggage, children, and boxes.

Mel ordered the boys to stay put until the other passengers boarded the train and then wait for his signal. Tawny quickly scanned the train and was amazed at its size. He also admired the train workers for getting so close to these massive machines. Mel led the boys into a car, which was dedicated solely for their use, and watched as they scrambled for seats. Mel took the front most seat in the car, and the big lady took the last seat at the rear. The porter quickly placed Mel's and the woman's bags in a storage compartment opposite the car's front entrance, and Mel handed the porter a piece of paper. The porter walked the entire length of the train car with his hands behind him looking for something wrong and finally left through the back door.

"Where we going?" called Jimmy.

Mel stood, turned around, and shouted, "We'll be two days to Toronto, lads. Relax, and enjoy the ride."

"Two days," said William, who sat next to Tawny.

The sun set over the horizon; they could see it from the windows. The train jerked and slowly started moving. Before long, the landscape changed from city to country. One thing was for sure, Tawny thought, Halifax was beautiful, but not very large when compared to London, the only city that the boys knew. The view from the train window was one of gentle, rolling, green hills; rocks; and pine trees in all directions. A porter carrying a large bag entered the car and handed out black and red boxes to everyone. The boxes, which were handed to everyone in the train car, contained lunch: a sandwich, a pickle, and a cookie. The entire train car seemed absent from talk as the sandwiches were devoured; the only noise heard was the clacking of wheels and the creaking of the wooden cars. About ten minutes later, the porter returned to gather the empty boxes and handed everyone a bottle of soda. They boys were glued to the windows, taking in the sights, but it was getting awkward to see through the dark. The train kept moving at a good pace and to Tawny, it moved very fast for its size.

"I'm scared," said Jimmy. Tawny turned around and said quietly, "Don't worry about it."

"I'm sure me Mum will find me," said little Jimmy, trying to hold back his tears.

"I'm sure she will, too," said Tawny, knowing in his heart she wouldn't.

It was a long night. The sleeping arrangements were terrible. The boys had to sleep sitting up on the hardwood benches. Morning finally came, and the sun peeked over the horizon and through the windows.

The porter entered, "Quebec City in twenty minutes!"

The train finally slowed and stopped, and the boys saw the station building, a huge mountain in the background, and crowds of people.

"Stay in your seats!" commanded Mel from his seat in the front of the train car.

The boys intently watched as another group of ten boys whom they recognized from the ship got off the train and were greeted by two, tall, dark-dressed men with buggies. From the windows, the boys watched the others climb onto the back of two horse-drawn wagons and leave. Before long, the train moved again. They were now paralleling a big river, even bigger than the Thames.

Farms were scattered all over the landscape, and each one had a big house and a bigger barn, surrounded by acres and acres of well-tended fields. The crops were bright green, and William said that everything looked better here than it did in London.

Tawny rose and asked Jimmy to change seats. Jimmy quickly sat in Tawny's seat next to William as Tawny now found the seat next to Billy, which allowed him the opportunity to finally get his concern off his chest.

"I don't know what you did with Ian last night," said Tawny. "I don't really care. I only want to protect Ian and my friends, I mean the friends from me orphanage."

"We had some fun, and we found something," said Billy.

"What?" asked Tawny.

Billy pulled a rag from his trousers, and after unraveling it, he showed Tawny the necklace that he and Ian had stolen.

"Where did you get that?" asked Tawny, now feeling a little agitated.

"From a rich family that didn't really need it," replied Billy, with a logic that confused Henry. "It was quite easy. The room was empty, and nobody was around. We didn't see anybody, so we took it."

Tawny held the necklace and admired its beauty and weight. He never saw anything this nice before, but he did remember a chain that Heddon had bought a year or so ago for his wife, but that it still didn't look this nice.

"It's wrong," said Tawny. "It's stealing."

"Yes, I know, but it was fun and exciting," replied Billy.

For the rest of the evening Billy and Tawny exchanged comments, feelings, and views on their early lives. It was strange that both of these boys had so much in common, but were completely different in values.

"I owe you," said Billy, "for sticking up for me."

"I can't believe your family just threw you out," said Tawny.

"Believe it. The streets are terrible," said Billy.

The rest of the day and the night passed so quickly as both of these lost souls talked and shared things while the train rumbled through the vast landscape. Tawny was curious how Billy could be so bold as to rob somebody, whereas Tawny himself would never think of doing something like that. Billy was shocked that Tawny's dad committed suicide. The sun started to rise, but neither Billy nor Tawny had slept.

Then, without warning, Mel sprang from a deep sleep, and shouted, "Stop that!"

Two boys in the front of the car were wrestling in the aisle. Mel stepped in to break it up, switched their seats with two other boys, and then returned to his own seat to finish his nap. Things were heating up between the boys for sure; close quarters usually does this.

The porter opened the door. "Kingston, next stop!" He vanished as quickly as he had appeared.

The train stopped and only a few people left and a few got on, but nowhere near the people who did at Quebec City, and there was no sign of other boys being picked up by wagons.

Quickly, the train again started. With a couple of loud blasts from its steam whistle, they slowly continued to move west. The porter appeared with his big tote bag and gave everybody another box, which, of course, held a sandwich. The hungry boys quickly devoured the egg-and-ham sandwich and waited for the porter to bring drinks. Eating the sandwich made Tawny think of Colin, and he wondered about his friend's body, which was for sure floating in the Atlantic Ocean somewhere between England and Canada.

"Three more hours," said Mel loudly, so that every one could hear him. He then leaned his head back to grab more sleep.

Suddenly, the train lurched to a stop; the cars jerked violently. Mel awoke from what seemed like a great sleep. The boys looked out the window to see if they could spot the reason why the train had suddenly stopped, but there was nothing to be seen.

"Look...Look!" screamed George.

"What is that?" shouted Thomas, now seeing it too.

"It's huge...and it's ugly," said Billy.

The porter opened the forward door and called out, "Relax, everyone. It's only a moose. We have to stop and let him cross. It's the rules. Only be a few minutes."

The boys were amazed at the size of this odd animal, this moose. Jimmy snickered at the name moose, and for the next hour or two, every other word out of Jimmy's mouth, then William's, and then everybody else's was "moose."

Ten minutes later, the train again moved slowly down the tracks. It wasn't long after that that the train again slowed and the boys, glued to the windows, saw rows of buildings, dirt roads, crowds of people, many horse-drawn buggies, and occasionally an odd-looking black machine with four spoke wheels and a seat with a canvas top covering it. These machines reminded Tawny of being back at the orphanage; he seen horseless carriages before but not one this small. He still was amazed that they could move under their own power, with no horse pulling.

The young porter poked his head into the train car. He looked at the boys and called out, "Toronto Station, next stop!"

Tawny looked at Billy and echoed, "'Toronto!'"

Chapter 11

The Train from Toronto to Waterford

After two short whistle blasts and then a third, longer, blast, the train quickly stopped in some kind of tunnel. The tunnel, it turned out, was the Toronto Train Station.

"Stay in your seats lads and wait for me," Mel shouted as he walked off the train.

The boys thought he looked a little upset. Mel held pieces of paper in his clenched fist. The boys watched the other passengers get off the train and walk away with their luggage and boxes. An hour or so later, Mel returned, entered the train car, and shouted, "Ok, lads, we're changing trains. Follow me, and don't get lost."

They gathered their few possessions and walked in single file down the boarding ramp only to enter a large common room with a lot of people milling about. Tawny noticed that the ceiling was curved and had a small window right in the center that provided light to the huge room.

"Next train doesn't leave until morning," said Mel.

"What are we to do?" asked the woman, fixing her blue-feathered hat.

"We'll stay here in the Toronto Station," replied Mel, checking out the benches, as though for possible sleeping arrangements.

"Ok, boys, take a seat," said Mel, sounding tired and agitated.

The boys grabbed bench seats along one side of the big room and watched the people come and go. Jimmy rose from his seat, went into the bathroom for a while, and returned to tell the others that it was the nicest bathroom he had ever seen. Mel, trying to compose himself, lined the boys up and told them to go one at a time and clean up. For the next several hours, Mel and the big lady watched as the boys went in and returned looking a little cleaner.

As the evening came and went, Mel gave the boys some local advertising pamphlets to read about Canada, Toronto, and other things that none of the boys could understand. He was visibly tired and seemed very uncomfortable. Tawny saw him drift off and then bob his head quickly and wake several times. Most of the boys curled up on the floor. Others just simply lay on the benches.

The night moved along at a snail's pace, and the big clock on the wall over the entrance never seemed to move. Billy and Tawny continued their discussions quietly in the corner, agreeing that they both had tragic lives. They also learned that they had things in common. Tawny still couldn't believe that Billy's parents had thrown him into the streets of London to fend for himself at the age of ten. Next to Billy and Tawny sat Jimmy and George, and they too were talking about their new lives in this new country.

Eventually, everyone slept, even if only for a few minutes. The ones who still slept were awakened by the sound of a cleaning cart being pushed past them on the way to the bathroom. Awake, they watched the elderly man push the cart. Rays of sunlight peeked through the window high up in the center of the ceiling. He knew by the light's color that it was early. He looked at the clock and confirmed that in fact he was correct. The hands read six o'clock. The boys were very hungry because they had missed dinner the night before. Their bellies, stretched out by the ship's meals, especially the last two, started to complain.

Mel rose, put his hand on his hips, stretched his back, and went for a walk, probably to get away from the complaints or possibly from the boredom of the train station. Mel returned after a little while with more crumpled pieces of paper in his hands. Tawny watched and thought by now Mel had collected a complete book. Mel yanked a single piece of paper out and straitening the corners he yelled, "Train leaves at eleven o'clock from track, umm, umm, track six."

"How may more train rides?" pleaded Thomas in a desperate voice to Mel.

"This will be the last one," replied Mel. He smiled mysteriously as he spoke.

The big lady stood, fixed herself slightly, and then sat back down. She knew that she had brought them on this journey to a better life in this new country called Canada, and this actually made her feel important. She waved and after a few seconds got Mel's attention. He walked toward her in a businesslike fashion, the kind of walk that warrants a straight back with arms swinging.

After a couple of minutes of quiet conversation, Mel returned, put his clipboard on the bench, and reluctantly said to the boys, "We can go for a walk through the city, but only if you behave and stay together. We will stay close to the station."

The boys all smiled a little, brushed off their wrinkled clothes, and formed their now-familiar single-file line.

"Ok, this way," said Mel, as he started to walk toward the exit.

The boys marched out the door into the bright sunlight and found themselves standing in a long line on a busy street. Buildings rose everywhere, and people were huddled on every street corner. Buggies and horses strolled around, and again they got to see a couple of those weird-looking black-painted machines with the four spoke wheels.

The air smelled cleaner to Tawny, and it definitely felt warmer than the London air. They walked down the street a mile or so and entered a park area that was well manicured and facing a big body of water.

"Is that the ocean?" asked William.

"Lake Ontario," said Mel, struggling to read the name from a pamphlet.

To the boys, it looked like the ocean, only greener and certainly not as wavy. For the next several hours, the boys sat on the grass, talked, and watched the waves of lake water gently crash on the shore. Tawny and Jimmy marveled at how well the park was kept and how clean it was. Perhaps, they had a work crew caring for it.

The morning passed quickly. Before long, Mel stood and shouted, "Ok, lads, let's go. We've a train ride to do."

The boys started their walk back to the station as the big lady counted heads. To Thomas, this had to be the tenth or twelfth time he had his head banged on.

"Thirty-six," she yelled to Mel. He waved like he was ignoring her.

As they entered the train station, Tawny heard a man yell, "Hamilton, Brantford, and Waterford—track six!"

Mel waved them on. "Ok, that's ours. Come on and let's hurry, lads."

By now, the boys knew exactly what to do. It didn't take long for them to get into single file and march to the train car. Soon, all the boys were again sitting in a train car, two to a seat. Mel took his now-traditional front seat, and the woman took the seat at the rear of the train car. The train moved slowly out of the dark station into the bright sunlight. The windows in this car were dirty and had smudge marks everywhere, and the seats were not as nice as the last train.

"How long this time?" asked William.

"Three hours or so," said the big lady. She took a rag and wiped at the window to see a little better.

The porter came around, this time wearing different colors and an odd-shaped hat, and again gave the boys a box that contained a ham sandwich.

"Tawny, Tawny!" called Mel. He stood and gestured to him to come forward.

Tawny stood, a little puzzled, went to the front of the train, and sat next to Mel.

"What's up, gov?"

"Have this for you. I almost forgot," said Mel, pulling an envelope from his jacket pocket. Tawny recognized it; the yellow envelope Heddon had given to Mel on the day they left the orphanage. Mel handed it to Tawny. On the envelope was written "Henry Dewberry."

"Go ahead, read it," said Mel, as he sat back and crossed his arms.

Tawny slowly opened the envelope and pulled out a single sheet of yellow paper. He looked at Mel.

"Go ahead...read it to me," said Mel in a quiet tone.

Dear Henry:
I hope your trip to Canada was a good one. I wanted to
write this letter to you to express my appreciation for your
loyal work at the orphanage. You have been a big help
over the past several years, and that is why I didn't send
you earlier. Remember that integrity, commitment, and honesty
are the three most important qualities of a successful man.
        Take care of yourself,
        Signed,
        Headmaster Heddon

"Only one," said Mel.

"What do you mean?" asked Tawny.

"You're the only one that got a letter. He told me so. He must have really liked you."

Tawny looked at the letter a couple more times and then folded it neatly and stuffed it into his pants pocket, taking extra precaution not to wrinkle it. It was the first letter he had ever received.

"Be off," said Mel, waving the boy away.

Tawny returned to his seat and stared out the window, now feeling better about himself. Deep in his heart, he had thought Heddon liked him. Now he knew for sure. Billy asked what happened, but Tawny just brushed it off by telling him that Mel wanted to know if the boys had any questions. Billy shook his head and said, "I have one. Where are we going?"

Before Tawny could answer him, the train stopped at the Hamilton station, and the boys could see lots of buggies and lots of people just standing still, watching the train. Several people left the train, toting luggage and boxes, but only five or six people got on. Then the train moved forward for another hour or so and stopped again in a town called Brantford, where the exercise of getting on and off repeated itself. The farm country was soothing to look at out the windows. Tawny thought, A lot of farms. For no logical reason, he had an awful feeling that the trip was coming to an end; he just felt it.

"Waterford, next stop," announced the skinny porter.

Mel stood and said a few words to the entire train car. Tawny thought he heard Mel mumble, "Good-bye." The big lady also addressed the boys. Her speech was very short. She definitely said good-bye.

"Where are we going?" asked Tawny, looking at Billy.

"Don't know," replied Billy. "I've been trying to find out for a week now."

From the storage compartment, Mel pulled a dusty old duffel bag and opened it. He withdrew rectangular pieces of wood with numbers painted on them. Each piece had a brown ribbon attached to either end. Every boy was handed a piece of numbered wood and was instructed to put it on around his neck. As Mel handed out the wood, the woman wrote on her clipboard. After a few minutes, every boy was numbered, labeled, and recorded.

"Sit still until I tell you," bellowed Mel. To Tawny, he sounded and acted like an army officer, the side of Mel that Tawny hated.

Tawny noticed that his number was 8, Billy's number was 30, and Jimmy's was 7. Thomas's was 14, William's was 15, and George's was 33. Tawny thought that the bag Mel had been toting around held clothes; now he realized that Mel had worn the same suit the whole trip. However, he had noted that the big lady was always changing her clothes and looked different each day.

Why are we wearing these stupid numbers? Tawny wondered. Something was about to happen. The entire train car of boys felt the nervousness that filled the air. Tawny knew something was going wrong here by the expressions on the boys' faces. Besides, he felt it, too.

At an arch, the train slowed to a stop. From the way the train had stopped, Tawny—with a little neck bending—could see the entire length of the train from his seat and started to count the cars. The fear in his stomach made him stop counting, and he noticed that the boys sitting on the left side of the train were straining their necks to see the entire length of the train. The view on Tawny's side, his right side, showed weeds, tall grass, and gigantic trees.

Mel stood and rumbled. "We'll be off in a minute or two. We have to wait for the others to leave first."

The boys sat straight in their seats, terrified, with no idea of what would to happen to them. Tawny noticed that even Billy was even acting strange. There were a few loud noises, and at each one of these noises the boys jerked in anticipation and fear. Tawny felt a terrible sense of emptiness overwhelm him, and he was not alone.

Chapter 12

The Final Stop

Tawny and the others sat in their seats like frozen ghosts. Tawny's palms were clammy, his eyes large, and he felt so empty. Billy looked at Tawny and said, "What's happening?"

"Don't know; just have to wait," answered Tawny, trying hard to do the same.

Mel was quickly glancing around from window to window, trying to see something and then finally Mel saw the wave from the station, which came from the man on the platform, "Ok, lads, let's go; follow me."

"Hurry, we don't want to keep them waiting."

"Keep who waiting?" belted out William. Mel didn't answer.

All thirty-six boys now stood next to the train on large gravel rocks as they stood in two lines of eighteen.

Mel scanned the formation and apparently felt it was all right to proceed. "Follow me." Both lines, with Mel leading the way, marched to the platform. The big lady followed behind.

"Don't talk," ordered Mel.

As they neared the platform, Tawny saw several wagons and horses, all in an organized row on one side of the station building.

"Me mum will find me, I know she will," said Jimmy, who was directly behind Tawny and feeling the anxiety. The boys quickly came up on the station platform and soon they all stood on the wooden planks, facing the hundreds of onlookers. The small black-and-white sign over their heads read, "Waterford."

Tawny looked around and saw many people staring at them, especially two young girls who were lying on the ground very close to the train. Tawny and the others were taking this seriously, and they all had the same question, "Why were the people staring at them?" and "What was going on?" He heard Jimmy whimpering behind him and decided that he had heard enough. He turned his head slightly then quickly grunted, "Stop that!"

Jimmy did not hear him, so Tawny turned his head completely around and, talking out of the corner of his mouth, said softly and sternly, "Stop that, Jimmy!"

Tawny saw the first wagon slowly make its way to the platform and a big man approached the woman and handed her something. She yelled four numbers out loud and Mel instructed those boys to leave their spots, go to the front of the line, remove their wooden plates, and then leave them with the big lady.

The first four boys, following directions, stepped out of line, walked down the platform, removed their tags, and got into the waiting wagon.

"Where are they going?" asked Tawny in a soft, scared voice that only looked for an answer, since he knew neither Mel nor the big lady would give him one. Billy yelled something from his spot at the rear of the line and, to Tawny, it sounded like, "How are we going to stay in touch?" or something like that. Mel quickly shouted, "Be quiet and stand still until your number is called." Tawny put his hand by his side and felt his loose pant leg and Heddon's letter that was still there, folded inside. He also felt the comb that he had crafted into a false key to use back in the orphanage. These were the only two things he owned other than his clothes and old brown shoes. Tawny occasionally stole a quick glance at the two girls lying on the grassy hill.

He saw them smile back a couple of times and thought that the one with the wide brown eyes and light brown hair was pretty. The surroundings looked much like England, but here there were many more horses, it was dustier, and the river was smaller.

The big lady called the next five numbers, and five more scared boys left the line for a parked wagon and quickly left. Then the next six numbers were called out and Tawny watched George walk past him and felt sad, as he might be losing another friend.

"Bye," whispered Tawny in George's direction. He hoped to see him and his other friends again, someday.

"Number 8!" When he heard the number, it seemed even louder than the train whistle, and Tawny left the line in a trancelike state.

Mel, under his breath said, "Bye, gov," and Tawny heard it, turned to Mel, and then smiled back at him. Tawny shook his head a couple of times to break the trance and then remembered the letter that Heddon had written to him and only him. He made himself change his demeanor and with a renewed confidence he walked toward the wagon, now realizing that Jimmy's number was also called and thinking that this was a good thing; at least he would have one friend with him.

Suddenly, Jimmy stumbled on his shoelace and, falling forward, crashed into Tawny. Tawny hit the gravel face first. He lay there for a second or two and then, as he regained his stance, finally truly saw the most beautiful brown eyes he had ever laid eyes on, and they were looking back at him. These eyes belonged to one of the two girls—just staring at him and, my god, it was a beautiful sight! Tawny smiled at her, even though it was only for an instant, then stood, brushed off the dust, and climbed into the wagon. He didn't even notice the small cut over his right eye. Instead, an unfamiliar warmth flashed through him. What happened next startled all five of the boys who now sat in the wagon. Not once but twice the farmer commanded the boys to remove their shoes. With no reason given to them, the boys handed their shoes to the farmer, who stashed them in a burlap sack.

Once the boys were situated in the wagon, the farmer drove the horses forward and, actually, the ride felt good as the sun beat down on their tired young bodies.

Tawny looked back at the platform. William and Thomas were still standing in line. Tawny tried to wave to them but they didn't see the gesture. Lying back in the wagon, knowing deep inside that he would never see his friends again, he forced himself to think about that cute girl he had just seen and the warm feeling returned, and he really needed it now. The surroundings, just like the hundreds of farms he had seen from the train, looked peaceful. Soon, he was almost napping.

The wagon moved down the main street, passing houses, and was now entering farmland. Jimmy noticed that George was waving from the wagon in front of them, so Jimmy kept waving back until the framer smacked his hand and told him to sit down. Jimmy looked back; the wagon following them had nobody he recognized. The evening air felt really crisp and clean. It even smelled nice, thought Jimmy, of grassy fields, animals, and plants.

After an hour of moving slowly over the gravel roads, Jimmy noticed that George's wagon was no longer in front of them. The wagon trailing was gone as well.

"Get up," said Jimmy as he nudged Tawny.

"What do you want," said Tawny rubbing his eyes and quickly coming back to reality.

"Sorry about the spill," said Jimmy, "I'm really sorry I fell into you."

"It's all right," replied Tawny, wiping at his dirty face with his shirtsleeve.

He felt a small stinging over his right eye; the blood had crusted over it. Tawny picked the small scab, pressured his finger on it, and then looked at Jimmy and asked, "Jimmy, is it all right?" He removed his finger only for a second, and Jimmy looked into his face. "It's fine."

"Just me and you, now," said Jimmy with sadness in his voice.

"Yes it is," said Tawny. "Just me and you."

The wagon ride was taking forever. How much longer? thought Tawny. Just then, the farmer grunted and pointed to the left. The boys looked in that direction. About a mile off, they saw a large red barn, a medium-sized dark red barn, several scattered small buildings, and a large white house, trimmed in blue. The wagon neared, the boys were looking at everything they could see since they knew that this must be the new life in Canada.

"Who's the oldest?" growled the farmer, making the turn into the farm.

"I think he is," said Jimmy as he pointed to Tawny.

"How old are you boy?" asked the farmer in a rough voice.

"Twelve," said Tawny, and then remembered, "almost thirteen."

The farmer pointed to each boy, and they all spoke their ages; Jimmy was nine, and the others were all ten or eleven. The land around the farm was well kept, and the barns wore fresh paint. The huge house was two stories tall and had a white porch surrounding the whole house. Jimmy saw a swing from a big tree on the right side of the house and imagined using it and having a good time, just like he used to do in England. The sun was setting slowly into a beautiful sky of pinks and blues.

"This looks like a nice place," said Tawny. Jimmy looked up at him and smiled, "Yes I think so." But neither of them really knew what to expect from this better place called Canada.

The wagon stopped directly in front of the big red barn. The farmer climbed down and opened the big doors. Inside was a neatly organized barn with tons of hay baled and stacked.

"In here," he shouted as the shoeless boys got off the wagon, entered the barn clumsily, and then found themselves standing in a semicircle facing the open doors. The farmer, reeking of bold confidence, spoke very loud and clear, "This is your home, you will sleep here, you will eat here, and you will work here. I'm the boss, and you will call me Mr. Lathrope. We will get up at sunrise, and we go to bed at sunset."

Lathrope cleared his throat. "We have well over two hundred acres to work, so I suggest that you get a good night's sleep." Lathrope laughed and returned to the wagon.

Jimmy looked up with tear-filled eyes and said, "This is our home? You mean in here?" Tawny smiled back at the little boy and said, "It could be worse; we could be outside."

Mr. Lathrope left in the wagon. All five of these young lost boys stood in a tight circle, feeling alone, shoeless, betrayed, and scared in the huge smelly red barn.

It didn't take long before they walked the entire length of the barn to check the place out. There were four huge brown horses, and each had its own stall. They were well groomed and had water trays and hanging feeders full of food.

Tawny noticed an upper loft that held nothing except hay. That's it, he thought. "We'll bed up there." One at a time, they climbed the wooden ladder to the barn loft. The loft was hot until one of the boys opened the small door at one end, and the welcome breeze actually felt good. Each chose his spot, flattened out hay, and made a bed. They began talking about their weeklong trip, and words like porter, moose, steward, dominion, and countless others were bantered around as they finally started to relax. Peter, a small boy, told the others where he came from, and Tom followed with his life story. Jack took his turn next, followed by Mark. Tawny went next, and then Jimmy went last. The other three had come from another orphanage similar to the one Tawny and Jimmy lived in. Over the next two hours, they shared their experiences.

Mr. Lathrope entered the barn, followed by an elderly lady in an apron who carried a large tray. "Here, boys," the farmer said, "you'll need this. Enjoy it!"

They came down the wooden stairs, like mice in search of cheese, and they found five glasses of milk and several large buns. Tawny had never smelled food this pleasing. And it tasted as good as it smelled. They quickly devoured the buns, and the milk tasted fresh. Leaving the tray on the ground next to the door, the boys retreated to the loft with full warm bellies and curled up on their hay beds. They continued to talk about the steamship, the train, the experiences, and the new place called Canada. Then after an hour or so, they nodded off to sleep.

Regardless of the conversation, and the great meal they just had, the boys were still wrestling deep inside for answers of why they were here in a barn working for a farmer thousands of miles from England.

Chapter 13

The Troublesome Walk Home

Lizzie and Clara lifted themselves up, brushed off the grass, and started back toward the town square. Most of the crowds had left the station, and it was now safe to leave the grassy hill.

"Where did they come from?" asked Lizzie.

"Why didn't they have any luggage?"

"What kind of English were they speaking?"

"Sounded like English, but not like us," said Lizzie, now full of questions.

"I'll ask my Dad," said Clara.

"No, you can't!" whispered Lizzie. "You'll get into trouble."

Clara shook her head and still couldn't get over the fact that her Dad had acquired more brothers for her. That her father had paid for these boys seemed to bother her.

"Lizzie!" yelled Mary, now standing on the corner by the General store. "I'm going home. Are you coming?"

"Yes," answered Lizzie, still dazed and confused.

"Clara, do you mind if I walk home instead of taking the buggy?" asked Lizzie.

"I don't mind. I'll see you at church tomorrow." They hugged.

"Bye," said Lizzie. Walking gave her more time to think. She needed to digest what had happened at the train station. She walked up Queen Street, toward the clock. The crowds in the town square had thinned; only a handful of people still moved about, finishing their business. Buggies moved in single file to Main Street as families returned to their homes carrying supplies and dry goods.

Which way did Tawny go? Lizzie asked herself. She grinned and thought, Such a funny name for a boy.

When Lizzie got home, she went directly to her room, changed into her everyday dress, and rinsed her face in the porcelain bowl. Mary was across the hall, doing the same. Lizzie couldn't remember when she was so puzzled. She couldn't wait to ask father about what she and Clara had seen.

Lizzie's mother had dinner almost made, and the aroma from the kitchen carried a hint of basil with the baked chicken and potatoes. Father had returned home, parked the work wagon, put the feedbag on Big George, and came in, tired and sleepy. Fred also followed his dad, went to change his clothes, and to also wash up for dinner. Arthur and Cecil were already primed for the evening meal and were playing in the living room with blocks of wood and a few other small toys.

Will entered the dining room, looking refreshed, sat down in his chair, and watched his kids playing on the floor.

"We lost two hours work today, Nell," said Will complaining about the picture-taking exercise. Nellie reassured him that everything was all right. Mary entered the room and looked at her father, "Is Hubrey Spence here yet?"

"No."

Mary, still in a world of her own, went into the living room and sat in a chair and watched Arthur and Cecil, who now were repeatedly peeking out the window. Uncle John arrived, exchanged pleasantries with Nellie, grabbed a bun, and then sat next to Will at the big table in the dining room.

Uncle John dropped a few pieces of his bun on the table. "Should be a damn fine picture."

"Lost two hours," said Will.

"Don't worry, you'll be paid for it," replied Uncle John.

"Fine. Want a drink, brother?" Will knew what his brother's answer would be.

"Sure. Sounds great," said Uncle John.

Will rose, made his way to a cupboard, and returned with a couple of glasses and a bottle of Canadian whiskey. He poured two glasses.

Lizzie entered the room looking very worried and sat at the big table next to her dad. She silently prepared for a lengthy discussion on what she had witnessed at the train station. "Daddy?"

Will looked down at Lizzie. "What is it, dear?"

"Why were farmers buying the boys that arrived on the train?" Lizzie looked deep into her father's eyes. Will returned her gaze with a wrinkled brow. This was the first time Lizzie had asked a question with so much intensity and passion.

"Honey, I don't really know. But I'll find out." Lizzie put her head down on the table and couldn't stop thinking about who had bought Tawny.

"Damn political people, damn those tobacco companies," Uncle John growled, sipping whiskey. "You know that the government and tobacco representatives are in bed together. They allow these young children to come here."

"Farmers need help to meet the harvest demands," said Will.

"Harvest is coming. Why don't they bring kids in from Toronto or from other Canadian cities and pay them?" asked Uncle John. "Not England; the way of life is so different over there. We have had nothing but trouble since this started ten years ago."

"Somebody is getting rich off those boys," said Will.

"The money is going back to England," Uncle John then added, "If Canada is to survive as a country, we need to keep the money here and use our own labor resources."

The knock on the front door couldn't have come a better time; the table discussion was surely going to heat up. Lizzie thought that she understood most of what her Uncle John and Dad were saying. Everyone stopped what they were doing. Suddenly, Mary bolted from her seat, fixed her dress in mid-flight, stroked her hair on the run, and then opened the door.

"Hello, folks," said Hubrey Spence.

"Hello," replied Mary. "Please come in."

Hubrey followed Mary into the dining room, waving at Will and Uncle John as if they were old friends.

"Here, these are for you." Hubrey handed Mary a couple of fresh-cut flowers. Lizzie watched and then laughed to herself; the flowers looked exactly like the ones at the Colin's house next door. She had passed the same flowers a few hours earlier on the way home, and she knew if she looked right now, the flowers would be missing.

"Thank you." Mary guided Hubrey to a chair in the living room. "I'll put these in water. Would you like a drink?"

"Sure," said Hubrey.

Mary left and, after a minute or so, returned carrying a green glass vase, which she placed on the coffee table, and handed Hubrey a glass of water.

"I'm sure the man would like something stronger," said Uncle John.

"Hubrey," said Will, "come here."

Hubrey went to the big table and then sat next to Uncle John. Soon, all three were toasting the town hall again, and again...and again.

"Mary," called Mother from the kitchen.

"Coming, Mom." Mary yanked Lizzie from her chair, and then they went into the kitchen. They all brought out plates while Mary made sure that the best silverware and linen were used; this was clearly a special meal, at least in Mary's view.

After dinner, Hubrey and Mary sat on the porch. They continued talking about the picture-taking process, his life in Brantford, his goals in life, and other matters that interested only Mary.

After the dishes were cleaned, Nellie came into the living room, sat in the chair next to the front door—her favorite—and began darning socks. Uncle John and Will discussed town matters and sipped on Canadian Club. Arthur and Cecil still played quietly on the floor, and Fred went to the shed to feed and groom Big George. Lizzie sat and stared at her Dad and her Uncle John. She wanted them to talk more about the incident at the train station and what happened earlier today.

"Daddy," said Lizzie.

"Yes?" Will answered; he knew the questions were going to come again.

"When you buy somebody, how long can you keep them?" she asked.

"You can't own a person," said Will. "It's against the law."

"The farmers are renting these boys for a while." Uncle John added, trying to help Will with the difficult explanations. "They will help in the harvest."

"Will they go home after that?" asked Lizzie.

"No, I don't think so," said Will. "They will probably stay at the farm and work the next year's crop as well."

"Who is Mr. Lathrope?" Her Dad and Uncle had been drinking and maybe the answers would be a bit more truthful.

"He's the new farmer. He bought the old Fell Farm a couple of years ago. You know, after old Marty Fell died." Uncle John knew everybody and everything that happened in the county. The Fell Farm, thought Lizzie. This must be where Becky Fell used to live, an old classmate of hers that she knew a couple of years ago, until she stopped coming to school. She was relieved and somewhat excited because now she knew where Tawny was.

It wasn't far away, probably the same distance as Clara's house, but the difference is that Clara's house is down the road and the Fell Farm is through the fields. It also bordered Clara's farm at one end.

Will glanced outside, apparently to see how Mary and Hubrey were doing, as he did every so often.

"Hubrey," said Uncle John. "We have your check ready."

"Hubrey opened the door and walked to the table. Uncle John pulled a piece of paper from his pocket and handed it to Hubrey and then stood and shook his hand.

"Thank you, sir," said Hubrey. "I will return next week with the pictures."

"That will be fine," said Uncle John. "Meet us here. One of the boys will come and get me; I live just down the street." Uncle John's words were slightly slurred. Lizzie knew that this was about the time he usually left and walked home.

"Bye." Uncle John staggered out the door and down the street.

Will retreated to bed after he kissed Nellie good night on the cheek. She continued sewing in the living room.

"I'd better be going," said Hubrey. "It's three hours to Brantford."

"It's a beautiful night for a ride," said Mary. "Wish I could come along."

"I'll see you again in a week," Hubrey said, smiling.

"I'll be waiting right here." Mary grinned from ear to ear, perhaps on one hand feeling excited and on the other sad to see Hubrey go. The young man slowly reached out, grabbed Mary's hands, and looked directly into her eyes. Then he leaned toward her. Mary knew what was going to happen, and Lizzie just watched intently as Mary closed her eyes and Hubrey kissed her gently on the corner of her mouth.

Hubrey then said his good-byes to Nellie. He turned and walked around the corner and shouted back to Mary, who was still standing and watching, "good-bye."

"Bye." Mary now stood in a daze; Lizzie giggled to herself as she watched Mary spin like a top while looking to the sky. Lizzie sat back down at the big table, now completely empty, and started to think about Tawny and the answers she had just heard from her father and Uncle John. These answers didn't help her, but they eased her mind a little. She thought of Clara and her new problem of having five more brothers that she didn't want. Lizzie had changed so much in the past twelve hours and really did not understand what was happening to her.

"Why don't you go to bed, sweetie," said her mother, who was still sewing and taking advantage of the peace and quiet that now filled the house.

"Yes, Mom," answered Lizzie. She walked slowly up the stairs, still thinking about the boys, the farmers paying for them, and then finally the blonde curly-haired boy with the deep blue eyes, the one named Tawny.

Chapter 14

The New Better Life in Bloomberg, Ontario, Canada

The barn doors flew open with an awful crackling noise and there stood Lathrope in the opening, with his hands on his hips.

"Get up, you lazy English bastards!"

The boys came quickly to their feet and climbed one by one down the ladder. They then stood in front of the farmer, hoping it was a dream, but it was not. Lathrope stood there, tall, rigid, and very intimidating.

"Got to go to work. Can't sleep all day," he barked. "Into the wagon." The boys piled into the wagon outside the barn doors, and they were off as the early darkness was replaced by a lighter gray dawn. It was damp this early in the morning, and the ground was mushy underfoot. They hoped it would warm up when the sun rose. Soon, the wagon stopped before a small square barn that had covered windows on both sides, which actually looked like a small replica of the big red barn that now was their home.

"We will be cleaning out these cure barns," bellowed Lathrope.

He told the boys how to clean a cure barn, but really didn't do a good job because it was too noisy during the short ride to the first cure barn. He stepped off the wagon and pushed Jack and Mark into the first barn, threw them a shovel, gestured with his arms for them to get started. Jack just looked at Mark in puzzlement. The wagon moved down the trail to the next cure barn, where Lathrope motioned for Peter and Tom to get out and threw them a shovel as well. Finally, Tawny and Jimmy were at the third cure barn and, yes, they had a shovel thrown at them. Tawny wondered how many of these little barns were there.

Lathrope quickly snapped the reins and the horse-drawn work wagon exited slowly.

It was a smelly job and the ground felt spongy to their bare feet, but it didn't take long to clean out these small barns from top to bottom. When this was done, a pile of sludge lay outside, next to the door opening, and the boys didn't know what to do with it.

Opening the two side barn windows was a little tricky, but Tawny, who had the height advantage, barely reached the hook and latch, and he opened the windows.

It didn't take long for Lathrope to return and soon he was there, watching the boys as they piled the brown sludge into the wagon.

"Hurry," said Lathrope, who seemed annoyed and nervous. After they loaded the sludge into the wagon, the boys had to climb in on top of it and, before long, they were soaked with the smelly wet brown stuff.

After all three small cure barns were somewhat cleaned, the wagon went to another field, where they had to spread the sludge over dirt. Lathrope, still sitting on the wagon, watched the dirt-soaked boys throw sludge over the ground and said, "Come on, hurry up; we have more to do."

The boys climbed back into the wagon as the sun rose in the blue sky, which made the barn sludge a little crusty, but still it smelled and felt terrible. Lathrope dropped the pairs of boys off again in front of three other cure barns, only this time he gave no instructions and just left, only to return a little later to pick up the sludge.

Ring! Ring! Ring! They heard a loud bell, and they looked toward the main house.

"Get in," said Lathrope.

On the ride back to the big barn, Tawny noticed that Lathrope was a tall, thick man, tanned and wrinkled. He had dark eyes and big rough hands, and he stood straight all the time. He never smiled.

Lathrope, without saying a word, dropped off the boys at the door to the big barn door and drove the wagon to the main house. The boys watched as several people scurried around the main house as Lathrope climbed down off the wagon. Jimmy commented on what seemed to be a slight commotion among several ladies who wore white aprons. Lathrope walked through the front door. They almost didn't see the tall lady who came out of the back door and approached them, carrying a large tray covered with a white cloth.

As the lady neared them, Jack turned to Tawny. She had a kind-looking older face. The woman set the tray on the ground in front of the boys and didn't say a word and didn't smile, but simply left. Tawny removed the cover; more fresh buns and several glasses of milk! It didn't take the boys long to eat their breakfast, despite how bad they all smelled.

The front door opened with a loud bang, and Tawny knew Lathrope was on his way. Lathrope picked up the boys in the wagon, and away they went to clean more cure barns. The entire day was spent cleaning these small cure barns and by Mark's calculations, he and Jack had done seven in total, which meant that they must have cleaned twenty-one barns.

It was very late in the day—almost dark—when the work wagon returned the boys to the big barn. They climbed off the wagon, their backs sore and their feet bloodied and aching, and they made their way into the comfort of the big red barn.

"Get in there and take off your clothes," yelled Lathrope, motioning to an area on the right side of the barn. Confused, the boys slowly entered and immediately started to remove their filthy clothing.

"Put them down here." Lathrope stood rigid, with his hands on his hips, and motioned to a spot on the barn floor.

The boys finally had all their clothes lying in a pile, and there they stood, all six of them, naked as the day they entered this world, stark white bodies and dark dirty faces, hands, and feet.

Puberty had already struck Tawny and Tom, and the other boys were trying hard not to look. Three ladies approached the door carrying buckets of water and soap as the first lady walked toward them and with a bristle brush she scrubbed their faces, hands, and feet. She was not a gentle lady; she made Tawny lift his arms and bristled his pits with tremendous effort.

Tom watched in horror; he knew he was next in line to receive a hellish washing. The next lady then rinsed them off with cold water by throwing it over their heads, quick and fast. Now, this part of the ordeal felt good, but there was still soap everywhere on them. The third lady repeated the rinse exercise, which managed to get most of the soap off, and she also handed each boy a fresh white towel.

After they were dry, the ladies returned to the main house carrying the old brown-stained smelly clothes and the used towels. The boys were still naked but much cleaner and a little colder. Tawny and Tom were also bruised by the scrubbing. Around fifteen minutes later, Lathrope returned carrying a bag, which he threw into the center of the barn. "Put these on!"

The boys quickly riffled through the bag and found pants, shirts, underwear, and hats, but no shoes. They must have looked like a pack of wolves eating a carcass. Some clothes fit and some had to be torn to fit, but most of all, the clothes were clean and dry and felt good on their skin.

The dinner lady, as they now called her, entered, dropped off a tray and when the cloth was removed, there were golden brown pieces of chicken, bread, and milk. Tawny enjoyed the slightly warmed chicken and couldn't remember the last time he had chicken this good. The chicken on the Dominion was just passable. After several minutes of thinking about food, he decided that it wasn't worth the effort. Besides, he was extremely tired.

He also enjoyed the milk because it was fresh and creamy and it simply tasted great. Tawny also now realized that the milk at the orphanage had been watered down.

Nighttime eventually came, the boys retreated to the loft, and one by one nodded off. Tawny couldn't recall when he had last felt so sore and tired. He simply closed his eyes and was out like a light.

The next morning came too fast, and so did the next five mornings, as the entire week was spent cleaning the cure barns that dotted the farm. Each day seemed identical to the previous one; the only difference was that, on two of the days, it rained a little. Tawny believed that it rained more in London than it rained here in Canada.

One night, Tawny overheard Jimmy whispering to himself just before he fell asleep, "You call this a better life?" Tawny and the others really agreed with Jimmy, but they didn't discuss it much; they were afraid that Lathrope might hear them. Tawny saw Lathrope sneaking around the barn a couple of times during the past few days. Trying to hear something, he figured.

Lathrope had promised the boys that on Sunday, their half-rest day, he would take them for a ride. The boys' excitement grew—they were going somewhere, maybe into town or, heck, just down the road would be fine!

"Where do you think he'll take us?" asked Jimmy.

"Don't know," answered Tawny, as he climbed down the loft ladder.

It was Sunday, and it felt really strange to them that they were awake and actually waiting at the barn door for Lathrope to arrive. They wanted their ride, and Lathrope was nowhere to be found. Usually, he shouted at them before they were awake.

After about an hour, the sun was in its full glory and still no Lathrope.

"What do you think they grow on this farm?" asked Tom.

"All I see is plants for miles and miles," replied Peter.

"Did you see those big ones with purple flowers out in the back field?" asked Jack.

"Yes, they were bloody beautiful, they were," said Mark.

"I heard Mister Lathrope say something about tobacco," said Tawny, who stood and looked out the barn door toward the main house.

"You mean cigarettes, like the ones my father smokes?" asked Jimmy.

"Yes," answered Tawny.

"How do they do it?" asked Mark.

"I don't know," replied Tawny. Just then, a wagon approached from the horse barn, a shorter but longer barn that housed the draught horses, work wagons, and a few cows.

The boys left the barn and were waiting outside in the damp cool air of this Canadian fall morning.

"Ok, boys, hop up," growled Lathrope. "I'm going to show you the farm boundaries. You better remember them, because if I catch you beyond them, you'll be in a lot of trouble. You don't want any trouble from me."

The boys just stared at Lathrope and in unison, shook their heads no.

The wagon moved up the entrance road and for a split second or two, it actually felt like the boys were going off the farm for their ride. Just short of the main road, the wagon turned right, and now they were riding on a small dirt road that paralleled the fence for a few minutes. Then the wagon made another right-hand turn onto yet another small dirt pathway.

"This is the marker road," grunted Lathrope at the boys. They rolled on for a couple of miles, and then turned right onto another dirt road and Lathrope pulled on the reins and the horses stopped.

"Do you see the white pole?" Lathrope pointed to a small white pole, half-buried in the ground.

"Yes," the boys said, almost in unison.

"That is the property stake. Don't go past it. I better not catch any of you past this marker."

Again the boys all shook their heads. If Lathrope was trying to instill the fear of God into them, it was working.

The wagon rolled on for a while longer, and then Tawny noticed that on their left was a small creek that was situated on the corner of Lathrope's land. The wagon bordered the creek bank for a long time and then it stopped. A huge elm tree grew on the bank of the creek.

"What do they call it?" asked Mark.

"You mean the creek?" said Lathrope.

"Yes."

"It's part of the Grand River system; I like to call it Lathrope Creek." The farmer seemed a bit proud of this and, for the first time in a week, they actually heard his normal voice.

"Nice here," whispered Tawny, looking at Jimmy.

"The creek is the marker," said Lathrope. "Don't cross it. Mr. Culmer does not like trespassers. Come to think of it, I don't care for them either." For the third time that day, the boys all agreed by shaking their heads.

To Tawny, this place was beautiful, with the big elm tree, the grassy bank, the big flowers, and the creek; it looked a like a little piece of heaven.

Is it the same river that flowed past the train station? he wondered. Water often flows in strange directions, another tidbit he learned at the orphanage. Tawny wanted to believe this stream was the same one.

Soon the boys had traveled the perimeter of the farm and it was nearing breakfast time, so Lathrope dropped off the boys at the big barn.

After Lathrope left, the boys knew they had some time to themselves, and soon the kitchen lady brought a tray out to the barn. They feasted on sticky buns and milk.

Tawny had mentioned to the others that they should find a lantern, some blankets, and other things to make their sleeping loft a bit more comfortable. Most of their free afternoon was spent salvaging through the barn, changing their bedding straw, fixing some wooden crates for tables, removing cobwebs, and trying to fire up an old lantern. They even found two old gray blankets that smelled like horses and a half-used bottle of whiskey stashed in the horse feeder tray. Soon satisfied that their new home was adequate, Mark and Peter were looking out the barn loft door and announced that several buggies were going down the main road. "Where do you suppose they are going?" asked Peter.

"Into town, of course," replied Mark.

The boys enjoyed using of their free time talking and learning more about each other, and they shared the experiences of their young but eventful lives. They even ventured out and looked in the other barn, which housed the workhorses, cows, and hogs, knowing that Lathrope had left with his family to join the other buggies, all going into town.

It took only a week to toughen the soles of their feet, and the hay now felt like dead grass instead of cutting blades. They talked about getting their shoes back, but none of the boys knew what to do about the situation. They all agreed they were trapped on this farm and even if they wanted to escape, they wouldn't know where to go.

"Do you think we'll ever get our bloody shoes back?" asked Peter.

"Probably not," replied Mark. "That's so we don't run away, you know."

"Hard to go anywhere with no shoes," said Jimmy, and then added, "Don't know where to go, neither." All they knew was that they were near a town called Waterford, in a vast country named Canada.

They did feel somewhat relieved in knowing that other boys were doing the same thing that they were doing, and that they probably felt the same way as well. Tawny had seen this behavior before at the orphanage, when the boys felt down and out; the only way to beat that feeling was to try and feel good about yourself.

"What are we going to do?" asked Tom, looking spent.

"Nothing, at least for now," replied Tawny, as he smiled a little. Tawny had developed a plan to make him and the others feel better and soon, he would share it with all the boys.

Chapter 15

The Sleepover

An entire week had passed, and each day, Lizzie thought about Tawny. It was Sunday, and Lizzie looked forward to her day at church, even though she only wanted to talk to Clara. She knew school was starting soon, and both she and Clara had only a week or two left for a sleepover. Perhaps she could find out what was going on with the slave boys.

Clara and Lizzie took their usual seats in the church, which allowed them to talk quietly to each other and catch up on the week's happenings. Finally, the service ended, and the girls made their way outside. They knew fall was approaching; the air was growing cooler and crisper.

"Maybe next week, one day?" asked Lizzie.

"I'll ask my Mom," said Clara, as she waved good-bye.

Lizzie strolled home, thinking of the boy called Tawny; he became the only thing she thought about when she was alone.

She even thought that there was something wrong with her, thinking about a boy a dozen times a day, and she confided in Mary about these new thoughts. Mary, who was very actively thinking about Hubrey Spence most of the time, only told her that it was normal and it was part of growing up. This helped Lizzie feel a little better. Lizzie walked home, which was only a few blocks away, and continued thinking about all that had happened over the past week.

Clara had told Lizzie what her dad had said, that the boys were farm help and that they would all be sent back after harvest. Clara also told Lizzie about a boy named Billy and how her father had complained all week over dinner about this boy and how much trouble he was. Clara had told Lizzie that her dad locked Billy in a cure barn for three days, with no food or water.

"Hello, Lizzie," said Mrs. Glimsky, who was sweeping her sidewalk.

"Hello," replied Lizzie, forcing her from her thoughts and back to the real world.

Lizzie entered the house and went to her room. She could hear Mary across the hall, getting dressed and doing the final preparations for her visit from Hubrey today. Soon, the whole family was downstairs, clamoring around the living room and ready for the Sunday meal. To Lizzie's way of thinking, dinner was almost ready only because of the way it smelled.

"Come eat," said Mary. Fred, Arthur, and Cecil took their seats, and father sat at the table head. Lizzie came to the big table, looked at the place settings, thought for a moment, and said, "Who's going to sit there?"

"That's for Hubrey Spence," chuckled Fred, loud enough for Mary to hear, although she was in the kitchen.

"If he shows up," added Arthur, even louder, holding a fork in one hand and the knife in the other.

Mary entered the room, carrying a huge plate of pork chops and applesauce. "He'll come and see me today; he promised."

Will said prayers, and they continued with their Sunday routine. If all was to plan, thought Lizzie, Uncle John should arrive in about fifteen minutes, just in time for coffee and crumb cake.

They were almost finished when there came a knock at the door. Mary leaped from her chair and opened the door.

"Hubrey," said Mary. "Please come in."

"Hello, folks," said Hubrey, as he handed Mary a box wrapped in a big red ribbon and bow. "These are for you."

Mary blushed a little, Fred and Arthur were snickering, and Cecil was oblivious to it all as he sucked clean a pork-chop bone.

"Sit here," said Mary. She directed Hubrey to the empty chair and slid the plate of pork chops in his direction. Hubrey apologized sincerely to Will and Nellie for his lateness and continued to eat his dinner with everybody watching him.

"I wish he would hurry up," whispered Fred to Arthur, knowing that they could not leave the table until everyone had finished. Mary just gazed at Hubrey, watching every bite he took.

Lizzie watched her big sister, and then wondered about Tawny again and what he might be doing.

Just like clockwork, Uncle John came in through the back door, shook Hubrey's hand, sat down, and waited for his usual coffee and crumb cake, which Lizzie's mother brought to the table.

"Look at this," said Hubrey, pulling a photograph from his satchel.

"Very nice," said Uncle John as he spit crumbs on the table and looked at the picture. "Look, Will; even you took a good one."

"Good coffee, Nell," said Uncle John as he sipped, looking at the paper that held his image.

Nellie and Mary took away the empty serving plates and returned with the crumb cake and the coffee pot. Soon, everyone was done and the talking started, only this time Mary was outside on the porch with Hubrey.

"Seems like a nice boy," said Uncle John, looking at Will.

"Yes, Hubrey does seem ok," answered Will, sipping his coffee.

"Want something a little stronger?" Will asked.

Uncle John smiled and said, "Of course." Will rose and returned with whiskey and poured a little in both coffee cups.

Evening approached, and the light faded in the room. Mary and Hubrey were talking up a storm as Lizzie, now sitting in the chair next to the door, gazed outside and noticed that neither one wanted to break for air. It seemed that every time there was a short silence, everyone looked in that direction to see if they were still there.

"Lizzie," cried Mary. "Come here, quick!"

Lizzie walked outside to find Mr. Nate standing on the porch, holding an envelope and smiling. He handed Lizzie the envelope. He tilted his hat, said good-bye and quickly left.

"Mom!" called Lizzie, as she came back into the living room, "Can I open it? Can I?"

"Ok, sweetheart," her mother answered, smiling at Lizzie, knowing exactly what the envelope contained. And Lizzie knew too; it was an invitation to Clara's for a sleepover. Mr. Nate always brought the invitation to Lizzie's house. She opened the envelope, ignored the nonimportant words and focused on "Tuesday and Wednesday!" Lizzie blurted as she ran upstairs, pulled her bag from the closet, and started packing. Nellie shook her head, laughed at Will, and then whispered, "Silly girl."

Mary and Hubrey excused themselves as they went for a walk to the town square for ice cream. It was routine for the people to do this on Sundays, and Lizzie usually went. On this day, however, she was busy. Nellie smiled as though satisfied with life. Fred and Arthur, with full bellies, napped on the sofa; Cecil quietly played with cards in the corner; and Will and Uncle John, drinking at the table, discussed the same old things.

Nellie figured Mary was now grown up and almost gone and Lizzie was trying hard to grow up. She realized that she had a normal family, and she loved it.

Mary and Hubrey returned to the house, and soon Hubrey left after saying good-bye to the family, at least the ones who were still awake.

"I like that boy," said Uncle John, now slurring his words.

"We'll be seeing a lot more of him, I think," said Will. They called it a night, Uncle John left, and everyone went off to bed.

Monday came and slowly dissolved into Tuesday. Lizzie was so excited—Mr. Nate would arrive soon to take her to Clara's. She was packed and ready to go and waiting by the front door. Finally, the buggy approached and before long, Clara and Lizzie were on their way to the Culmer Farm.

Along the way, they noticed that each farm had several boys working in the fields, and Lizzie knew that these were the same boys they saw at the station. They could not see the Lathrope farm from the main road, but Lizzie tried hard as they passed by. As they passed the road that led down to the Lathrope Farm, Lizzie strained extra hard to see down that road and maybe, just maybe, catch a glimpse of Tawny.

No luck. Besides, the old Fell Farm was at least four miles further down the road. The buggy turned into the Culmer driveway, and Lizzie saw boys working close to the little barns scattered throughout the fields.

"Where do they sleep?" asked Lizzie.

"In the big barn," replied Clara, "with the animals. Dad won't let them in the house." Then she added, "They are a bad influence on us; he has told me several times."

"Hello, Lizzie," said Mrs. Culmer as she greeted them at the front door.

"Hello, Mrs. Culmer," answered Lizzie.

"Come in, girls," said Mrs. Culmer, "and have some cookies and milk." The girls sat at the kitchen table and ate cookies and drank a glass as they exchanged small talk and a few giggles. Once in Clara's bedroom, they sat on the bed looking out the window toward the barn. Lizzie couldn't wait any longer.

"Where's the bad one?" asked Lizzie.

"Around somewhere," said Clara, and then added, "it will be breakfast soon. They will all run up to the barn as soon as the bell rings."

The girls waited patiently, and then a loud bell sounded, and just as Clara predicted, the boys ran to the barn.

"That's him, that's him," whispered Lizzie. "It's number thirty, from the station. The one who waved to Tawny. He must know Tawny." Lizzie was rambling on and on as she grew more excited.

"Be quiet," said Clara. "Take a deep breath."

Lizzie thought to herself, he was only a hundred feet away from her and she couldn't talk to him. How she was going to see him and ask him about Tawny fully occupied her mind. "Clara, help me."

Clara thought about the whole idea, and after a couple of minutes she told Lizzie what to do, explaining that they would go outside for water and

Clara would distract her dad while Lizzie spoke with number thirty. Both girls came outside, carrying one bucket between them as they passed the boys, who were eating lunch, and, just then, Clara turned and faced her father. "When are you going to get my school things?"

"I don't know," said Mr. Culmer, looking bothered by the question at this time. "Go ask your mother, she takes care of that sort of request."

"Daddy, can we go for ice cream after dinner tonight?" Clara was trying desperately to keep her father's attention. Meanwhile, Lizzie made her way to number thirty and boldly asked, "Who is Tawny? Where do you come from?"

"England," answered Billy, still standing by himself and not even looking at Lizzie. "Now go away; you'll get me into trouble, and I don't need it now."

Billy returned to the pack of boys, who were still eating and drinking as they all watched Lizzie walk away to get the bucket of water.

The girls finally got to the bedroom and started to look outside at the pack of boys sitting and eating.

"Is he the bad one, the one named Billy?" asked Lizzie.

"Yes, the tall one," said Clara, pointing through the window. Lizzie thought that later tonight, she would get her answers about Tawny. She would climb out the window when everyone was sleeping and satisfy her desire about the boy they called Tawny.

Chapter 16

The Special Place

Monday morning came—just like every other morning—and the boys were hard at work cleaning the last few cure barns. Tawny couldn't stop thinking of the big elm tree and the creek bank that he saw yesterday. It looked so peaceful; he thought that it would make a great hideaway and he then remembered that back in the orphanage, he had a place where he would be by himself. The only difference was that the furnace room in the orphanage—where he used to hide or just get away—was noisy and dirty, but the big elm tree was outside and provided shade and quiet. The morning meal bell rang and the boys scurried back to the barn for breakfast. The midmorning skies were cloudy; rain was coming. Tawny thought that if it rained hard, not a drizzle, but a big rain, what were the boys going to do? Last week during a brief drizzle, the farmer kept them working in the small cure barns.

After eating, they returned to the cure barns, and about an hour later the skies opened up, flooding the landscape in a heavy downpour. The boys all scattered back to the big barn, soaking wet and trying to shake the water from their clothes.

Lathrope finally entered the barn, shaking the water off his hat and stared at the dark sky. "We'll wait here; it should pass."

The boys watched the rain fill up the small ditches in front of the barn, and it wasn't long before everything was waterlogged.

"Come over here," said Lathrope motioning them to form a circle. The boys quickly formed a semicircle and were looking at him with anticipation.

"We are going to start suckering the plants," he said.

"As soon as the rain lets up, I'll show you. Wait here. I'll be right back."

Lathrope grabbed his hat and ran through the rain for the main house. When he was out of sight, Jimmy laughed, "Suckering the plants."

Tom laughed along with him and before long, all of the boys were laughing.

"Suckering the plants," said Tawny. "Sound s really funny."

They all sat close to the barn door and watched the rain, relieved that they didn't have to work in the smelly cure barns. It rained all afternoon, giving Tom and Peter a chance to nap. Jack and Mark were busy talking and looking around the barn. Jimmy spent the afternoon staring outside, acting as if he wanted to go back to work.

Tawny loitered around the barn, thinking about that special place. Suddenly, Lathrope ran back into the barn with his head covered by a newspaper.

"Ok, boys, I don't think it will let up," he said.

"Stay in the barn for the rest the day," he said sternly and then quickly left, only to return to the main house.

Tawny decided this was the perfect time to go to the special place. Besides, nobody would try and find him, especially in the rain.

"Jimmy..."

"What, Tawny?" answered Jimmy, still staring outside.

"Come with me. I want to try and find something."

Jimmy looked confused, wrinkled his little face, and asked, "In the rain?"

"Come on, you'll be all right," said Tawny, looking directly into Jimmy's eyes. Suddenly, both of them made a dash out and around the barn and headed down a pathway through the fields, wiping the rain from their faces every few feet.

"Where are we going?" asked Jimmy.

"This way!" exclaimed Tawny.

They kept on running, and Tawny thought of how good the rain felt on his feet, and then finally Tawny stopped and leaned against a big elm tree and Jimmy followed suit.

"How much further?" asked Jimmy, panting like a dog who just had a long walk.

"Right here," said Tawny, who was out of breath but still smiling.

Tawny scanned the countryside carefully and knew that this was the best place he had ever seen. It's about seven minutes from the barn if I run, probably twenty if I walk, he figured.

They sat down. The ground beneath them was as dry as a bone because the big tree provided shade in the sun and cover from the rain. Tawny and Jimmy gazed into the creek, watching the water run over the rocks with a tranquil gurgling. Suddenly, the rain stopped, and they looked at each other in panic.

"Come on," said Tawny. "We have to go."

Jimmy and Tawny ran back to the barn as fast as they could, retracing their original steps, and hoping they wouldn't get caught.

"Were did you go?" asked Tom.

"To the place," said Tawny, wiping the mud from his feet on a pile of hay close to the door.

"What place?" Asked Jack.

"You know, the one I was telling you about," said Tawny, happy and grinning.

"Oh, yeah," said Jack.

Almost immediately after Tawny and Jimmy had returned, Lathrope entered the barn, smiling from ear to ear.

"Come on, boys," he said, walking away from the barn. The boys followed without hesitation.

"This is a sucker." Lathrope held a piece of plant that was growing between the leaf and stock. "Just snap it off without breaking the stock."

"Remember, check between all the leaves, starting at the ground and working your way up."

"Tomorrow, you will be removing suckers," said Lathrope, then added, "A little late in the season, but I'm banking on a long Indian summer."

Tawny looked puzzled at Jack and then mouthed the word that made him feel uneasy, Indian. Jack simply shrugged his shoulders and made a funny face.

They returned to the barn as Lathrope made his way back to the main house. Dinner was served earlier than usual, but the boys didn't mind and expected that it be done this way, because of the rainstorm. Usually, Tawny preferred eating at the same time each day, like at the orphanage, but he also knew that the meals tasted much better here.

After the kitchen lady picked up the dinner tray, the boys were sitting around feeling as if they had a day off, kind of like yesterday afternoon.

"If it rains, we get an early dinner," said Tom, rubbing his belly and laughing.

"Sure looks like that," answered Tawny.

"Look!" said Jimmy, pointing to the main house.

The rest of the boys looked out the barn door and saw four buggies coming down the long driveway. Once in front of the house, the buggies were abandoned as the people went inside the house, and the horses were tied to the white fence pole.

About an hour later, the boys heard noise coming from the main house, and they saw light beaming from each window.

About two hours of daylight left, thought Tawny, and the air was cooler now, after the rain.

"Come on, lads," said Tawny.

"Where?" asked Jack.

"Just follow Tawny; you'll like it!" said Jimmy, excited.

All six of them made their way around the barn and through the fields and in about seven minutes or so, they were there.

"Isn't this bloody beautiful?" said Tawny who stood with his arms on his hips.

The others stood around, taking in the scenery and one by one, they dropped to the ground and sat in front of the creek.

"Listen," said Jimmy.

The boys listened carefully; the creek made soft rippling sounds.

"This is the special place," said Tawny. "This is our place, and nobody knows we are here. We'll keep it that way, right?"

Jimmy stood up and threw his fist in the air, adding, "Right!"

The others took Jimmy's lead and soon they we all in agreement and were really enjoying this temporary freedom they had made for themselves.

Jimmy pointed to a large upright pole. "Look over there."

About two hundred feet away stood a dead hollow tree trunk, about ten feet high, with several holes dug out at the top. Probably animals, thought Tawny. Tawny removed a nail he found in one of the cure barns from his trousers and started to engrave something on the trunk of the big elm tree. Jimmy strained to see Tawny carve something. After a few minutes, Tawny stepped back, and there it was in a fresh-cut look: "HD" in small letters.

"I'm next," said Jimmy, as he took the nail.

Soon, the bottom portion of the tree trunk was covered with small initials, and the boys were proud of what they had accomplished.

The western sky quickly turned deep purple and orange, and Tawny began feeling a little anxious about being away from the barn.

"Come on, lads. It's time to go back."

The boys made their way back down the trail toward the big barn, and as they entered, they sat back down and acted as if nothing extraordinary happened. The noise from the house grew louder until it sounded like a dull constant roar. Suddenly they heard, "Where in the hell were you bastards?"

Lathrope appeared from behind them, holding a half-empty bottle. "Do you think you can just come an' go as you please?" He slurred his words slightly.

"Just went for walk," said Jimmy calmly.

Lathrope cut him off quickly and roared, "You don't ever leave the barn!"

It was obvious that he had been drinking. Tawny had seen this behavior before, once when Mel and Heddon got drunk, argued a lot, and Mel passed out in the fourth-floor hallway. Thinking about it, Tawny knew that the entire house had been drinking, since the voices got louder and louder, just like Mel and Heddon did that one night.

"Whose stupid idea was this?" asked the staggering Lathrope.

The boys just stood like stone and said nothing. Jimmy glanced over at Tawny and just as Jimmy looked at him, Lathrope, in his drunken state, caught it.

"You!" he screamed, pointing at Tawny. "Come with me!"

"The rest of you stay here, and I really mean 'here.'"

Lathrope pulled Tawny by his shirt and dragged him off into the field and soon they were out of sight from the rest of the concerned boys. A little while later Lathrope returned to the main house weaving and mumbling to himself and Tawny was not with him, which scared little Jimmy.

"Where's Tawny?" cried Jimmy, now looking panic stricken.

"Don't know," said Tom, trying desperately to remain calm and wishing to see Tawny coming back to the barn, but he didn't. They were all confused and wondered what happened to Tawny. Jimmy finally said, "Should we go and find him."

"Are you crazy?" shouted Jack. "No. We'll stay right here. You heard Lathrope."

Not another word was spoken as the boys retreated to the hayloft and kept to themselves. It was hard to sleep that night, and Jimmy felt so bad about his friend not being there.

Chapter 17

The Questions and Answers

The cool evening air filtered through the open window in Clara's bedroom. Lizzie couldn't wait until the entire house was quiet so she could sneak out and get answers. Both she and Clara were still under the blankets, and occasionally, they would whisper and giggle quietly.

"Ready to go," Lizzie said softly into Clara's ear.

"I don't know about this," said Clara.

"Come on," said Lizzie, as she threw off the sheet and climbed out of bed. Clara and Lizzie, wearing only their nightshirts, put on their slippers, descended the stairs to the main floor, and went directly into the huge kitchen.

"We will sit here for a while," said Lizzie, pointing to the chairs around the wooden kitchen table. Clara sat quietly, still feeling scared. She had never snuck out of the house before and thought that her father would kill her if he found out. They sat motionless but fully awake at the kitchen table, and then Lizzie stared at the back Dutch door. Clara watched Lizzie but for the most part was too involved with herself as she tried desperately to hear something, or perhaps she was only looking for a way out of this plan. Outside, it was extremely quiet, except for the crickets, which were chirping.

"Do you think that's long enough?" whispered Lizzie.

Clara shook her head. "Give it a few more minutes. "Remember, the bottom door is the one that opens."

Lizzie nodded her head and they waited a few more minutes until Clara gathered enough courage. They both padded softly to the half-door and pushed the bottom. It opened slowly and quietly; it was perfect so far.

"That's enough," whispered Clara.

They left the main house, taking a few steps, stopping, looking around, and continuing, like two mice hunting for food. As they came to the barn door, the ground still felt wet from the rain earlier. They pulled, and finally the door moved just enough for them to slip through.

They stood for a few moments to become accustomed to the dark. The inside of the barn smelled musky and old, thought Lizzie, when they heard a slight creaking sound. The noise they heard came from above, on the left side of the barn. Lizzie climbed the wooden ladder, which only took about six steps, to find five boys sleeping on hay beds. She stood motionless and watched for a while, feeling excited about being so close to her answers.

"Billy..Billy..Billy!" she said, getting and more demanding louder each time.

"What do you want?" said a voice from one of the beds.

"Come here," said Lizzie.

Billy rolled over to see a small head staring at him from the ladder.

"What?" he said, yawning.

"Tell me about Tawny," Lizzie said.

"Met him at the docks, great boy, you know in South Hampton. Just before we got on the ship. Tough boy," explained Billy, rubbing his cheek and thinking about the fight they had almost two weeks ago, "Strong too. We talked a lot on the train ride, you know, we became pretty good friends." Billy yawned again, looked at Lizzie in a different way for a moment, and then decided she was a little too young for him, "We came from the same background."

"Lizzie, Lizzie," cried Clara, still standing at the barn door. "I hear something."

Billy with his eyes wide open now asked, "Do you know where he is?"

"Yes," replied Lizzie. "The old Fell Farm."

"Where is that?" asked Billy.

"Right behind this farm." said Lizzie. "Two or three miles back. If you see him, tell him I said hello. My name is Lizzie, the girl at the station.

"Ok," answered Billy. "Now get out of here before you get us into more trouble."

Lizzie climbed down the ladder and felt a little more satisfied about Tawny, but she still didn't know if he was thinking about her too. She also thought that Billy seemed like a nice boy.

"What did he say?" asked Clara.

"I'll tell you later," said Lizzie.

Clara yanked Lizzie's nightshirt and they stumbled back to the main house; but as they approached the back door Clara yanked on Lizzie's nightshirt for the second time only this time it was much harder.

"What do you want?" whispered Lizzie stopping and turning around.

"Look at our slippers," said Clara, pointing to the ground only for them to find out that their slippers were all covered in mud and hay. Both of them sat on the porch steps very quietly, removed their slippers, looked at each other in a small panic, and then smiled like little schoolgirls with a secret. Clara looked around and finally stood, went to the rain barrel and said, "Put them in here." Both Lizzie and Clara dropped their slippers in the rain-filled barrel and it did not take long before they were back in bed, giggling, and trying to sleep.

The rooster started to crow, which everyone knew marked the beginning of the day and Lizzie glanced outside: The barn door was wide open. Lizzie panicked and shook Clara "Did we forget to close the barn door last night?"

"No," said Clara, "Dad and the boys have already left for the fields." Lizzie felt relieved.

They went down to the kitchen. The kitchen workers were busy making bread and preparing food for the day's meals. It smelled so good in the kitchen! Lizzie loved baking, and she always took the time to watch the older ladies ply their trade. Mrs. Culmer came in through the back door, with her head tilted back slightly and toting a brown burlap bag.

"Clara," said her mom, "what is meaning of this?"

Clara peeked into the bag and saw the soaked slippers. She swallowed hard, and then she looked quickly at Lizzie.

"Thank you," said Lizzie. "We put them in the rain barrel last night. Clara and I were walking around, and we didn't want to bring the mess into the house. We're sorry." Now looking back at Clara, she grinned deviously.

"That's thoughtful," said Mrs. Culmer. "Clara, you should be more considerate, like Lizzie." Clara was amazed at her friend's way of turning things around, and realized that she had never heard Lizzie lie (or at least omit the complete truth) before.

Martha entered the kitchen and sat down next to the girls. "Good morning." The whole room answered her back as the girls poured themselves a glass of milk, while Martha retrieved a coffee, and the three walked through the house to the main porch, where a table was set up.

"Keep away from those boys," said Martha, holding the hot coffee mug close to her lips.

"What do you mean?" asked Lizzie.

"They are trouble. They were raised with different standards," said Martha. "Do yourself a favor; stay away from them."

Now Clara was really confused. On one hand they almost got caught because of the slippers and on the other hand, Martha likely knew something. Did she see them last night? Clara looked at Lizzie, wondering what to do, and Lizzie smiled back with confidence, deciding that saying nothing was the best solution.

Martha smiled coldly. "I saw you go into the barn last night; I saw Clara standing guard at the door."

"I just wanted some information on a boy named Tawny," said Lizzie. "I saw him at the train station last week, and he smiled at me."

Martha sipped her coffee twice and sat the cup down, leaned forward, and with a stern matronly voice said, "Last year, three girls from school got pregnant. I'm sure they were smiled at too. They had to drop out of school. Two were sent away, you know. Never came back." Martha leaned back in her chair and took another sip and gazed out at the green fields.

"You never saw your friends again?"

"No, Clara, never again. Their parents sent them away to relatives or a school for unwed mothers to avoid the shame. They had babies and stayed away."

Lizzie suddenly remembered about a talk she and Mary had about six months ago, where Mary said the same thing. It had to be true.

"Just be careful with the boys," said Lizzie.

"Right, we must be careful," agreed Clara. Martha shook her head and rolled her eyes, but she didn't realize that the girls might know more than she did. Lizzie only knew that the day she saw Tawny, she had strange feelings, feelings she liked, and feelings she wanted to have again. She tried to explain this to Clara, but Clara didn't seem ready to understand; she called Lizzie stupid for feeling that way.

Mrs. Culmer interrupted them with some fresh rolls, creamy butter, and a slice of cheese. The rest of the morning was spent in Clara's bedroom talking about Tawny. Clara was sick and tired of hearing about Tawny. It was Tawny this and Tawny that, and at one point, Clara even thought that Lizzie had lost her mind.

"Do you like Billy?" asked Lizzie.

"He's ok," answered Clara, who was sitting on the bed.

"I think he is really nice," said Lizzie.

Clara had noticed that their last sleepover, three weeks earlier, wasn't like this one. Lizzie's changed, thought Clara. Boys had replaced dolls; there was lying and covering up the lies, and most of all, this boy Tawny had taken over her mind. Clara became concerned for her best friend. The only other person she knew who acted like this was Mary, and now Lizzie was doing the same thing. Perhaps they were both crazy.

Chapter 18

The Big Surprise

Tawny jerked up from the cold damp floor of the cure barn, brushed the dirt from his trousers, felt a small pain in his cheek, and then fixed his hair. It was much darker inside the barn at night. Tawny thought that he would just push the door open, return to his friends, and be back before daylight. The door wouldn't move. He pushed it again, and it still didn't move. Finally he had realized that Lathrope had locked him inside the cure barn. Tawny tried the windows; they too were securely fastened. He was trapped inside the small barn, a prisoner. Tawny scratched his ear and felt a needle-sharp pain and thought, This is where Lathrope hit me, as he gently fumbled around the ear to see where it hurt the most. Tawny remembered that the driest part of the barn was next to the door. He kicked some hay and dirt to one side and sat down with his back against the barn wall.

Jimmy was wide awake back at the big barn, thinking about Tawny, and he stirred at every sound, regardless if the noise came from inside the barn or outside. Jimmy had opened the barn loft door slightly so he could see outside. To the right was the main house, and to the left was a cure barn in the distance, perhaps where his friend was.

"Get some sleep," said Tom. "I'm sure he's all right."

"Lathrope was drunk," said Jimmy. "Maybe he hurt Tawny."

"Be quiet and go to sleep," muttered Mark.

Jimmy lay back down on his hay bed and spoke to himself quietly, "Me mum will come for me. I know she will. Me mum will come soon. I hate this place. I miss me mum."

"What?" asked Peter.

"Nothing," replied Jimmy.

"I heard something about 'me mum,'" said Peter, now crawling closer to Jimmy.

"Do you think your mother is coming here to get you? Is that it?" asked Peter.

Jimmy's eyes filled up with tears and his bottom lip started to quiver. If Tawny were here, Peter wouldn't have said anything.

"Me mum will come," said Jimmy.

"Leave him alone." Tom glared at Peter in the dim light, and with that, Peter rolled over to face the barn wall.

Jimmy rolled over and looked outside through the crack in the barn loft door. The moon was full and bright; Jimmy could see the dirt road that brought them here, way past the main house.

He thought about leaving, and then reality set in. Where would he go? How would he get there? Finally, exhausted and sad, Jimmy fell asleep.

"Bang!" Jimmy opened his eyes. He looked outside; Lathrope walked through the fields at a fast pace. He must be going to get Tawny, thought Jimmy. As his eyes adjusted to the light, he could see a bag under Lathrope's arm. Jimmy opened the loft door a little more and now was watching Lathrope approach a cure barn, unlock the door, and open it. He saw Lathrope throw the bag into the barn, close the door, and lock it. Jimmy felt a little relieved knowing his best friend was still alive and in that barn. Lathrope returned to the main house, and Jimmy knew that the workday would soon start.

What was in the bag? thought Jimmy. How long is Tawny going to be in there?"

It wasn't long after that Jimmy and the others were jolted by Lathrope's booming shout.

"Get up, you lazy bastards," Lathrope roared. "Time to go suckering."

The boys were dropped off in the fields two to a section and were told to yank off the suckers that grew between the stalk and leaves. Soon Lathrope was gone and Jimmy wandered toward the cure barn that held his friend prisoner. He thought if he bent over a little, nobody could see him because he was small.

"Tawny, are you all right?" asked Jimmy as he peeked through the crack in the door.

"I'm fine," said Tawny. Then he added, "Get out of here, Jimmy, or he'll lock you up too."

"What was in the bag?" asked Jimmy.

"Potato peels," replied Tawny. "Go back. Go back before he sees you."

Jimmy returned to his place in the field and suckered plants, feeling better that Tawny was all right. The loud bell rang from the main porch, and the boys hurried back to the barn. The boys liked the kitchen lady and by now had her smiling at them when she dropped off the tray, but only if Lathrope wasn't with her. The tray contained fresh buns and milk for breakfast, which seemed to be an everyday occurrence. Jimmy was swallowing the last bit of bun when he heard it and couldn't believe his ears.

"Get that boy out of there, you animal," said a loud lady's voice from inside the main house.

"He has to learn a lesson. He can't take off when he wants, and he certainly can't take the others with him when he wants."

"You lost the last one you locked up," said the lady's voice.

"I need to teach this one a lesson. He's the leader of this bunch."

Jimmy figured out that the Lathropes were arguing about Tawny. Then the arguing abruptly stopped, and Jimmy heard the front door slam shut. They all could see Lathrope approach them, and Jimmy knew by his face that he was very angry.

"Come on, you...boys," bellowed Lathrope. "Get back to work!"

The boys ran back into the fields. Lathrope went into the big barn. Jimmy wondered what Lathrope was doing in the barn, and then he remembered the last time Lathrope was in the barn. He was drunk, and Tawny got into trouble; Jimmy suddenly felt scared.

The sun quickly heated the fields, and soon the boys had their shirts tied around their waists. Jimmy kept looking back at the main house, noticing children playing on the porch and a couple of older ladies supervising and drinking something.

He remembered not so long ago when he was the one playing on the porch with his mother watching and sipping tea with her friends. These thoughts gave him a warm feeling and yet a feeling that Jimmy tried hard to forget because it made him cry. Suddenly, Jimmy saw Lathrope come out of the big barn and walk directly toward the cure barn that held Tawny. It looked as though his head was trying to beat his feet in a race. His arms were swinging hard.

Lathrope tossed the door aside, yanked Tawny outside, and then threw him against the wall. Lathrope had one hand on Tawny's neck and the other hand was pointing directly at Tawny's head. Jimmy knew words were said, but he couldn't hear them. Jimmy saw Tawny's eyes squinting, and then Lathrope let Tawny fall to the ground as he walked back to the main house. Jimmy watched his friend get to his feet and walk slowly back toward the main barn, occasionally stopping and suckering the plants, just like the others.

The afternoon dragged on, and it even seemed to get hotter as Lathrope kept appearing, then disappearing, all afternoon like a jack in the box. He's watching his plants really close today, thought Jimmy, who wanted badly to talk to Tawny, but wouldn't take the chance of being caught. The afternoon ended, and soon they all returned to the barn and were cleaned and fed. Jimmy noticed a bruise on the side of Tawny's face, close to his ear.

"What happened, Tawny?" asked Jimmy.

"Nothing much; he tried to hit me, and I ducked and turned me head. He must have hit me on the ear. He told me to straighten out or he would kill me." Tawny drank his milk slowly.

"Kill you!" e xclaimed Jimmy, his eyes wide.

"He was drunk and didn't know what he was saying." Tawny knew he now had an audience. The others sat in amazement enjoying Tawny's version of the story and started to laugh at the telling.

"Tawny, Tawny," said Jimmy.

"What?"

"He killed someone before." Jimmy now put an end to the fun that they were having. Immediately, the boys became still. They stared at Jimmy.

"What are you talking about?" asked Mark.

"I overheard Mrs. Lathrope tell Mr. Lathrope that he lost one before. I'm sure they were talking about a boy," said Jimmy.

The festive moment faded. The boys were truly frightened. "Are you sure what you heard?" asked Tawny.

"Yes. They were yelling at each other about you, while we were eating this morning." Jimmy took a deep breath and then continued. "Mrs. Lathrope wanted you out of the cure barn and told him to take you out, but he told her he had to teach you a lesson. She then said, 'remember, you already lost the other one you locked up.'" The boys went silent.

"I really don't know how long you can stay in one of those cure barns without dying," said Tawny. "It gets really hot in there."

The evening passed quickly and soon the boys were sleeping, scattered and all curled up in the loft. The morning came, and again the boys went to the fields to continue suckering tobacco plants. It was definitely hotter than the previous day. Jimmy nursed some cuts on his hands. Late in the afternoon, Tawny and Jimmy worked the backfields and were getting close to the special place and soon Tawny saw that the spot in daylight was more beautiful, and the recently cut initials were still visible in the big tree. Tawny couldn't fully understand why he needed a place where he could go to be by himself, nor did he feel the need to explain it to anybody else. He simply needed this place, and that's all there was to it. He started walking toward the special place.

"Where are you going?" asked Jimmy.

"Come over here and sit for a while," said Tawny, as he leaned against the tree trunk. Jimmy sat next to Tawny, and both of them just stared at the creek that slowly ran past them. Tawny realized that this place was truly spectacular and so peaceful. The best spot on the whole farm, thought Tawny.

"Look!" Jimmy pointed across the creek.

"What?"

"Over there. See him?" asked Jimmy.

"Yes. I do," replied Tawny. They stood and were looking hard across the creek. They had noticed a boy, around Tawny's height, working the other farm and they watched the boy bending and picking, probably doing the same as Tawny and Jimmy.

Suddenly, Tawny froze and stared at the black outline of a boy across the creek and then for some strange reason he started to walk toward the creek bank slowly. Tawny smiled, cupped his hands over his mouth, and shouted, "Billy! Billy! Billy!"

Then, to Tawny's amazement, the boy looked up and yelled back, "Tawny...is that you?"

Tawny, full of warm feelings, grabbed Jimmy's shoulders and started shaking him at first; then they both jumped up and down. "It's Billy! It's Billy!"

Chapter 19

The Departure

Lizzie and Clara spent the entire afternoon and evening talking about all kinds of things, including Billy, Tawny, what Martha had told them earlier, and finally the strange feelings Lizzie had experienced last week. They went to bed late that night, and Clara begged Lizzie to stay inside and forget about talking to Billy again. Besides, Mr. Culmer was still up, working on farm finances. Early in the morning, they awoke to sunshine streaming through the window, and it didn't take them long before they were eating sticky buns and sausages and drinking milk. Clara kept glancing at Lizzie; some of the things they talked about last night were a little frightening.

After breakfast, the girls spent the morning on the porch mostly talking about school, which would start in a few days, and about the new teacher. They compared notes about clothes and meeting arrangements because Lizzie walked to school and Clara had to be driven. Still, they were both ready to tackle the new school year, but Lizzie, knowing she was changing, wondered whether Clara was ready for her.

The girls positioned themselves on the front porch by moving a couple of chairs and enjoyed their drinks while watching the boys eat their morning meal outside the barn door. Lizzie determined that of the bunch, Billy seemed to be the leader, and Clara realized that Lizzie was looking harder and harder at these boys. Three weeks ago, Lizzie would have glanced at the boys once or twice and that would have been the end of it. Clara grew more concerned for her best friend; Lizzie's mind was changing drastically.

Clara's mother stepped through the door. "Lizzie dear, it's time to go home."

"Ok." Lizzie and Clara went back upstairs, gathered her things, and then returned to the porch to wait for Mr. Nate.

"Thanks for letting me come and stay." Lizzie took a last look at the boys, who were returning to the fields for their day's work.

"You're always welcome here," said Clara's mother.

Mr. Nate drove the buggy around to the front of the house. Soon, both Clara and Lizzie were on way back to Lizzie's house.

Clara even noticed that every time they passed a farm with boys working the fields, Lizzie bobbed her head, bouncing from side to side. Clara thought that she never wanted to act this stupid, especially over boys, but deep down, the change in Clara was brewing. It was only a matter of time before it surfaced. The girls hugged good-bye, and Mr. Nate turned the buggy around.

Lizzie strolled through the house saying hello to her mother and brothers, and then she made her way upstairs. She quickly unpacked her bag, brushed her hair, and found herself sitting on the bed staring outside through the window.

The next few days were routine. Lizzie had to prepare her closet for school, gather her books and paper, buy pencils, and get a sharpener. She also helped clean the house, bake cookies, and go for errands, but one thing Lizzie didn't do was talk to Mary. Mary wasn't around and Lizzie honestly didn't even miss her.

On Friday morning, around nine o'clock, Mary came home and started shouting at her Mom. Lizzie listened from her upstairs room and noticed that that the yelling quickly turned into crying.

"Lizzie!" called Nellie. "Come here." Lizzie ran downstairs into the kitchen to find out what happened.

"Guess what?" asked her mother. To Lizzie she seemed happy and sad at the same time; this really confused Lizzie.

"What?"

"Hubrey Spence has asked your sister to marry him."

"Is she moving out?"

"She's moving to Brantford on Sunday," said Nellie. "She's staying with cousin Vera. Hubrey got her a job at the photo gallery."

Lizzie was happy for her sister, but she was sad to see her go.

"Where is Mary now?"

"She just left for the Town square, Lizzie. I guess to pick up a few things," replied Nellie. "She will be home soon because I need things to finish dinner."

"When are they getting married?" asked Lizzie.

"Next spring," replied Lizzie's mother, wiping at her tear-filled eyes.

Lizzie went outside and sat on the stoop, thinking about her new role in the house and all the new chores that she would have to do, but then she thought about the chores she could pass off to her brothers. This exercise of receiving and passing off chores equaled itself out, and Lizzie grew more comfortable about Mary leaving. Besides, Lizzie liked Hubrey Spence.

They make a nice couple, she thought. Lizzie laughed quietly and then began crying at the same time. Her sister was leaving tomorrow for good. Lizzie had one day—actually, only a half-day—with her big sister.

Mary returned from the square and the two sisters excitedly began talking about the wedding, the dress, the shoes, the wedding night, and then the fact that Mary was moving to a big city. Just before Lizzie went to bed, she realized that this was the first time she and Mary actually enjoyed everything they talked about. The next morning began like every other Saturday morning, except father was a quiet, and Lizzie noticed his eyes were slightly red as he left the house for work.

After breakfast, Hubrey's buggy rounded the corner. Mary and Lizzie went to greet him. He stopped in front of Lizzie, and she shuddered at the sight of the big horse; she couldn't help it, she still feared horses.

"Hi, Lizzie, or should I say, 'hello, sister'?"

"Call me Lizzie; that's just fine," said Lizzie as she ran back to the house. Hubrey jumped from the carriage and kissed Mary. Hubrey parked the buggy, entered the house, hugged Nellie, and sat down at the kitchen table, with Nellie serving him coffee and a cookie.

Mary ran back upstairs and quickly returned, carrying several bags, and one by one showed off what she had purchased, smiled, and then kissed Hubrey. Mary sat on Hubrey's knee and started to tell him all about the things she had bought yesterday and how much she saved.

Right in the middle of a sentence, Mary looked over at Lizzie and sternly said, "Mr. Owen needs you right away; he told me yesterday." Lizzie's eyes opened wide and she thought to herself, I finally have a paying job!

Lizzie still had ample time before dinner, so she excused herself and made her way to the town square. Mr. Owen was pleased to see Lizzie so quickly and before long, they forged an arrangement of times and rate of pay. Lizzie thanked Mr. Owen and left the bakery for home, now feeling proud and responsible. Father came home early and cleaned up. They all sat down to a meal of pork, potatoes, gravies, buns, and turnips.

Lizzie's father even brought out the good whiskey that he kept under the hutch. Hubrey and Will sipped whiskey, and Fred was sent to retrieve Uncle John. Soon Uncle John joined them and tried to catch up.

Hubrey became talkative after a few toasts, and Lizzie couldn't stop laughing at his slurred words. Fred pled his case to mother as to why he should take Mary's room and that Arthur could have his room. Nellie just smiled at Fred—in fact, today she smiled at everyone. Her daughter was getting married and moving away to start a new life.

Hubrey slept on the sofa, snoring a little, but mostly breathing hard. He had had a lot to drink; besides, Mary and he stayed up talking on the porch well into the morning. Uncle John entered through the back door, tossed his paper on the coffee table, and poured a cup of coffee. He sat facing the sleeping Hubrey Spence; suddenly, Hubrey opened his eyes and quickly sat up; apparently, he wasn't used to people watching him sleep.

"Sorry, didn't mean to frighten you."

"It's ok, John," said Hubrey wiping his eyes.

"Get a cup of coffee—best in the land." Uncle John hoisted his cup.

"Sure, thanks." Hubrey stood, went into the kitchen, and returned with a hot cup of coffee.

"Great coffee," said Hubrey.

"Told you so."

Mary came downstairs, dressed and ready for whatever the day would bring, Fred was outside feeding the horses and cleaning the street. Arthur was helping as much as Arthur could, and Cecil still slept and probably would for another couple of hours. Mother soon was preparing breakfast, and Will joined the men for coffee.

"Want some?" Will pointed the brown bottle to Hubrey.

"No, thanks, Will," said Hubrey. "Had too much last night."

Uncle John stretched his cup to the bottle, and Will poured a shot.

Uncle John stood and raised his cup. "Here's to Hubrey and Mary..may they live well."

Hubrey toasted with his coffee and smiled. Breakfast was served as Lizzie assumed her new role of meal server. She took her time and placed the plates in the same location on the table as Mary had. Everything went smoothly until Lizzie tripped, and a bowl of strawberry preserves went flying right into Hubrey's lap. He jumped back and Mary started wiping the red sticky syrup.

"I'm so sorry," said Lizzie. "I'm really sorry."

"Don't worry about it," said Hubrey "I'm sure they will clean up."

After breakfast was done and Hubrey's pants were somewhat cleaned, Lizzie and Mary packed Mary's suitcases and hatboxes. Hubrey prepared the buggy and turned it around. The boxes and suitcases were packed neatly and still had room for both of them to sit. The time had come. Tears were flowing all over the place, even Cecil cried, but he surely did not know why. Nellie's eyes were bright red, Will kept dabbing his eyes, and even Uncle John was sobbing. Mary hugged Lizzie tight and whispered, "You're the big sister now; I will miss you."

Lizzie cried like a baby. Mary was crying too as she hugged Fred, Arthur, and then Cecil. Will handed Mary an envelope, which Lizzie knew held money, as he hugged her. Nellie hugged her one last time, and then they were off as everybody waved and waved. Soon, they were out of sight, and everybody was back in the house, trying to compose him- or herself.

Lizzie helped clean the house and realized she had experienced a completely new set of feelings. She was happy for Mary, but she was still sad to see her go. Also, Lizzie now had a paying job, which would start in a few days. She stood in the kitchen, looked out of the window, and thought, I'm the big sister now.

Chapter 20

The Storm

Billy dropped his bag that held the plant suckers and ran as fast as he could through the plants, trampling everything in his way, when he suddenly stopped on his side of the creek and smiled. "Tawny..nice to see you again."

"Great to see you too, Billy. Doing all right?"

"Yeah. There's a girl asking questions about you."

"Who?"

"A friend of Clara's, the girl who lives here. I think her name is Lizzie. Yeah, Lizzie."

"What does she want?" asked Tawny.

"She wants to know about you; saw you at the train station, I guess, the day we arrived.

"Big brown eyes?" Billy nodded. "Must be the one I saw lying on the grass." Tawny rubbed his forehead. Billy suddenly turned in the direction of a noise. Tawny heard a horse grunt and knew it was time to go. "Later, governor."

"Meet me tonight," said Tawny. "After dark."

"Sure," called Billy over his shoulder as he retreated to his assigned work spot.

Tawny and Jimmy started to walk toward the barn, occasionally yanking a leaf or two from the plants and, as they got closer, the dinner bell rang. After dinner, the boys sat in a semicircle, discussing the day's business. Tawny stayed quiet about Billy, since none of the other boys knew him. Jimmy also kept quiet, but only because Tawny had told him to.

The nightly baths had slowed down now that the cure barns were cleaned; however, suckering plants brought another set of misfortune. The boys all had a slight discoloration on their hands, a few minor cuts, and sore backs.

"Tomorrow, Lathrope said we are topping," said Mark, stretching his aching back.

"What's topping?" asked Peter.

"Don't know," said Mark. "Just heard him talking about it."

Tawny rose, walked outside the barn, and looked toward the house. Where was Lathrope? Where was his family? Would he come later to check on the boys?

All these questions didn't really matter since Tawny was meeting his friend Billy soon and nothing would stop him, not Lathrope and certainly not the boys. Jimmy came outside and stood next to Tawny, who was still "looking the situation over" (as he called it) and couldn't wait until the main house went quiet.

"Is everything's ok?" asked Tawny, smiling at Jimmy. "You know the plan?"

"Yeah. Wish I could come."

"Too dangerous for you. Next time."

Tawny led the boys up into the loft by pretending to yawn a few times, and it was strange that his plan worked because soon they were sleeping, except for Tawny, who was wide-awake and ready to leave.

"Jimmy. Jimmy." Tawny gently tugged Jimmy awake.

"Ok." As part of the plan, Jimmy moved over onto Tawny's bed and then curled back up and fell asleep.

Tawny crept out of the barn and made his way through the dark landscape to the special place, which didn't take too long now that he knew the shortest way. Tawny approached the big elm tree and then sat and listened to the creek. It was even louder at night, and the crescent moon reflected on the water. Then he heard a noise from the far side of the creek bed, looked up, and peered into the gloom. "Billy, is that you?"

"Yeah. Where are you?"

"Over here..follow my voice," said Tawny.

"How do I cross this creek?"

"Don't really know," said Tawny.

The creek was wide enough that nobody could run and jump over it. Also, they couldn't cross the creek on foot since getting wet would give them away; besides, they didn't know how deep the water was. So, they had to devise a plan. For the next three hours, they stood on each side of the creek and talked as they compared farm owners, habits, food, sleeping arrangements, and finally Lizzie.

Tawny was satisfied and relieved to know that the Culmer farm was the same as the Lathrope farm, and they chuckled when they found out that both of them had been locked in a cure barn. They agreed that the food was all right, and Billy told Tawny that his orphanage friend Thomas was on the Culmer farm, which excited Tawny. He told Billy to bring Thomas next time.

"Tawny, when do you want to meet again?"

"Tomorrow night's alright," said Tawny.

"Yeah, sure, ok, see you later," said Billy.

"Bye. Don't forget to bring Thomas."

They waved and Tawny returned to his barn slowly and quietly. When he neared the barn, it was getting closer to daylight and the temperature was very warm. Tawny climbed up the loft ladder, lay down on Jimmy's bed, and slept for only a couple of hours.

Morning came too fast. Again, Lathrope stood in the door and belted his usual good morning, which happened to be something about being lazy and English. Tawny struggled to rise, only for a little while, and soon they were all working in the fields again, topping. It was hot and muggy, even at six in the morning, and it was obvious that topping plants was so far the easiest job for the boys. Lathrope kept the boys close to the main house during the morning so he could keep an eye on them; the topping work was new to them, and he had to watch to make sure they didn't ruin the plants.

The morning meal bell rang and the boys ran back to the barn. After the morning meal, Tawny and Jimmy were again given the backfields to work, and they walked toward the creek and started topping plants as they were instructed. Tawny knew that Lathrope would make a round in about an hour, so he and Jimmy had to get as much done as possible if they were to enjoy the special place.

Lathrope suddenly appeared from nowhere and approached the boys as Tawny and Jimmy were snapping off the flower pods as fast as they could.

"Pretty good," said Lathrope. He watched for a few minutes, and then left while looking to the skies. The clear skies from yesterday were gone and now replaced with dark, hard angry-looking clouds. It was very hot and humid, and Tawny felt the storm and it was coming fast.

Suddenly, the dinner bell rang and rang. Both Tawny and Jimmy knew something wasn't right as they started to run back to the barn. The others also ran back, and soon they all stood at the open barn door, wondering what was happening.

Lathrope entered the barn, looking frightened and sweaty. Those who stood closest to Lathrope heard him mumble "I'll lose it all." The rain and wind started, and then after a few seconds, the heavens seemed to crack open. It rained and blew in a hellacious frenzy.

The boys watched the water quickly fill the yard and form thousands of tiny lakes. Tawny had seen this kind of rain back at the orphanage, but what he saw next was his first. In the distance, toward the back corner of the farm property, Tawny saw a dark gray funnel cloud coiling, touching the ground, and then moving in a jagged line.

"Look. Look!" Tawny pointed.

Lathrope's chin dropped as he watched along with the boys. "It's a tornado, damn it!"

The long funnel cloud only lasted about ten or twenty seconds, and then it disappeared as the wind blew the rain sideways at times and slightly slanted at other times.

About thirty minutes later, the storm blew itself out and the sun actually started to show itself as the air temperature dropped. Lathrope, who was visibly shaking, quickly fetched his wagon, demanded the boys climb in, and they made their way through the fields stopping every ten seconds to check the damage. Lathrope was still mumbling, and often the boys could make out the word ok. Most of the plants survived the wind and rainstorm; however, once in a while, usually on the outer edges of the fields, a plant or two was bent over. Lathrope continued his damage survey, taking his time, as he scanned the fields carefully.

"Tomorrow, we gather the damaged plants," said Lathrope.

The wagon turned a corner and as they neared the creek; a small section was leveled to the ground in a cluster of green leaves and stems, which protruded upright in all different angles. Lathrope stopped the wagon, got off, rubbed his head, and walked forward. The part of the field that was damaged was right next to the creek bed. Tawny swallowed hard as he slowly turned his head to the right. The big elm tree was still standing.

"No!" shouted Lathrope, as he kicked leaves about, like a little boy throwing a tantrum.

"We'll pick up these leaves tomorrow morning, first thing." The wagon returned to the barn and the night was over. Tawny decided not to go tonight, but he could possibly go tomorrow night, and realized that Billy was probably thinking along the same lines.

Lathrope woke up the boys a little earlier the next morning, and soon they were in the damaged field, picking leaves and stacking them in the wagon. It didn't take long to fill it up. Lathrope told Peter and Mark to lie on top of the leave piles to hold them in place so they wouldn't fall out of the wagon. After they reached the cure barn, the closest one to the main house, Lathrope showed the boys how to hang the leaves and tie down bundles.

For the rest of the day, the boys prepared the cure barn with the first batch of tobacco leaves. Lathrope showed them how to open and close the vent doors, which was a little tricky but easy.

Lathrope used the word kiln several times, but neither of the boys asked him about it because he was still in a foul mood. Then the dinner bell rang just as Lathrope stood back and marveled at his first hangings of the year. They ran back to the barn and were served dinner. Around thirty minutes later, they saw the bucket brigade appear from nowhere and they knew then that it was bath night.

The boys, now a little fresher and cleaner, talked about the storm they had witnessed yesterday and the damage it had caused and also wondered if this was a normal thing for Canada.

Tawny thought maybe tonight he could meet Billy, but he'd have to wait until the right time to make his move, not to mention having Jimmy or somebody else cover for him again. Tawny smiled at Jimmy and knew what he was thinking—he was hoping that he could go tonight. Once everybody fell asleep, Tawny rose and nudged Jimmy. Jimmy quickly sat up and said, "I want to go tonight."

Tawny took one last look at the main house, shrugged, and then said, "Why not." Tawny grabbed a pile of loose hay and made a sort of replica of himself and Jimmy followed suit and before long, if someone looked at it in the dark, their beds really looked like two curled up sleeping boys. They crept out of the barn like burglars stalking the night and ran through the fields to the special place.

Chapter 21

The Bakery

It felt a little strange not having Mary around. Lizzie would often look into Mary's old room, which now was empty, and wonder how her big sister was doing in the big city.

Lizzie slowly opened her eyes. Today was the first day of her job, and Mr. Owen told her to arrive first thing in the morning. Lizzie looked at the mantle clock on her shelf: 5:30. She rolled out of bed, stretched, and made her way to the outhouse. She held her breath. At other times she would take a handkerchief and cover her face.

Lizzie went to the kitchen, poured a glass of milk, and sat at the big table in the dining room, feeling so excited about having a paying job. She was thinking of all the things she could buy and all the things she could do. Suddenly, she stopped, went blank, and realized that she was acting just like Mary again! A small grin grew as she continued to daydream. Fred and Arthur were awake and stirring around the house while father was outside, preparing his work wagon.

Lizzie's mother was making breakfast and, before long, the whole family sat down to eat. Uncle John finally showed up for morning coffee and was acting pleased that Lizzie was working at the Owen Bakery. He sipped his coffee, took a bite of cake, and lectured her about work ethics, loyalty, and honesty. Lizzie had heard all this from Mom and Dad just yesterday, but she nodded politely as her uncle finished.

She also remembered how Mary would leave the house, how she would dress casually but always had her hair up in a bun, except on Sundays, when she would wear her hair down. Lizzie grabbed her own hair and realized that it was down and messy. She quickly went to her room and returned a little while later with hair that looked neat and proper, just like Mary's, and everyone knew Mr. Owen would be impressed.

Nellie and Will commented to Uncle John how much Lizzie had matured over the past couple of weeks, and Uncle John agreed while sipping coffee and eating cake.

The walk to the bakery was short. As she enjoyed the early morning air, she noticed that it had grown cooler in the past few days. She also noticed tree limbs that were broken by the storm two days ago. People used the word tornado a lot since then, and to her recollection, it was the only time she had ever heard of a tornado in Canada. She would have to ask her Uncle John about it later.

"Good morning," said Mr. Owen as Lizzie entered the bakery. "You can use the back entrance, Lizzie. It's a shorter walk—you don't have to walk around the entire building."

"Thanks," replied Lizzie.

Mr. Owen gave Lizzie an apron. Lizzie tied it around her neck and waist. It was larger than she was used to, but with the right tugs and ties, it felt perfect.

"What are we making this morning?"

"Hot-cross buns, Lizzie" said Mr. Owen, and then added, "and the normal bread, of course."

After ten minutes, Lizzie and the two elderly ladies were covered from head to toe in flour. It smelled so great after the oven doors were opened; the whole room filled with the sweet smell of baking.

"Good job," said Mr. Owen.

"We'll find out soon enough," said Lizzie looking at her first unbaked tray of rolled dough. Time flew in this bakery, but one thing troubled Lizzie; the two elderly women would always speak in a foreign language, and Lizzie didn't know what it was. She knew it sounded funny and she tried to pick out recognizable words when they spoke. Lizzie shrugged her shoulders; this was just another thing she would have to ask her father about.

When Lizzie's rolls came out of the oven, they were plump, tanned, and beautiful. Mr. Owen nodded appreciatively and commented that Lizzie was a chip off the old block. I guess he's talking about Mom, thought Lizzie.

Soon the morning baking was complete, and the two elderly women— Lizzie hadn't learned their names yet—sat and had a cup of coffee and continued talking in that odd language.

People came and went in a steady stream buying and paying for breads, rolls, cakes, and specialty items. The only conversation was the about the tornado sighting. Lizzie overheard that it tore up fields, ripped out fence posts, and overturned an old wagon.

It seemed that everyone was affected in some way by the tornado. It wasn't until Mr. Fletch came in and actually told Mr. Owen that the tornado was a rare event in these parts that Lizzie was relieved to know that it probably wouldn't happen again for a long time.

Mr. Owen handed Lizzie a handful of change at the end of the day and told her she did a good job. He also told her that she would learn the cash register next so that she could take money on Sundays.

Lizzie returned home with $1.28 in her pocket. She worked out the math and figured that she was earning sixteen cents an hour. If she saved it all, it would grow fast, and then she could buy so many things! She stopped, angry with herself, and thought again, I'm thinking like Mary.

Lizzie waited at the big dining room table for her father to come home. She had a few questions for him. Soon, Will came in, washed his hand and face, and then sat next to his daughter.

"What's on your mind?"

"You know those two older ladies at the Bakery?"

"You mean Gretchen and Madeline?"

Lizzie nodded. "Where do they come from?"

"Germany. Baden–Baden, Germany. They are German, just like me. Their father and your grandfather came to this part of Canada, together, around fifty years ago," explained Will.

"Thanks," said Lizzie. She stood and retreated to her room; another mystery had been solved.

The next day at work, Lizzie spent time learning the cash register. Afterward she helped prepare the day's special and she figured out how to ring a sale and pop open the large wooden door. It wasn't too difficult, but Lizzie had to stand on a footstool to reach the big white buttons. Several years ago, Mr. Owen had built a stool for Mary, and he pulled it from the storage closet and brushed it off. It worked very well.

Lizzie couldn't wait for Sunday so she could tell Clara all about her new job and her new personal bank, which now was filling with coins.

Lizzie was getting good at figuring, multiplying numbers, and adding amounts. This occupied part of her time when walking to and from work and at night, just before she drifted off to sleep. The other part was devoted to Tawny.

"Lizzie!" called Clara, as she approached the church.

"Clara!" Lizzie exclaimed as she ran to her friend. They hugged, walked into the church, and sat in their usual favorite spot—the last row on the left side. This was the best spot to talk and not be heard if they whispered.

The service started, and between the standing and the sitting down a few times, it was quickly over, and the girls went outside to continue their discussion in the cool breeze.

They talked about school, Lizzie's new job, the tornado, and finally about Billy. Clara told Lizzie about talking to Billy a couple of times during the week, doing it exactly like they had done before, when everyone was asleep. Lizzie looked at her best friend in a whole new light.

Lizzie was totally amazed at Clara for what she had done. Clara told Lizzie that the harvest had started. Pretty soon, winter would be on them, bringing snow, ice, and miserable cold for three or four months. Lizzie dreaded the winter months, but maybe this year it would be different; she had a paying job, a big sister in Brantford to visit, and a new interest named Tawny.

"Did Billy say anything about Tawny?" asked Lizzie.

"Yeah, he said he saw him," said Clara "Told me to tell you too."

"Your farm borders the old Fell farm, right?"

"Yeah," replied Clara. "Only in the back, along the creek, for a hundred yards or so."

"That's where they must have seen each other." Lizzie felt proud that she figured this out on her own.

"Probably," said Clara.

"When you see Billy again, tell him to say 'hi' to Tawny for me." Lizzie grinned.

"Sure," answered Clara, "Next time I see him."

Something in Clara's voice made Lizzie think that Clara was starting to like Billy...that and that Clara's cheeks reddened when she talked about Billy.

"He's so cute," said Lizzie, and Clara agreed with her.

Lizzie now realized that Clara, even though she was six months older than Lizzie, was now catching up to her in the department of boys. Lizzie now understood that this school year would be a completely new and different experience for both of them.

Richard P. Tanos

Chapter 22

The Find

Tawny pulled Jimmy by the jacket sleeve toward a clearing that led directly to the special place. The moon was bright and supplied a little light that added an eerie glow to the creek and the rocks on the creek bed. The storm didn't hurt the big elm nor did it hurt the immediate surroundings. It was still peaceful. It did knock down a few smaller trees, however, and uproot lots of plants.

Tawny heard a noise to his left. He gulped hard, leaned against the tree, and peered so hard into the gloom that his eyes watered. Jimmy had heard the same thing and now cowered directly behind Tawny. Tawny could make out two forms coming slowly at him on his side of the creek. Tawny could feel Jimmy shake behind him. It wasn't until the two forms were almost on top of them that Tawny knew.

"Billy, you surprised me," said Tawny, as he stepped out from behind the giant tree.

"How did you cross the creek?"

"Down there, governor, about two hundred feet." Billy pointed. Tawny looked downstream, but it was too dark to see anything.

"Tawny, good to see you," said Thomas, who quickly peeked out from behind Billy.

"Good to see you too," replied Tawny as they hugged and clapped each other on the back.

"Hi, Thomas..Hi, Billy," said Jimmy, as he too appeared from behind Tawny and the four of them sat around the big elm tree talking, laughing, and just plain being boys.

"How did you cross the creek?"

"The storm a couple of days back," said Billy. "You know the tornado? Well, it dropped a big tree across the creek. Saw it yesterday, while I was working."

"Thought it was a perfect bridge," added Billy. "You never know when you might need a bridge to leave this prison called Canada."

121

The four rose and started toward the fallen tree trunk around two hundred feet downstream and Tawny slightly remembered looking at the big dead tree trunk when Lathrope took them for the boundary tour. Also, Tawny remembered that if he was coming from the left side the dead tree made a great marker. Not any more.

Finally, they stood and looked at what Mother Nature had done. She had provided a natural bridge that the boys could use to go back and forth. It had fallen perfectly and linked the two properties. It also fell in a well-hidden location.

"Somebody up there likes us," said Thomas, gazing into the heavens.

"Bloody right," said Jimmy.

The boys walked to the creek's edge and examined the dead hollow log. On Tawny's side, the bank was uplifted a little but not too badly; on Billy's side, there was a small indentation made by the impact of the fall.

"The storm must have stopped right after it hit the tree," said Billy.

They could see that on one side of the dead tree were a lot of torn-up plants and pieces of tree branches strewn about, whereas on the other side, there was no damage at all.

"Watch," said Billy, as he ran across the dead tree.

Thomas followed, then Tawny, and last, Jimmy.

It was different now that they stood on the other side of the creek. It felt strange to Tawny that they could come and go so easily. They all crossed again and again—it became a game as they laughed at each as they crossed. After a few times of running the crossing, they felt comfortable and confident. When Jimmy was making his last crossing, he hit a knot in the tree and went tumbling to his left and hit the ground, which made the other three boys laugh hysterically. Jimmy rolled over, sat on the ground with his legs crossed feeling foolish, and brushed the dirt off.

"What is that?" Jimmy stared at something sticking out from one end of the tree trunk.

Tawny came closer, knelt down, and then stuck his hand out to move some grass.

"It's a hand, a damned bloody hand." Billy bent forward for a closer look.

Tawny and Billy quickly backpedaled a couple of steps. Thomas was trying to get a better look and started prodding to reveal it more fully.

"You're right...it's a hand." Jimmy, now standing, began to shake uncontrollably.

They looked, trying to figure out exactly what this skeleton hand was doing there. Tawny was the first to get a really close look at it.

"It's wrapped in burlap," said Tawny poking and moving it slightly.

"It's a hand, all right. And it's attached to a body. Move over." Billy nudged Tawny away. He touched it a few times. After examining the hand bones and after tugging at the burlap a bit, Billy had managed to pull out a good portion of the skeleton. All the boys gasped when several small bones from the fingertips dropped to the ground.

"It's really small," said Thomas, backing away.

"Get it out," said Tawny. He knelt and tugged. There it was, a fully wrapped skeleton of a small person, with one hand sticking out. The remaining finger bones were slightly curled, as if it was trying to hold an invisible ball. The burlap wrapping that covered the body was loose.

Tawny thought that the burlap coat was loose because the boys tugged on it trying to get it out of the hollow tree trunk and never thinking that the person wrapped in it had a full body that would disappear over time, causing the burlap to loosen.

"Unwrap it," said Jimmy.

"I wonder who it was," said Thomas.

"Jimmy, lie down next to it," said Billy.

"You're, you're, crazy," replied Jimmy, backing up quickly.

"Yeah, it's a great idea," said Tawny. "This way, we can tell about how old the kid was."

Jimmy layed down next to the wrapped skeleton.

"Put our your hand," said Thomas.

Jimmy stretched his hand out, visibly shaking, and after a minute he quickly got up.

"There, I hope you're happy." Jimmy brushed himself off, obviously angry.

"It's about your age," said Billy. "Eight or nine."

Tawny and Billy started to unwrap their new discovery and it was hard because the burlap was brittle and disintegrating. They took their time and soon, there it was, the complete skeleton of a child, around the same size as Jimmy. The boys examined the skeleton carefully. Small holes appeared in the skull, and the jaw gaped with the yellowed teeth. They couldn't tell if it was a boy or girl.

"Lathrope killed him."

"Jimmy, what are you talking about?" Tawny looked puzzled.

"It was when you were locked in the cure barn. I heard Mrs. Lathrope...remember? Telling Mr. Lathrope about the one he lost."

"This must be the one he lost," exclaimed Tawny.

"The tree was on his property," said Thomas.

"Look. Look," said Billy. He reached down, and between the bones pulled out a silver object and held it up to the moonlight. "It's a Saint Christopher medal. I've seen these before."

"Something about traveling and God," explained Billy.

"Keep looking," said Jimmy.

Tawny examined the medal carefully. There were no significant marks visible, except for a small semicircle piece missing from one of the ends. The boys poked and felt the bones. Tawny slid the medallion in his pants pocket and said, "Let's put the body back."

"What?" said Thomas. "Why don't we throw it in the creek"?

"You heard me; put it back."

Billy and Tawny carefully rewrapped the body and stuffed it back into the tree trunk. This took a while because the arm sticking out would not go back into position, and they really did not want to break the skeleton more than they already had. Billy sat on the ground and, with his legs, pushed the skeleton deeper into the tree trunk.

Crack, crack. The joints were breaking.

Tawny hefted a boulder from the creek bed and wedged it into the hollow tree trunk to cover their find. Jimmy kicked dirt into the trunk to cover the rock.

"Just make it look normal," said Billy

"Wonder how long it has been there?"

"Don't know, Jimmy," said Tawny.

"Who put it there is a better question," said Thomas.

"Keep this to ourselves," said Tawny. "Just the four of us ." Tawny stuck out his left hand and almost in a flash, the other three did the same, and they just smiled at each other.

The boys all agreed to tell no one nor even talk about it. It was their secret.. and, obviously, somebody else's. After a quick examination of the fallen tree trunk, the boys said their good-byes and agreed to meet Sunday afternoon, which was a good time because the farmers' families went to town for church. They walked away from the special place, leaving by two different directions but now with one common bond, the skeleton.

Richard P. Tanos

Chapter 23

The School

Lizzie was excited about the first day of the new school year, not only because she would see her friends again but also because everyone would talk about what they did on their summer vacations. Mostly, Lizzie was happy that she could see Clara every day and that they could talk freely. For Lizzie, the walk to the school was short, but Clara had to be driven by Mr. Nate. Lizzie would take Arthur to school each day, and next year, she would have to take Cecil as well. Lizzie would first drop off Arthur at his seat and then go outside to sit on a low stone wall that surrounded the schoolyard and wait for Clara. Lizzie's father and some other stonemasons built the wall two years previously. Lizzie remembered that her father and Uncle John argued about how high it should be; to Lizzie it looked just fine the way it was.

Lizzie looked forward to meeting her new teacher. She'd heard Uncle John say that the town had hired her from the city of Hamilton, which Lizzie knew was north of Brantford, but had never been there, to replace old Mrs. Johnson, who retired last year.

Clara finally arrived, and after hugging each other, they entered the school and took their seats.

The school had only one classroom, separated by a huge space providing one area for the younger children and another for the older students. The children entered one at a time, and soon everybody was seated, even Greta, the German girl. There were also a few new students. After scanning the classroom, Lizzie saw five classmates she knew and six whom she didn't. After a quick count, she figured that seven girls and five boys were in the older class and the rest were new.

The new teacher entered the room. "Hello, my name is Miss Kemp."

Miss Kemp was a young, tall, well-dressed lady; had flowing shoulder-length blonde hair; sported stylish black glasses; and wore very little if any makeup. Lizzie liked her as soon as she saw her.

The first morning was taken up by Miss Kemp, who asked each student to stand and tell the class all about his or her summer.

Lizzie sat next to Clara; they had done so for several years, and often smiled back and forth to each other, sometimes getting into trouble with the teacher.

"Ok, it's your turn, Missy." Miss Kemp nodded at a new girl in the front row. Missy was dressed well. Probably upper class, thought Lizzie.

"My name is Missy Lathrope," said the new student.

Lathrope? Lizzie looked at Clara, her big brown eyes even wider and now probing.

Lizzie listened carefully and heard everything Missy said. She even jotted down a few things on paper. Missy was around nine, thought Lizzie, and had a long neck with short hair. Missy said that she had spent the past three years living with her aunt and uncle in Buffalo, New York. Missy's father had owned the farm for three years and that they came from Eastern Canada—she thought she heard the word Cornwall.

Missy had two younger brothers and a younger sister, but she never heard Missy talk about Tawny or the other boys. In fact, Lizzie had never heard any of the farm children in school talk about the boys working on their farms.

Lizzie remembered last year seeing a couple of boys in school wearing rubber boots but only during the winter months. Could these be the farm boys? Maybe Tawny would show up for school this year. For a moment, Lizzie got excited.

"Lunch time," said Miss Kemp.

Lizzie and Clara rose from their seats and walk toward the lunch table.

"Did Tawny say hi?" asked Lizzie. "You know, did you tell Billy I said hi to Tawny?"

"Not yet," replied Clara, "Couldn't get out." Clara grinned and then whispered, "Maybe tonight."

The children fetched their bags and began eating. Afterward, Lizzie and Clara took advantage of the great weather and strolled around the schoolyard talking about Tawny and Billy.

Clara was now paying more attention to the topic of boys. It was only last week that Clara didn't care about boys at all. Today, Clara had already asked three questions about Billy.

Lizzie noticed that Missy Lathrope was sitting on the steps along with Greta. All the boys were young and really didn't interest Lizzie and, as of today, they didn't interest Clara either.

The afternoon flew by, and soon the children were leaving for home. Miss Kemp said good-bye to each child and made sure the children took their belongings and homework. Clara and Lizzie would always stand out in front of the school and wait for Mr. Nate. Sometimes he would be there first and other times he would be just a little late; nevertheless, he always showed up. Lizzie and Clara, while waiting, would always spend their time talking or playing. Now, they added boys to their list of topics.

Mr. Nate finally showed up. Clara climbed aboard and started to wave from the buggy. Lizzie returned the wave and walked home, all the while thinking about Tawny. She wondered what he was doing; if he was safe; and, most of all, if he was thinking about her.

"Lizzie, how was your first day at school?" Nellie was pounding a huge piece of red meat.

"Fine, Mom." Lizzie sat at the kitchen table, watched her mother, and had a glass of milk with an oatmeal cookie.

Lizzie spent the entire week going to and from school and trying to find out each day if Tawny had been told that Lizzie said hello. Each day, Clara had a reason for not telling Billy, and this bothered Lizzie. The only highlight of the week was that Mary and Hubrey were coming home this Sunday for dinner, and Lizzie couldn't wait; she knew that she would be working all weekend at the bakery and wouldn't be home until late Sunday afternoon.

Lizzie got up early Saturday morning and got ready for work by putting her hair in a tight little bun. Actually, she was getting good at it and often she would thank Mary, silently of course, for showing her how to do it. She went down to the kitchen and joined her mother for a cup of tea.

Lizzie knew that her mom was waiting for Uncle John to bring the local newspaper because the coffee was ready and a single piece of chocolate cake sat on the counter. Lizzie was sure this cake had Uncle John's name on it.

"Good morning," said Uncle John as he wiped the grass from his shoes on the mat outside and entered through the back door.

"Hello," replied Nellie and Lizzie.

Uncle John hung his jacket on the hook next to the back door, picked up the plate with the single piece of chocolate cake, nodded at Nellie, and started to eat the cake even before he reached the table. Lizzie's mother always seemed amazed that her brother-in-law loved to eat cake and pastries so much. Nellie's question was why then hadn't he married someone who would give him those things?

"Where's Will?" asked Uncle John, showing tiny pieces of brown cake between his teeth.

"Already left for work," said Nellie, laying a napkin on the table hoping Uncle John would use it either to wipe his mouth or catch the flying debris. "You know...the county job."

"Yeah, I forgot. They should have that sign done by tomorrow," said Uncle John, stuffing more cake into his mouth.

To Lizzie, Uncle John, was a great man. He was a fantastic listener, a knowledgeable man, and a good friend; but there was one thing that he was terrible at—eating: slurping soups, talking with his mouth full, and often spraying and spitting at anyone who would get close enough. Lizzie was amused at times, especially when guests were at the house and Uncle John came over after dinner to eat cake and then would speak at the same time, which did not happen too often, but when it did, it was a spectacle.

After Uncle John had sipped his coffee a few times, Lizzie took a last glance to see if his plate was empty and she knew it was safe now to ask a question.

"Uncle, can you tell me about the boys working on the farm?"

"What do you want to know?"

"Where do they come from? How long will they stay here? Do you know the framer named Lathrope?"

Uncle John sat back in his chair and glanced over at Nellie, perhaps to get Nellie's blessing before he answered. Nellie blinked, and Uncle John smiled. "Most of them come from England, the ones with no parents, the ones in trouble with the police, and the ones born into poverty. Canada allows these children—honey, we call them immigrants—to enter the country. In fact, Canada advertises in other countries to attract people to occupy the new territories."

Lizzie listened intently to her uncle, but she only wanted to hear something that pertained to Tawny or Lathrope. Because she was brought up correctly, she continued listening to the same old story that she had heard several times before.

"Damn the tobacco industry and those representatives who set up this thing with the farmers. They bring over these kids to work and use them as slaves. They are supposed to go to school...Yeah. Can't see that happening." Uncle John shook his head as he stood and poured a second cup of coffee.

"Any more cake?" he asked.

"No," replied Nellie and Lizzie in unison.

"Just simply moving too damn fast—the whole country is moving too fast. I heard that they are working on labor laws for the country. Let's see what kind of things the government can do."

Lizzie, now realizing that Uncle John wasn't going to answer her question because he had gone off on a tangent, decided to let it go.

Maybe it would be better if she asked one question at a time, but she also knew that her uncle, once started, could talk with the best of them and usually was not the first to stop.

Lizzie abruptly and politely thanked him, said good-bye, and then started her walk to work.

"Slave," she said to herself, and then again, "slave."

This word kept running through her mind over and over, like a Gatling gun, and grew louder each time she thought it. This distressed her, that her Tawny was labeled as a slave.

Lizzie walked to work and was surprised to find herself at the rear door to the bakery; she had no recollection of how she got there.

"Good morning," said Mr. Owen.

Lizzie walked right past him and hung up her jacket, not moving her head at all and not blinking. Mr. Owen stared at her and shook his head, thinking that it was possibly too early in the morning for Lizzie.

Mr. Owen put his hands on his hips, drew in a huge breath, and then repeated much louder, "Good morning."

"Oh...hello, Mr. Owen." Lizzie was now coming back down to earth.

"Are you all right?" he asked.

"I'm fine; sorry, Mr. Owen," she said, and then added, "My mind has been really busy this morning."

"Ready for a big day, Lizzie?" asked Mr. Owen.

"Yes, I am."

She had no idea of how big a day it would be.

Chapter 24

The Harvest

Every farmer looked forward to this time of year, and yet at the same time, they dreaded it because harvest was hectic and tiring. The harvesting of crops usually took four to eight weeks and had to be completed before the first snowfall. It was a gamble and this year, Lathrope had gambled with one week; most of the other farmers started a week earlier.

The weather was changing fast and no one really knew what to expect from day to day, but the first order of business was to get the leaves in the cure barns as fast as possible. However, the first order of business for Lathrope was to go to town on Saturday and pick up a delivery of cordwood just to be ready in case of a severe cold that could damage the leaves in the cure barns. Saturday morning came and Lathrope had resolved to get a wagon of cordwood from the general store at the square, because the temperatures seemed to be dropping. Besides, he had waited an extra week to start his harvest.

"Tawny, come here." Lathrope stood at the barn door looking as he always did first thing in the morning.

"Ok." Tawny rose and donned an extra shirt because the air felt unusually cold. Lathrope had picked him because he was the biggest of the bunch; he would obviously be the strongest; and, because cordwood requires a lot of muscle to handle, Tawny was the logical choice.

They took the wagon, with Tawny sitting in the back and Lathrope driving, and they headed toward the town center. Tawny noticed very little activity in the fields, probably because it was so early in the morning. It took less time to get to the train station than when they were brought to the farms. Lathrope took the wagon directly to the general store as Tawny took in the sights.

"Wait here," said Lathrope as he jumped off the wagon and tied the horses to the post before entering the store.

Tawny looked around at the buildings. There was the train station; now it seemed a lot smaller than he remembered.

Lathrope returned to the wagon and instructed Tawny to start loading the pieces of cordwood that were stacked next to the back door. It took about an hour or so, and the wagon was piled high with cut pieces of wood that had sap oozing out from every piece and, by now, it was all over Tawny's hands and arms.

Lathrope motioned for Tawny to get into the wagon. They were on their way home when suddenly the wagon stopped on the main road. Lathrope said, "Wait here."

Lathrope entered a store that had a sign that read "Owen Bakery."

Meanwhile, Tawny just sat on the back of the wagon with his legs dangling over the edge, doing exactly as he was told, waiting for his boss to return.

"Bang, bang." Tawny heard a noise coming from his right. It sounded like a quiet tapping. He looked around and to his amazement there, peeking through the glass window, was the little brown-eyed girl he had seen a few weeks ago by the train station. He could never forget those brown eyes. He quickly smiled, waved, and actually felt a little embarrassed sitting on this wagon, acting like he was guarding a pile of wood. Lizzie smiled back with a look that melted him. Suddenly, Lathrope returned with a bag of pastries, and the wagon was off. Tawny and Lizzie waved until they could no longer see each other.

Tawny sat back against the wood and felt warm inside, knowing that he knew where Lizzie was and that she had asked questions about him. The ride back to the farm seemed shorter than before, perhaps because he was preoccupied with thoughts of this young girl who liked him. He knew now that he liked her, too.

Tawny and Jimmy removed the wood from the wagon and piled it next to the small barn that was only twenty feet or so from the main house, the one that housed the animals.

It started to rain, and Lathrope told the boys to wait for him in the barn. After about ten minutes, the skies opened up again and the rain pelted down hard and furious as Mark, Peter, and Tom ran back, soaking wet.

"Where did you go?" Mark shook the water from his hair.

"Got some wood." Tawny was still thinking about Lizzie.

The rain stopped almost as fast as it started, and Lathrope returned to the barn to gather the boys; harvest was going to start.

The boys were dropped off in the field next to the main house. Lathrope showed them how to pick leaves and store them on the wagon without damaging them. After the wagon filled, the leaves were taken to a cure barn, piled and tied, and then hung to dry. They had worked at this for about three hours and had only made a tiny dent in emptying the fields; Tawny hadn't realized how many leaves these tobacco plants had.

The dinner bell rang, and the boys walked to the barn and, like clockwork, the kitchen lady brought them their tray of food. Picking leaves took longer than any of the other chores they performed, but except for minor cuts and staining, the work was relatively easy.

The problem Mark and Peter had was tying the leaves into bundles and hanging them from the roof of the cure barns. Jimmy was too small to hang leaves but Tom picked up on this trade easier than anybody else. Night came and the boys slept in their hayloft, enjoying the cool night air.

For the next few days, the work routine was identical; the entire farm had to be picked clean and the cure barns loaded with thousands of leaves. To Tawny, it seemed that he was doing nothing but sleeping, picking, and tying. Lathrope seemed to be concerned only about the weather and didn't bother the boys too much about the picking and tying exercise because they knew how to do it and they were doing it well.

After a week of yanking leaves, the boys were still harvesting tobacco as Lathrope and his family had left for church early in the afternoon for a day in town.

Tawny, who was feeling very tired, sank to the ground and started thinking about Lizzie. Out of the blue, he started thinking about his thirteenth birthday, which by his calculations had to be within several days, and thought about the night he found his file and almost burnt the orphanage by not putting the candles out properly. He knew his birthday was on the 26th of September but had no idea of what the actual date was today. None of this really mattered to him; birthdays were always unimportant—not a big deal.

The boys kept at it, still yanking leaves off the big stems of the tobacco plants. As it grew dark, they waited to hear the dinner bell ring. After it rang, they scattered back to the barn and ate; right in the middle of eating dinner, the family buggy returned. Lathrope quickly scanned the fields, which were close to the main house, and approached the barn only to tell the boys that they were doing a decent job and for them to keep it up.

For the boys, the following days flew by as did the next several days; this harvest was both boring and tiring. The boys filled the cure barns as fast as they could, and as far as Lathrope was concerned, they were sure it wasn't fast enough. On the other hand, the boys stayed out of trouble only because they were extremely busy picking, stacking, tying, and hanging big green leaves. Perhaps it was Wednesday afternoon, or close to it, that

Tawny was hanging a tied bunch of leaves in one of the cure barns, the one that was closest to the farm boundary with the white pole, when he dropped a pile of leaves. When he picked it up he noticed something. He bent down and picked up a silver chain, wiped it off, and realized that it still had a piece of metal attached to it. After examining this thing for a while, he reached into his pocket and pulled out the medal they had found on the skeleton from the hollow tree trunk.

"Good God." The two pieces fit perfectly. His mind raced, and it felt spooky knowing that the skeleton was here before it became a skeleton. He quickly put the chain in his pocket along with the medal.

Mark looked at Tawny. "You're sure acting strange. What's going on?"

"Nothing." After the barn was fully loaded, the boys headed back to the fields, only to start the process over again. The best thing about the boys working the harvest was that now both Tawny and Tom had learned how to drive the wagons and the horses. That night after dinner, the boys noticed that the fields looked really bare, almost like that field they saw after the tornado had hit it, only this time the boys had cleared the fields.

Lathrope seemed to be keeping a close watch on the boys; he didn't let them out of his sight, and if they did wander off, he surely stopped it quickly.

Tawny crawled into bed and covered himself with one of the horse blankets that they had found weeks before and started to think about Lizzie. Tawny fell asleep curled up in the hay bed.

The boys continued the harvest without incident for the next several days. Lathrope was too busy trying to get the leaves hung within the next week. Tawny knew that if they were going through the harvest, then Billy and Thomas were also going through the same thing on their farm.

Lathrope took each of the boys into town, one at a time, except for Jimmy, to gather cordwood for the upcoming winter, as he told each of them. Tawny's birthday came and went; the harvest was too time consuming, and the boys had no idea what day it was. They knew only that the air became cooler and the days were less humid and shorter. Tawny had completely forgotten about his birthday.

Chapter 25

The First Kiss

Lizzie was working at the counter on this Saturday, taking in money and working the big wooden cash register. Normally, Lizzie worked the register on Sunday, but Gretchen was sick and since Lizzie knew how to work it, it was hers for the day; besides, Lizzie really loved to work the large buttons that made the tray pop open and sound the bell. Business was slow on this morning but Mr. Owen was sure it would pick up later, and Lizzie actually found herself a little bored just waiting for customers to come in and buy baked goods. She often stared out the window that faced the grassy park and the Grand River thinking about many things, including Tawny.

Mr. Owen called from the back of the store. "Lizzie, Lizzie, come here." She left the front counter, after she made sure the cash door was shut, and stood in front of her boss.

"Help me glaze the buns," he said, pointing to a pail full of white paste. Both of them quickly glazed the buns, prepared them on a sheet, and stuck them in the rack in the front of the store. Lizzie walked back to the cash register, wiping her hands off on her apron.

The door opened and a tall man entered looking weather beaten and tired. He looked at the trays, and then Mr. Owen said, "Hello, Mr. Lathrope, how are you?"

Lizzie almost gasped.

"Do you have that cake ready?"

"Right here," said Mr. Owen, as he pulled from the top shelf a white cake with the words Happy Birthday Carol on it. Lizzie remembered assisting Mr. Owen in preparing the cake earlier this morning and applying the frosting around the edges.

"How's harvest coming?" asked Mr. Owen.

"Just fine. We should be done in a week or two."

Lizzie had a strange feeling come over her as she turned her head slowly and there he was, as big as life, sitting on the back of the wagon, her newfound interest in life, Tawny. He was just looking at the ground swinging his feet, which dangled from the end of the wagon, and not paying attention to anything. He's so cute, thought Lizzie.

She tapped the glass a couple of times. He looked up, saw her, and smiled. She smiled back, wanting so desperately to just go outside and talk to him. Lathrope left the store, and before long the only thing she had to remember was a smile and a wave or two.

It was a good thing that business was slow because Lizzie was in a daydream. Lizzie couldn't wait to see her big sister tomorrow and catch up on all what was happening in Brantford and with Mary.

Sunday morning arrived windy, but sunny. After breakfast, Lizzie walked to church and waited there for Clara. Then they took their usual seats and whispered about what happened yesterday to Lizzie, and soon Clara knew all about it and was really happy for her best friend. Clara shared some news herself; Lizzie was invited to spend next Friday and Saturday nights at Clara's. At first, Lizzie said yes without thinking about her job, then sat back and cursed a little, and then asked for forgiveness.

"I'll let you know Tuesday at school," said Lizzie. "I'll ask Mr. Owen right after church, when I go into work."

Clara left the church and Lizzie made her way to the town square and entered the bakery only to find Mr. Owen standing in the door, probably wondering if business today would be any better than yesterday.

"You look really nice today," said Mr. Owen.

Lizzie smiled. "Thanks."

It took her around an hour to get up the nerve to ask for Saturday off because she didn't work on Friday; besides, other than Saturday, she didn't come into work until Sunday after church. She desperately needed Saturday off. Lizzie approached Mr. Owen—she was good at things like this. In record time, Mr. Owen had given her the day off and also told her any time she needed a Saturday off, just let him know in advance.

Lizzie returned home to find Mary and Hubrey sitting at the big table talking to Mother and Father. Mary ran to Lizzie and hugged her hard. Lizzie noticed a new fragrance and then, to her surprise, realized Mary had brought her a bottle as well.

For the next hour, everyone listened to Mary describe her new life in the city, working at the photo gallery and learning all about photography. She briefly described her life with Cousin Vera and then moved the conversation directly to the wedding, which seemed to be all planned, only it wouldn't happen until sometime next year. Nellie and Lizzie brought dinner to the table, and Mary commented several times on how much she missed Sunday dinners, but to Lizzie's recollection, Mary had missed only one Sunday dinner. Regardless, Nellie loved the fact that her daughter said it, so it didn't really matter. After dinner, the talking started back up again, only this time Uncle John joined in. Lizzie and Mary retreated to the solitude of Lizzie's room. Lizzie told her sister about Tawny, about the feelings she had for him, because Lizzie knew that Mary was the only one around who might understand.

Mary really didn't take Lizzie too seriously because it was Lizzie's first love, and Mary seemed to believe that others would come along. Mary tried to tell Lizzie about "so many fish in the sea" and other things that Lizzie didn't understand. Lizzie knew only what she felt, and she wanted to keep feeling that way.

The girls came back down in time for a story that Hubrey was telling about one of his cousins in Toronto who played ice hockey and lost his pants while playing. Lizzie acted as though she was paying attention, but she didn't hear a word; her mind was focused on Tawny. When everyone laughed at the story, Lizzie laughed along to be polite.

Evening came, with Mary and Hubrey saying their good-byes and leaving to go back to Brantford but not before telling Will that if the weather was good next week, they would be back; otherwise they would visit again in two weeks. Lizzie waved and then went back upstairs to bed.

The next week passed slowly for Lizzie, She was so excited about spending Friday and Saturday at Clara's—she would be close to Tawny. This made her feel warm. Finally, Mr. Nate took the girls to the farm, and as they stopped in front of the main house, Mrs. Culmer came running out to greet them. The sky was bright blue and cloudless but the air was cold, even colder than normal, and the harvest was almost over. Even Mr. Culmer was smiling and acting happier than usual when he said hello to Lizzie and, as usual, took her bags.

The girls sat on the front porch and Lizzie tried to see Billy, who was out in the fields doing what they do for harvest. The days were getting shorter now. Soon the dinner bell rang, and the boys came running back as the skies darkened.

Mr. Culmer lit a huge fire in the pit behind the house. Clara had warned Lizzie about the wiener and marshmallow roast that was planned. After dinner, the entire family sat around the fire, each holding a small willow branch, which was sharpened at one end. Mrs. Culmer came outside with a tray of sausages and soon everyone was holding the meat sticks in the fire and turning them from a raw pink color to all shades of black. Occasionally, Lizzie noticed that the boys were peeking through the loft door in the barn, and she wasn't sure if it was Billy or not. As the evening ended, Mr. Culmer put out the fire with shovels of dirt. The girls said good night and went upstairs to Clara's bedroom, where the activity started. Lizzie and Clara locked into a discussion that lasted for two hours about kissing, boys, Billy, and Tawny. They decided that they would go to the barn later and see Billy.

They opened one of the big barn doors just enough to squeeze through. Lizzie ran up the ladder and started whispering, "Billy, Billy." but there was no response until somebody in the corner said, "He's not here."

Lizzie said, "What do you mean he's not here?"

"He left about an hour ago with Thomas. They go somewhere at night sometimes." Lizzie could not see who was talking, but it came from the corner of the barn loft. Lizzie returned to Clara and asked her if she knew where they had gone so late at night. Clara had no idea and knew if her dad found out, there would be hell to pay for sure. The girls returned, upset that they were missing out on something but realized that it was probably for the better, not knowing. Lizzie tried to stay awake to catch them coming back, but it didn't happen and the next thing she knew it was morning.

Saturday was as beautiful as Friday, only it felt a little warmer. Mr. Culmer asked the girls if they wanted to go into town and pick up a few things. Soon were on their way to the town square.

While at the square, Lizzie and Clara devised a plan that, if all went well, they would learn where Billy and his friend went. It was a beautiful afternoon, and the girls bought ice cream. Lizzie stayed away from the bakery.

Mr. Culmer rounded up the girls, and they returned home with bags of goodies and supplies. They spent the evening talking on the porch and confirming what they were going to do later. Finally, Mr. and Mrs. Culmer went to bed. The last thing Clara's dad said to her was, "Don't stay outside too late."

They unlatched the Dutch door in the kitchen for an easy exit and put a blanket on the ground in front of the porch area that could not be seen from the barn. They put a bag of clothes next to the porch post and acted like they were going upstairs to bed, but only Clara went upstairs Clara shut her door, then opened it quietly, and crept back downstairs in her socks. Lizzie and Clara changed their clothes and kept an eye at all times on the barn door.

As soon as the candle went out in Clara's mom and dad's room, the barn door opened, and two of the boys ran down the trail. Lizzie rose and grabbed Clara, and they started to run behind the boys. The boys were extremely fast and the girls only hoped to catch up. After about ten minutes, the girls stood, breathless, at the edge of a field.

Clara said, "We lost them."

Lizzie yanked on Clara's arm and they slowly walked along the creek only to hear a noise, which was definitely boys' laughter, and then they stood still and watched for a couple of minutes. They saw where the boys had crossed the creek using the fallen tree trunk, and they decided to join them, even though Clara told Lizzie that she was scared. Lizzie led the way, and soon they were standing behind the boys, only ten feet away, and could hear everything they were saying and doing.

"Hi," said Lizzie. The four boys jumped to their feet and stared.

"What in the bloody hell are you doing here?" asked Thomas.

"Don't ever sneak up on someone like that," said Jimmy, as he sat back down on the grass.

Tawny looked hard into Lizzie's eyes. "It is you, isn't it?"

"Yes." Lizzie now moved a little closer to the tree trunk. Before long, the two girls had joined the club, knew where the meetings were held, and knew how to get there. Lizzie sat next to Tawny, and they talked a little, but Lizzie found his English accent at times difficult to understand. She often made him slow down or repeat something he'd said. They laughed at this and exchanged words that meant the same thing and again found it amusing. Billy and Clara were also sitting and talking about the farm, school, and the upcoming winter. It was a good night, thought Lizzie, until Clara stood up and said, "We have to go now." Lizzie knew in her heart that leaving was the right thing to do, but she also wanted to stay all night.

Jimmy agreed and he too indicated that they should go back, and it wasn't too long before they were all standing up and ready to leave.

"Next week, right here," said Billy.

"Sure," said Tawny. He and Lizzie walked to the hollow tree trunk bridge and started to say good-bye to each other. Clara went first over the bridge, followed by Thomas and then Billy. Now, they waited for Lizzie, who still stood next to Tawny and Jimmy. Tawny suddenly bent over and kissed Lizzie on the mouth so quickly that if you blinked, you missed it. Lizzie was speechless.

"Bye," said Tawny as he and Jimmy left in a hurry.

"See ya," said Lizzie, turning slowly and walking toward the bridge.

"Be careful," called Clara, as she watched her best friend walk across the tree bridge and not falter once. They quickly ran home, and soon were in bed trying to sleep. Lizzie thought that tonight was perfect and things couldn't get any better.

Chapter 26

The Pumpkin Festival

Tawny and Jimmy returned to their barn loft and talked a little about Lizzie. Jimmy admitted that she seemed nice. Tawny wondered why he kissed her and always came up with the same conclusion: There was no reason; it just it felt right. He started smiling and thought, When will I see her again? In his heart, he knew that he wanted to see her again.

Lizzie and Clara, now back upstairs and in bed, couldn't sleep. Lizzie's eyes stayed open; she knew that sleep wasn't in the cards for her but it didn't matter. When the sun came up, there were six children in Waterford who were still tired; but to them, it was just another night of having fun, feeling good about themselves, and just being children.

Mr. Nate dropped Lizzie off at work after church, and Clara went home. The afternoon dragged on as Mr. Owen's smile had been replaced by a half-smile. Lizzie knew he was upset that business had slowed. When Lizzie asked, he explained that harvest usually did this to him for three weeks or so, and according to Lizzie's estimate, he had another week to go.

"Hello, Mr. Owen." It was Mrs. Cott, a rich, very plump lady who owned three farms a couple of miles beyond Clara's and was a prime target for gossip since her husband had left her a year ago. Her children no longer went to school because they were older now, and they did most of their business in the city of Simcoe because it was a little closer than the town square in Waterford.

"Do you mind if I hang this in your window?" asked Mrs. Cott.

After a quick glance at it, Mr. Owen nodded. "No, please go right ahead." Mr. Owen glanced at Lizzie and rolled his eyes. Mrs. Cott thanked him and quickly left without buying a thing.

Lizzie went outside to read the flyer. It announced the Annual Pumpkin Festival, which would be held on Saturday, October twentieth, at the Simcoe fairgrounds. Lizzie knew that she had to go, and she had a strong will to bring Tawny with her.

How can I pull this one off, she thought, as she reentered the bakery and then realized that it didn't matter because she still had several weeks to plan for it. For the rest of the afternoon, Lizzie's mind working furiously, and she nearly had the plan formulated, but she needed to talk to Clara to put it all together.

On Monday morning, Tawny felt exhausted from the last two days of not getting enough sleep. He started to work in the fields along with Jimmy; it seemed that both of them were paired for the duration of the harvest. Harvest, however, was coming to a close because the fields were getting sparse.

During the next week, Tawny noticed that the leaves they had loaded up in the cure barns a couple of weeks ago were turning brown and produced a smell that he could not describe. He knew that the weather had changed; the days were much colder than before, and the boys sometimes had to wear two shirts just to keep warm as they worked the fields. Their feet were getting raw and hard because the ground always felt cold and damp, and Tawny knew if he kept moving it felt a little better.

Lizzie spent the next week at school, working a couple days through the week and wondering how she could get to see Tawny again. She asked Clara to have another sleepover, but Clara didn't respond and kept telling Lizzie "soon." The girls looked forward to the upcoming festival in Simcoe and agreed to go, but wanted to get Billy and Tawny to go as well. So far, however, they had no real plans.

The Simcoe fairgrounds were about fifteen minutes from Clara's house by buggy, and her parents were going because it marked the end of harvest. Besides, Clara's Uncle Todd and Aunt Grace would be there because they lived close by. Lizzie also knew that her parents planned on going and that it would be very difficult to bring Billy and Tawny along— they would probably get into trouble if they were seen with these boys. They had to come up with a plan so they could enjoy the event with the boys and not be seen.

Lathrope entered the barn and roused the boys for the day's work. It was much colder now, and the skies had gone gray with rain; regardless, they had things to do, and eventually they were all working hard, caring for the hanging leaves. Then a huge wagon came down the road with the writing "Michigan Cigar" on its side. Three men entered the big barn asking for Lathrope.

The boys spent the next few days removing the bundles of brown leaves from the cure barns and loading them into the big wagon. Tawny at one point thought about his birthday, but wasn't sure whether it had passed him by. With all five of the boys loading the big wagon, it really didn't take long before the cure barns were empty. The fields were stripped completely bare, and the only things still standing were thick stalks. They also noticed that Lathrope was extremely happy over the past several weeks and guessed it was because the crop was good and that he made money on the harvest.

The boys got together at the special place during a weekend and talked about the harvest, the hard work that was required to get the leaves ready, and the cold weather setting in. They all knew about England's weather, where it sometimes got cold and it always rained, but where snow was a rare occurrence. Billy and Tawny talked about Clara, about Lizzie, and the skeleton that they had found. Jimmy went to the hollow tree and looked at the end that they had packed with a boulder and dirt.

"Come here!" said Jimmy in a panic.

"What?" said Billy, as all four of them walked toward the tree trunk.

"It's gone." He pointed to the boulder that now sat next to the tree trunk, the boulder they'd used to hide the skeleton.

"What the—?" said Tawny as he inspected the site.

They all felt weird, as just a couple of weeks ago it was there. Now, it was gone. Jimmy shook his head. "Lathrope probably took it!"

Tawny told the boys that it was not their problem, and whoever took the skeleton was the same one who put it there and that they shouldn't concern themselves with it. Tawny felt a little sick as he touched the chain and medal in his pocket. He hadn't shared his find with anybody, and decided that he wouldn't.

Tawny was the only thing Lizzie thought about, except for her job. At church on the following Sunday Lizzie told Clara with her plan about the festival, and Clara quickly agreed. First, they had to tell the boys about it. This was Clara's department because she could get to Billy easily. One night, Clara made her visit to the barn and told Billy about the upcoming Saturday night and the plan for them to visit the festival and have fun. He was to tell Tawny. They were supposed to meet at the old burned-out house just before Simcoe on the main road, about five miles away. Clara had seen this old abandoned house several times when she had gone to Simcoe for supplies with her mother and sister.

Billy agreed and told Clara that he would pass the idea along to Tawny the next time he saw him, which was probably tomorrow night. The next step was to have Lizzie stay the weekend with Clara and persuade Mr. Culmer to take the family to the festival, which wouldn't be a problem since they usually went every year. The plan was in motion, and the only thing left was waiting.

Mr. Nate brought the girls to the farm after school on Friday and they were ready, anxious, and excited, giggling at every moment. Lizzie wanted to talk to Billy, and she also wanted to go the special place to see Tawny, since they hadn't seen each other in about four weeks but decided it was best to stick to the plan. Saturday came and the girls pretended it was just another day, doing what they always did, sitting, talking, eating, and generally being adolescent girls.

As the evening approached, Mr. and Mrs. Culmer instructed the girls to gather their things because they were off to Simcoe for the Pumpkin Festival. Lizzie and Clara were the first ones at the front porch waiting for the buggy. Before long, the family moved down the road to the festival. Mr. Culmer was talking about getting one of those Hungarian sausages on a bun smothered in horseradish; the girls didn't really hear him. Their minds were mainly focused on one and only one thing. They passed the burned-out house; they looked at it in anticipation. In the distance, they could see the fairgrounds with all kinds of activities and large crowds of people. The buggy stopped, and Mr. Nate helped everyone down. "Have a good time; I'll be right here, waiting."

Lizzie could see that it was not completely dark yet and that they had about and thirty minutes before they were to meet the boys. She and Clara were scared and excited at the same time.

The girls quickly ran around the grounds seeing and being seen, as part of their plan. Then they left and walked through the field that led to the old burnt house a half a mile back down the road. Just as it turned dark, the girls stood there waiting at the old house away from the road for the boys to arrive.

With help from Billy and Thomas, Tawny and Jimmy made their way through the fields and up to the Culmer farm; it was their first time to visit the Culmer farm. Billy took control and led a small work wagon and a horse from the barn. He adjusted the reins and prepared the horse for the ride. All four of them, now sitting in the wagon, trotted down the strange dirt road. They worried about running into the farmers at the festival, but what they didn't know was that the girls had this planned so that they would see and hear the festival but they would not actually be there.

It was a good thing that Billy and Tawny had some experience in handling horse-drawn buggies; it was also a good thing that everyone was still at the festival and finally that the road was empty. Eventually, they saw in the distance a black and half-burnt building just off the main road.

"There." Jimmy pointed to the house. "That has to be it."

"Yes, over there," cried Tawny. The girls stood to one side, peeking down the road, waiting for the boys. Billy maneuvered the wagon close to the house and tied the horse to a big oak tree trunk. It was dark enough that anyone would have a hard time seeing the wagon from the main road. They all knew that their time was limited and they would have to leave before the others did, but for now, it didn't matter.

They started talking and heard the festival taking place behind them in the distance. It felt, to them, that they had their own little festival happening.

"So far it is a good night," thought Lizzie. It was the second time she had seen Tawny, but she knew he was the boy she wanted to be with.

Chapter 27

The Night in Simcoe

The warm night air provided a soothing background to the prearranged get-together that Lizzie and Clara had organized. Lizzie thought, so far, so good.

The muffled music and the vibrant sounds in the background coming from the festival a half-mile away added a carnival-like atmosphere. Tawny reached out and took Lizzie's hand as they walked toward the main grounds. Soon, they were standing only a hundred feet away and could even make people out who Lizzie knew. Tawny would ask her about a person, and Lizzie would tell him what she knew. It felt as though they were watching people act out their lives in a mirror because they knew that they had to stay in the shadows, keep quiet, and just watch people be themselves.

"Who's that?" Tawny pointed to a person in the distance.

"That's Mr. Bennett. He runs the hardware store at the town square; nice man but drinks way too much, according to my Uncle John."

They played this game for a while as they stood and held hands and Tawny got to know the entire town in one evening. Lizzie felt the strangest when she introduced her parents to Tawny. Using a comedy of politeness, she removed the tension by starting the conversation, "Mom and Dad, I would like you to meet my newest friend from London, England, now working at the Lathrope Farm, the one, the only, Tawny." Then she reversed the roll and answered for him in a crude version of the English dialect, "Nice to meet you Mr. and Mrs. Lizzie's mum and dad." Tawny was laughing so hard at this little brown-eyed girl who was capturing his heart. For the moment, this new country called Canada was a better place. Tawny wiped tears from his eyes when he felt a tap on his shoulder. He turned quickly; it was Billy and Clara.

"Do it again; you know, show Billy," said Tawny, begging Lizzie to act out her introductions again.

Lizzie laughed. Clara and Lizzie had played this game for years.

"Move back," said Billy, as he saw Mr. Culmer walk past eating something wrapped in a napkin.

"It's ok," said Clara, "He can't see you tonight. Anyway, looks like he's too busy enjoying his Hungarian sausage sandwich."

Lizzie looked into Tawny's eyes. "What is your last name?"

"I...I've almost forgotten —Dewberry." He felt almost ashamed to say it. He couldn't explain or even understand this sudden mix of shame and joy that overcame him.

The four of them held hands and watched the festivities, commenting on almost everything they saw. Tawny noticed that Lizzie's little hand was so smooth and he apologized for his being so rough and scabby.

"That's what they are supposed to feel like," said Lizzie, knowing full well that the harvest could do that to a person. Besides, as long as they were not as rough as her dad's, she was happy.

Jimmy and Thomas suddenly showed up after having discussed what they thought actually happened to the old burnt-out building and were laughing and having a good time.

"Thanks Lizzie, thanks Clara," said Jimmy. "You know, for setting this up for us. It's more fun and a lot better than the barn loft."

Lizzie smiled at Clara, who also smiled. "You're welcome."

Clara pointed to Miss Kemp. "Look, look over there."

"She's our teacher, you know."

"She looks nice," said Billy, as he winked at Thomas in appreciation.

She did look beautiful strolling through the dimly lit fairgrounds by herself, swinging her purse, and allowing her skirt to flow in the gentle breeze. Lizzie knew right then and there that she wanted to be exactly like her when she grew up.

"When she grew up," echoed in her brain. The inner voice sounded like Cecil, or even Arthur, had said it and it made her feel so young; but she didn't care because tonight was theirs, and nobody was going to take it away from them.

A lot of people whom Lizzie didn't know were at the festival, probably because the it was held closer to Simcoe than Waterford, but nevertheless, when somebody walked by that she knew, the group knew as well.

"Move back," said Clara, who waved at the group to step backward. They hadn't realized that they had inched up, around ten or twenty feet or so, and were much closer to the people they were watching. If Clara hadn't noticed, they would have joined Lizzie's parents, Mr. Bennett, Miss Kemp, and others for a stroll through the fair and conversation.

They all stepped back, where it was safer, and continued their discussion, their laughter, their small talk, and their generally being kids.

At one point, Lizzie thought that Tawny was a real down-to-earth person who put on no airs or tried to be someone he wasn't, and this made her feel comfortable.

"Aren't your feet cold?" asked Clara, looking at Billy's dirty bare feet.

"You get used to it—you have to," replied Billy, trying to brush it off as being nothing so as to avoid bringing the group down.

The six sat in the field and enjoyed what was left of the evening and knew they would have to say good-bye soon. The boys had to get the horse and wagon back to the barn before Clara's mom and dad left, and Lizzie and Clara would have to devise a plan that would make out like they were on opposite sides of the fair for the entire night. This would be the reason why they didn't run into each other.

Tawny and Lizzie were talking about the orphanage, his friends there, the classes he took, and life in general under Heddon. Lizzie was fascinated that Tawny had spent almost his whole childhood in an orphanage, and now he was thousands of miles away in a field, enjoying her company.

Lizzie pointed to a bright object in Tawny's hand. "What's that?"

"It's a chain and a medal. I found them at the farm."

Tawny considered sharing this story with her and decided that if he clouded certain parts, it might be all right. He pulled her away from the others and started walking with her back to the burnt outhouse as he told her about how, after Billy had spotted the medal, they found the skeleton, looked at it carefully, and then put it back. He then added that, as of last week, the skeleton was missing from the tree trunk.

Lizzie listened to Tawny's story not so much for content but more for how he told it, enjoying his accent and mannerisms on certain words and phrases. She then told him that she knew nothing about it and, as far as she was concerned, it probably happened too many years ago and that the farmer probably spotted it and decided to get rid of it. Nevertheless, she did say she wanted to see where it was the next time they got together at the special place. She really wanted an excuse to meet Tawny.

"That's him," shouted Jimmy as he spotted Lathrope walking around the fairgrounds by himself. Tawny and Lizzie had returned and Tawny told Jimmy to keep his voice down.

Lizzie told Clara about the skeleton that used to be in the hollow tree trunk and now was missing. Clara couldn't believe it.

Billy and Thomas were studying Lathrope carefully and both agreed that he reminded them of Clara's dad, the way he dressed, the way he stood, and his expressions.

Jimmy overheard the girls talking about the skeleton and offered his two cents by saying, "He killed that kid, I know he did. I heard Mrs. Lathrope say so. I know he's a murderer."

Tawny looked down at the younger boy. "Jimmy, be quiet. Don't ruin the night with talk of killing or murder."

Jimmy left with Thomas and they went a little closer to where they were not supposed to be, acting older but showing everybody that they were still children at heart.

Tawny and Lizzie continued to enjoy the evening by strolling through the fields and talking.

Lizzie would often peek to see if Clara and Billy were doing the same, and they were definitely not since Billy was paying a little more attention to what the other two boys were up to. Billy quickly tracked them down, brought them back to safety, and then told them to stay put and be quiet.

Thomas pointed to a buggy moving down the road with three, maybe four, people in it. "Look, over there." For a second or two it frightened the boys; but it really scared Clara, knowing that one of her dad's buggies and horses were there only because of her.

"I think we should go," said Clara.

Lizzie agreed and said bye to Tawny. She pulled him down, kissed him on the cheek, and told him that they would see each other again, maybe next weekend, and Tawny smiled as if to say all right.

The girls quickly left and walked back to the festival grounds as the boys watched them. Billy whispered, "Come on, lads, we had better get the buggy back."

The boys ran to the burnt outhouse, untied the horse, and then started their fifteen-minute trip back to the Culmer farm. Tawny and Jimmy felt a little more comfortable now because they had just seen Lathrope and he looked normal and not angry. Jimmy sat and watched to see if any other buggies were approaching them and so far, the coast was clear. Billy was driving the wagon perfectly, almost like he had done this, his whole life. Thomas was amazed and Tawny agreed.

Crash! The sound came as the wagon tilted at one corner and came to a complete stop. They jumped out and stared numbly at the broken wheel, half wedged into the wagon and half hanging out in midair. They weren't going anywhere.

"God help us," cried Billy as he peered down the road to see how far they had to go and, to his luck, the Culmer farm could just be seen in the distance; it was a clear night.

Jimmy started jumping up and down until Tawny grabbed his shoulder and told him to stop or he would hit him. Billy kicked the wheel and looked confused and anxious.

"We have to get the horse back to the barn," said Tawny. "That's the most important thing."

"Yes, you're right." Billy unhooked the straps and freed the horse. "Thomas, come here." Billy handed the reins over to him. The other three boys decided that they should hide the wagon off the road so no one else could see it, because the entire town would shortly be coming this way.

"Good idea," said Billy.

The three boys dragged the wagon off the road and into a field, which had been picked clean of leaves, and they left it.

"Go back to the road and tell me if you can see it," said Billy, as Tawny ran back.

Tawny returned a moment later. "A little more." The three of them moved the small wagon a little further into the field. "That should do it," said Billy. They walked back to Thomas, who still stood, holding to the reins of the big horse.

"We'll tell him we don't know where it is," added Billy.

"Yeah, a good idea," replied Thomas. "Let's get back right now."

The four boys and the horse walked back to the farm. Billy and Thomas locked the horse in its stall, sent Tawny and Jimmy back to the Lathrope farm, and then climbed into the loft only to wait their now-clouded future. They would know tomorrow, as soon as the sun shone light on their misadventure.

Chapter 28

The Wrath of Culmer

The ride home from the pumpkin festival seemed slow, because the girls were happy that they had spent the entire evening with the boys and that Mr. and Mrs. Culmer didn't know. They passed the spot, not even noticing the abandoned wagon, and soon they were at home in the house, enjoying a drink and a cookie, talking about the night. Mr. and Mrs. Culmer excused themselves to bed; Mr. Culmer complained about an upset stomach, because he was burping all the way home and still was.

Mrs. Culmer folded her arms and looked at her husband. "How many of those things did you have?"

The girls went to bed and shared things that had happened to each of them; it seemed that if Lizzie knew it, so did Clara and vice versa. Clara opened her window to let in the night air and took a quick peek toward the barn loft door. It was closed. The laughter gradually stopped, and only an occasional snicker remained, as they laughed on the bed only to fall asleep.

Clara and Lizzie woke to the sound of the front door banging and just looked at each other, surprised. The girls fixed their night shirts and went downstairs to the kitchen where, as usual, there were plates of dark brown rolls with thick, white icing. Clara grabbed a piece for her and one for Lizzie as they sat and enjoyed the bounty of the Culmer kitchen. Clara noticed that the back half-door was fully open. "I guess to cool off the kitchen," said Clara. The ovens were fully stoked on this cool October morning.

"What's that?" asked Clara as she approached the Dutch half- open door and spotted a small black object in the distance in the middle of a field. Lizzie followed, looked, and then stared at Clara, as if to give her a silent warning.

"It's a wagon...look, see the wheels," whispered Lizzie, only to find Clara's eyes now drifting to her left at the small wagon and horse barn.

Lizzie pointed out two men walking toward the abandoned wagon and watched as they stopped. She took another long, hard look and then glanced back at Clara. "It's your dad and Mr. Flood."

The girls watched Mr. Culmer and Mr. Flood walk around the wagon, tilt it up a little, try to roll it, and then just stand next to it and exchange words. Mr. Flood was a younger man, stout for his small size, and always kept to himself; his farm bordered Clara's farm on the west side. Everybody seemed to like him, and he was considered the new farmer; he was referred to as such by other farmers when they got together to discuss their farms.

Finally, the two men split up, and Clara watched her dad, seemingly calm and walking at his regular Sunday stroll, with his head down, arms behind his back, and slowly strutting.

"It's mine alright," he said, as he entered the back door and started to fix a cup of coffee. "Wonder how it got there?" Lizzie's heart started to pound so hard that it actually made her shake, and there was no way she could stay in the same room as Mr. Culmer and not give everything away. She left and dragged Clara with her as they went to the front porch. They spoke in low whispers about how the wagon got into the field, if the boys knew how to handle these things, if the horse fell, or if they had an accident. Clara quickly rose. "I have to go see," and started to walk away, when Lizzie grabbed her tightly by the arm and pulled her back into the chair.

"We'll stay right here. Let's not give it away."

"You're right." Clara took a deep breath. They heard a small noise and looked over to see the barn loft door had opened a little more. There stood Billy and Thomas, stretching in the sunlight. Clara shook her head. There were more important issues to be handled, like the wagon.

Thomas was pointing to the wagon in the field. The girls also saw Billy grab Thomas's arm and quickly bring it back into the barn as the two boys sat down.

Mr. Culmer went outside, made his way toward the little storage barn, and then opened the door. He was almost certain that the wagon in the field was his; he just had made sure. It was. He took two of the boys from the barn; they retrieved the wagon and placed it in front of the small storage barn. Billy and Thomas had made sure they were not seen when Culmer came into the barn and grabbed the other two boys. Culmer looked at the wagon carefully as Billy and Thomas watched from the loft door. He studied the broken wheel for a while, went into the barn, and returned with another wheel. He took off the hub and quickly changed wheels. The wagon was now back to normal, with three dirty wheels and one clean one.

Mr. Culmer went back into the house and had another cup of coffee. He then sat on a chair on the front porch and just stared at the bare fields.

Clara knew that her dad was angry and was on his third cup of coffee. Clara knew trouble was brewing; it was only a matter of time before he would erupt. She had seen this happen a few times before. The girls slowly left the porch and went back upstairs where it was safe, or safer, at least for the moment.

"Those little liars!" Mr. Culmer rose from the chair. "I'll kill them all!"

"Calm down, calm down!" Mrs. Culmer quickly ran to the porch and tried to sit her husband back down.

"I'll fix them; I'll show them to respect my property!"

He showed no sign of calming down. Clara was frightened.

"Do they think they can just take a buggy any time we're out?" Mr. Culmer waved his arms wildly.

The tirade lasted about thirty minutes, and then Mr. Culmer continued sitting and having yet another cup of coffee, probably to calm him down, but Clara knew nothing would do that now.

Mr. Nate made his way to the front porch and spoke for a long while with Mr. Culmer. Then he shook his head and left to tend the horses and move the broken wheel back to the small barn. The boys watched as Mr. Nate rolled a metal barrel to the side of door that led into the big barn and filled it with wood to start a fire. Mr. Nate didn't seem at all happy to be performing this task. White smoke plumed into the air and soon a full-scale inferno raged, with the yellow flames shooting into the air.

The family prepared for church as Mr. Nate brought the big dark blue buggy to the front of the main house, stood next to it, and waited. Lizzie and Clara dressed for the day, and Lizzie grabbed her bag. They waited on the front porch, saying nothing and feeling guilty for what they had done the night before. It was close to noon, and soon the family left for the church in town.

It was a normal Sunday except for one small detail; Mr. Culmer did not attend church. He had stayed home and, by the concern in Mrs. Culmer's eyes, the girls didn't know what to expect when Clara would return home later that afternoon.

Everything happened in the next twenty minutes. Mr. Culmer rose from the front porch, rolled up his jacket sleeves, and went to the little storage barn. There, he retrieved a long piece of iron and brought it to the fire barrel. He stoked the fire and left the iron in the barrel and stalked toward the boys. From the large barn, the boys saw that the farmer also carried a rag tucked under his arm.

"Get down here, now!" His shout vibrated through the open barn doors.

Billy, Thomas, and the others quickly made their way to the front of the barn door to confront an angry man. "Who took the wagon last night?"

The boys stood perfectly still for the next two minutes. Culmer grew even more agitated as he moved from side to side in front of the red-hot barrel and his eyes grew wider. "I said, who took the wagon?"

No one answered. The younger boys knew too, but they were not going tell on their friend Billy. Culmer unraveled the piece of rag. It was Billy's jacket!

Billy had left his jacket in the horse barn when he had strapped the horse to the wagon. The boy's stomach ached, and he wondered if he could make up a story to get out of this situation. No. He couldn't bring Clara and Lizzie into this mess. His mind went blank, and he just stood there numb.

Culmer approached Billy and now was standing directly in front of him like a man possessed, a man with a mission. He reached out, grabbed Billy by the shirt, and dragged him to the front of the fire barrel.

Now Culmer and Billy stood on one side of the barrel, and the others watched intently on the other side. Culmer threw Billy's jacket to the ground. "You can't take what is not yours." Billy swallowed hard.

He grabbed Billy's left arm and put an arm lock on it so Billy could not move it. Billy felt the pain and knew that if Culmer had put any more pressure on it, it would surely have broken, probably at the elbow or forearm.

Billy, terrified, never imagined Culmer's next move. It happened in an instant. Culmer, who wore one thick large glove on his right hand, removed the bright red iron from the fire and quickly laid it onto Billy's outstretched hand.

Billy's scream could have been heard three farms away. Pain mixed with the inarticulate sounds coming from the boy's mouth diminishingly echoed inside the open barn. The others watched in horror as their friend fell to the ground, awkwardly clutching his left hand. The burnt skin hung like pieces of torn, wet paper.

Culmer calmly put the iron rod back into the fire, almost as if nothing had happened. The gathered boys smelled burning flesh as Billy, rolling on the ground, continued to scream. His friends could do nothing, nor did they want to, for fear of receiving the same punishment. Thomas cried as if he too could feel Billy's pain.

"Let this be a lesson to you all. Don't take what is not yours." Culmer removed his glove, threw it on the ground, and stalked back to the house as if nothing out of the ordinary had occurred.

Richard P. Tanos

Chapter 29

The Harsh Winter

After church, Mr. Nate dropped Lizzie off at the bakery, and the Culmers returned home. Mr. Culmer still sat on the front porch with a drink in his hand and gazed out at the bare fields. Clara quickly ran upstairs to change her clothes and then decided not to return to the front porch. She just stayed in her room and waited for any lecture or punishment that might come her way. She did notice that her dad was angry, but that it was not directed at her, so she felt a little safer. She opened her door, sat on her bed looking at the now-vacant loft opening, and just waited for what would happen next. Waiting for punishment was the worst thing, she thought, and eventually Clara nodded off to sleep, curled on her bed.

Lizzie spent the afternoon working at the bakery, oblivious of what had happened at the Culmer farm. Tawny and the boys were busy at the Lathrope farm, cleaning the barn and learning how to sharpen the plows.

Thomas looked at Billy's hand and felt sick. His friend's hand looked like red meat and the skin hanging around it resembled a cobweb. One of the other boys handed Billy an old shirt, which he quickly wrapped around his hand, which now started to form hundreds of blister bubbles.

"It hurts so bad!" Billy groaned and gritted his teeth. The others just watched, silent. They didn't know how to comfort Billy. The kitchen lady brought the dinner tray to the barn, but on this day, the boys stayed in the loft. The tray remained on the ground, and the lady returned to the kitchen. Thomas noticed that she looked as if nothing terrible had happened.

The Culmer house seemed normal, as the family enjoyed a Sunday meal. All sounds coming from the house were normal and did not seem out of place.

Eventually, the boys, except for Billy, ate and retreated back to the loft to comfort Billy, who was still in agony. Billy was in too much pain to eat.

The dinner table in the Culmer's dining room was quiet on this night; Martha wasn't home. She had left a few weeks earlier to work on her uncle Todd's farm because a hired hand had quit, and she was needed to fill in. After dinner, Mr. and Mrs. Culmer went outside and talked for a while as Clara listened carefully to learn what happened. She was angry that she couldn't just go to the barn and talk to the boys. Instead, she had to wait for another opportunity to see Billy. Mrs. Culmer was not herself; she had been angry ever since she and Mr. Culmer spoke that morning. Mr. Culmer continued to drink heavily throughout the evening.

Late that night, when everyone was asleep, Clara put on her robe and made her way to the barn loft. She didn't really care whether she was caught.

"Billy? Billy, are you there?" she said, gazing at what she knew were boys sleeping in curled mounds under their blankets.

"Yes, I'm here." Billy's voice sounded hoarse.

"What happened?" she asked. "My dad is acting like I've never seen him act before."

Billy crawled on two legs and one arm over to where Clara was. "Look at this."

He unwrapped his hand and shoved it close to her face.

"Oh, Billy!" Her eyes widened as she stared at a hand that seemed to be falling apart.

"My dad did this?"

"Yes, he burnt me hand. Hurts like bloody hell, it does."

Clara didn't know what to do at this point as she felt like hugging him at first and then decided that it was not the best thing.

"I'm so sorry!" She said. Then she quickly left the barn and ran back to the house. How could her father have done this horrible thing?

At school the next day, Lizzie and Clara talked about what had happened. Lizzie's stomach turned as heard. Clara's description was frightening and soul wrenching.

The skies were a bright blue and the air was frigidly crisp, and they all knew that winter was near and that once it hit, the town and farms would close down for four to five months. This bothered Lizzie a bit since she would not be able to see Tawny until next spring. The sleepovers would be limited, and they might manage one at best during the winter months, but even that was a remote possibility. However, the holiday season might give them a chance to see their friends, but this too wasn't likely.

Winter had saved itself for that Tuesday morning. It hit suddenly and with a fury as winds blew cold air down from the north, the sky clouded, and the ground turned hard and crispy. It was the start of a long, cold season of snow, ice, and storms. The boys were stranded in the barn lofts, wrapped in thin and scratchy blankets. Tawny thought that, in some ways, it was like living at the orphanage: confined and isolated. Lathrope gave each boy a pair of rubber boots and a pile of rags to wear as socks for the winter.

The boys' only task was to retrieve cordwood to be used in the barns and the main house. Whenever a day was clear, the farmer would take a couple of the boys into town to pick up cordwood that arrived by train. Their hands were cold and cracking because Lathrope gave no gloves to the boys.

The meals, which were cut back to once a day, would arrive cold, and they weren't really enjoyable and were nowhere near what they were used to. The snow piled up, and one job was to keep the barn doors clear. The boys used the shovels almost every day. Life at the farm was dreary and cold, with most of the days spent just huddling around each other to keep warm. The entire town was housebound except for times when the sun shone and the square opened for business, even though business was slow and almost nonexistent. It felt as though someone had thrown a blanket over the entire region to protect them from the elements and that they all had to wait for spring for life to return.

Christmas came and went, with families exchanging gifts and eating bountiful meals, except for the boys at the farms. They were treated to their now-regular once-a-day meal and a holiday piece of fruitcake that was hard and not really tasty. Thomas really liked this cake, however, so he ate almost everybody else's.

Clara's birthday, in February, came. It fell on a day on which a major snowstorm dumped four feet of snow. Lizzie was supposed to come over, but those plans were quickly changed. At school one day, Clara had told her about the small party she had with her parents. Often, Lizzie attended school more than Clara—many farmers wouldn't take out their buggies in the cold weather—because she had only a few blocks to walk. She had actually seen her best friend only two or three times over the entire winter.

One day, the second time that Clara made it to school—and, then, it was only for a half-day—Clara bragged about getting a brassiere for her birthday from her mother. Lizzie and Clara were coming of age, and Lizzie thought about her thirteenth birthday, and she wondered if she would get one too. The thoughts about Tawny were constantly there, and she was finding it extremely hard to suppress them.

Billy's hand had healed nicely, showing only three or four marks of white scar tissue on his palm. Tawny still didn't know what had happened to his friend, nor would he know until the temperature rose, the snow had cleared, and they could meet at the special place.

The farmers had readied their spring planting tools and were anxious to start the next year's crop. For the most part, they stayed away from the boys. The rubber boots helped ease the frigid air somewhat, but still their toes often lost feeling, and they needed a lot of rubbing and movement to prevent frostbite.

The horses were fed three times a day and were growing fat in the stalls from hay and other feed, which the boys had to get from town. Tawny told the others that the horses were treated better than they were -- everyone agreed.

Easter approached and the weather broke. The snow melted slowly. One Sunday, the Lathrope farm filled with people whom Tawny had never seen before. It must be a party, or a special occasion, he thought. Anything out of the normal boredom was appreciated and welcome.

This day Tawny would remember because the meal, served late that afternoon, was the best he'd ever had: ham, mashed potatoes, gravy, creamed corn, and fresh, hot bread. It must have been Easter, Tawny decided; it could have not been any other day because the meal was extraordinary.

To the boys, the winter months were hard and boring, and they could only look forward to an end of the bad weather and getting back to a regular work schedule.

Tawny also thought about the special place, and how he'd tried to reach it one day. He had to give up because his boots filled with snow. He remembered that on another day, while Mark shoveled snow away from the barn door, a small piece of the boy's right ear fell off. Tawny knew that that piece of ear would never grow back. Tawny realized now that life in the orphanage was not this brutal, and once in a while, he wished that he was back there. He decided that Canada was a horrible place. Then he thought about the warmer months. For this, he would wait it out.

In late April, the ground finally showed itself—brown, flat, and demanding attention. It wasn't long before Lathrope returned to the barn early in the morning, screaming at the boys again to start the new crop. Tawny felt better because now the days would move along quicker, the temperature would rise, and they would get two meals a day. His mind started to shift to the special place and he knew it was very soon that the boys could meet there and resume what they had last summer. He wondered about Billy, about Thomas, and definitely about Lizzie, whom he had thought about hundreds, even thousands, of times over the winter months.

It didn't happen all in one day, but soon the boys were back at the fields, learning how to plow and sow. Jimmy had only three attacks of missing his mother and father and still vowed that they would come for him. Jimmy had grown during the winter; his voice even changed, and Tawny recalled teasing him about it. He'd told the younger boy it probably would stay that way, but it didn't. Things were slowly getting back to a familiar norm, and to the boys, they were ready, not only to tackle the new growing season, but more importantly, to get back to the Special place.

Chapter 30

The New Crop

It was late April, and Tawny knew that Lathrope was anxious to plow the fields and to start planting the new crop. Tawny also knew that it was time to get back to the special place to be with his friends. Early one morning, Lathrope woke the boys and took back the rubber boots. He made each boy toss them down, a pair at a time, from the loft. Lathrope also gathered the plowing tools and got the boys ready to work the horses and fields. The crisp air reminded Tawny of last fall, although the trees that bordered the farm were gray bare now, and the spring buds were sprouting but not yet visible from a distance. Tawny and Mark were ordered to fetch and bring back three horses from the barn, and Lathrope attached each of them to the three plows. Each plow had a harness attached to a couple of very long, wide, and heavy leather straps.

Tawny stood and attached the horse to the harness, holding the wooden handles of the large V-shaped plow. Both Tawny and the implement were hitched with heavy leather straps to the horse fifteen feet in front. The other boys stood and watched. Lathrope barked a command, and the horse jerked forward. Tawny went face first into the hard dirt and was dragged for a few feet until Lathrope ran up and stopped the horse. Peter and Mark laughed and then quickly stopped as Lathrope glared. "Don't laugh, boys; you're next to learn this!"

Tawny stood again, wiped the dirt from his face, turned and faced the others, and glared. That generated more laughter. Lathrope didn't appreciate it. "Pay attention!"

The farmer now instructed Tawny to prepare himself for the sudden jolt. "Try it again."

Now that Tawny knew what would happen, the second time was easier, and the plowing began. The others clapped and then stopped when Lathrope leered at them. It was difficult to time the expected sudden jolt. Leaning back and letting the horse and plow do the work is the secret, thought Tawny. He couldn't wait for the others to try it. Lathrope shouted at them all day as they took turns working the plow, falling, getting up, and trying again and again. By the end of the day, the boys had successfully learned the craft of plowing.

Because the weather had improved and Clara now regularly made the trip to town, Lizzie and Clara met at school nearly every day. Their conversations still included Billy, Tawny, Mary in Brantford, Martha in Buffalo, how bad the winter had been, and a new topic: Clara had started to develop into womanhood.

Lizzie kept asking Clara about having another sleepover, possibly one to mark the beginning of the crop season. Clara knew that she would soon have to arrange one just to stop her best friend from hounding her.

One day at school, Clara informed Lizzie that she and her mother were going by train to Buffalo to visit Martha, who had moved there during the winter to take a job. Clara knew little about this move, but she was glad Martha was gone because it made life much easier. Lizzie knew that Clara no longer had to deal with her older sister every day; besides, she had a handful just dealing with her two younger brothers when they were around.

"Oh, yeah, I almost forgot. Mother said we can have the sleepover on the holiday weekend in May," said Clara. "I think it's the holiday that celebrates Queen Victoria's birthday. You know, the royal who died a few years ago."

"That sounds great; I'll make sure I take that Saturday off," said Lizzie, now thinking about the upcoming visit.

Lizzie knew about Clara leaving for a three-week visit with her mother, but didn't expect it would be so soon. She was working at the bakery on the next Saturday when Clara entered the store, dressed in a pink dress with a matching hat trimmed in lace. She informed Lizzie that they were leaving in about an hour and wouldn't be back until the week before the holiday. Lizzie grinned, and they smiled at each other, knowing full well what was being planned and that they would get together at school before the next sleepover.

"Mr. Owen has given me the Saturday off, but I have to work on the following Sunday, after church," explained Lizzie. Clara nodded, smiled, hugged Lizzie, waved, and then was gone.

By now the entire region was executing the largest field-grooming exercise in Canada. Everywhere, brown and gray dirt was turned into beautiful brown mounds of soil. The trees grew greener each day, and they provided a vibrant backdrop to the plowed fields.

The local people thought that this was no doubt the prettiest part of the crop season and would actually take day trips out to the farmland just to see the well-tended fields of brown dirt, bordered by a sea of bright, light green.

Tawny now handled the horse and plow with ease because he'd done nothing else for three weeks—sometimes from morning to night and even late into the evening. According to Lathrope, the fields had to be ready before the May holiday weekend, when the seeds planting began. Lathrope even gave the boys rags to wrap over their hands because holding the rough oak handles gave them blisters. Before they went to sleep each night, the boys pierced their blisters with their teeth to drain them. For Tawny, it reminded him of the harvest, when he worked all day and slept all night, and there was no time or thought for himself or the special place.

The only time Tawny had to himself was when he walked behind the horse, and even then, his thoughts were constantly being interrupted by the horse, rocks, the straps, turning, and the speed. Nevertheless, Tawny was developing muscles in his chest and arms from this work, as were the others. One day, Tawny wondered about Billy, whether he had mastered plowing, and how he was doing. He decided to go to the special place on the first mild Sunday evening that they weren't plowing. He picked Sunday because last year that was the day they usually met; besides, he hoped that Billy, thinking along the same lines, might pick the same day.

It was the only time of the year that rain was welcomed with open arms. It provided a natural soil-softener and made the plowing easier. It also prepared the soil for the planting process. Tawny knew that Lathrope had set up a table in the small barn with little seeds scattered around on a piece of paper, and he seem to be guarding them with his life.

The next step in the crop season was the smelliest, but definitely not the hardest, chore. A huge pile of horse manure, once covered by snow, was now fermenting behind the small barn. Lathrope grabbed Jimmy and Peter and drove a wagon to the dung mountain. There, they loaded the wagon and headed out to the fields, where they scattered it all over the ground. Lathrope made sure that the main fields next to the house got treated first and, if any was left, that the back fields would get some.

Plowing wasn't really a dirty job; however, when Jimmy and Peter entered the barn or just came close to the others it was bad enough that the others told them to stay away until they were bathed. Tawny didn't like the winter, but he did like working long hours into the night, which melted the time away. He often thought about Lizzie. He tried to keep those thoughts during the day because at night, these thoughts stopped him from sleeping.

It wasn't long before all the dung had been spread over the fields and the time to plant approached. Lathrope had told the boys that they would start sowing around the end of May, but if the weather was warm enough and if the chance of frost was small, they might start a week earlier. It was growing close to the planting time because the nights were warmer and the days were great, even when it rained.

It was a Monday, toward the middle of May, when Lathrope retrieved the boys from the barn loft. Soon they stood in the main field next to the house. He handed Mark a hoe and started to show the boys how to sow.

Mark had to drag the hoe through the soft earth to make a small trench in a straight line. Tawny was next; he had to place two small seeds next to each other in the trench and then repeat the seed placement every six to eight inches. Jimmy and Peter followed Tawny, walking along each side of the dirt mound that now had a trench running through it with seeds placed every so often. Their job was to kick the dirt into the trench. Jack followed next by walking on the now-covered trench to pack the seeds into place and make a small indentation that would hold water. Tom was last, carrying a bucket of water to soaked the seeds with as much water as Lathrope had showed him, about one handful per seed. This crude production line ran smoothly and was halted only when they had to wait for Tom, who regularly fetched more water from the wagon. Another small problem for the boys was waiting for Lathrope to bring seeds, but Tawny believed that Lathrope wanted it this way to control how many seeds were planted and ensure that seeds were not wasted.

It took about an hour to do each row, and there were several rows they had to do, so Lathrope made them work late into the evening on the nights that had a full moon. The planting cycle actually worked well and every once in a while, the boys would change places when Lathrope wasn't around. Lathrope had already told them not to change positions because it might alter the seeds and the crop would not grow. Tawny heard that this planting season was the best ever because they had two days of drizzle right at the end of the planting days, which, according to Lathrope, provided the correct amount of water to make the plants grow.

The weekend approached, and Tawny knew it was the holiday weekend because Lizzie had told him all about it, which made him think about London, the orphanage, and the friends he left behind almost a year ago.

Early on Friday morning, Lathrope took Tawny into town to pick up groceries from the general store. While at the store, Tawny noticed George was also there, along with another smaller boy, waiting for his farmer. Tawny tried to tell George about the special place and that it was on the creek somewhere between two farms. George really had no idea of where he was or how to even start to get to the special place, but promised Tawny he would try something tomorrow night. They spent the next twenty minutes trying to describe to each other what they had seen on their respective farms, but neither could agree on a match until Tawny mentioned the tornado. George knew about it because he too lost some plants. The boys cut their conversation short because Lathrope returned, and he and Tawny left immediately to return to the farm.

Tawny, after helping bring the bags to the kitchen door, went back to the fields. The boys had to water two sections of field according to Lathrope, and it needed to be done early, because the next chore was to fetch water from the creek and fill two enormous tanks that were delivered to the farm yesterday.

"Just saw George," said Tawny, and then he thought Jimmy might not remember the boy.

Jimmy smiled. "That's great. Do you know where he is—I mean do you know what farm he's at?"

"No, just the framer's name—Fraser, I think." Tawny then added, "His farm was also hit by the tornado, so it must be close. I told him to try and come to the special place tomorrow night."

"Do you think he will come?"

"I hope so, Jimmy, but I don't think he'll be able to find it."

Chapter 31

The Two Books

Clara returned to school three days before the arranged get-together on Saturday, and knowing that her friend was back made Lizzie feel much better. Lizzie also couldn't wait to see Tawny again.

"Did you tell Billy?"

"Yes, everything should be fine," answered Clara, now acting more mature and wearing new undergarments. Lizzie noticed that even her makeup was a little heavier than usual, but quickly brushed this off as Martha's doing.

"How is your sister?"

"Martha's fine. She's doing well at her new job in the library." I asked her if I could bring you next time for a visit."

Lizzie's chin dropped to the floor, "What did she say?"

"She thought that maybe this fall, just before school starts, would be fine," said Clara.

Miss Kemp pointed at Lizzie and Clara. "Stop talking." Lizzie looked over at Clara, and they both smiled with anticipation.

Lizzie took her bag and went to school on Friday, feeling even more excited than she felt before the Festival outing last fall. The day crept by until mid afternoon, when Mr. Nate arrived earlier than expected. Clara noticed him standing outside waiting and she poked Lizzie to tell her. The last twenty minutes seemed to take forever; when Lizzie stared at the hands of the classroom's clock, they never seemed to move.

It was a lovely late spring day when the girls returned to Clara's house. Mrs. Culmer had cookies and milk waiting for them on the front porch, their favorite spot.

"Hello, Lizzie," said Mrs. Culmer, seeing her for the first time in six months. "Don't you look nice. You hair is longer, and you've grown a couple of inches, haven't you?"

"Hello, nice to see you too," answered Lizzie. "I heard your trip to see Martha was enjoyable."

"Yes, it was," chimed in Mr. Culmer, as he was just leaving the house for the day's work, "Thank you for asking."

Mrs. Culmer smiled at her husband and then—as usual—grabbed Lizzie's bag and had one of the kitchen help, a new girl Lizzie had never seen before, put it into Clara's room. Meanwhile, the girls sat outside in the chairs and watched out of the corners of their eyes for the boys, who were nowhere to be seen. Lizzie and Clara started talking about what was going to happen tomorrow night and they hoped that things would work out and that it would not rain. Clara informed Lizzie that tomorrow, her Uncle Todd and her cousins were coming over to spend the afternoon with the family.

"When did you tell Billy about tomorrow?"

Clara sat back in her chair, looked up, and said, "I told him the night I got back from Buffalo; I think it was Tuesday."

"Does Tawny know about tomorrow?" asked Lizzie in a soft voice.

"I'm sure Billy will try and let him know," said Clara, whispering even more quietly than Lizzie.

Lizzie and Clara went into the kitchen to watch the help prepare the evening meal while they sat at the big table and had a second glass of milk.

"Who's that?" asked Lizzie, now pointing her nose at the new lady in the kitchen.

"That's Gwen," said Clara, "She started a month ago when old Mrs. Thompson had to stop because of her back troubles."

Lizzie looked at her and knew that she had seen her somewhere before, possibly at the bakery. Gwen was young, in her early twenties, definitely younger than Mrs. Thompson. Gwen was thin and had blue eyes; curly light blonde hair pulled back under a white hat; soft-spoken; and very pale, probably a result of the long winter, thought Lizzie.

In any event, Lizzie liked her because she smiled most of the time, whereas the older kitchen help would always look at you in a way that made you feel that you did something wrong or made you feel the urge to reveal something deep inside of you.

"Gwen, this is my friend Lizzie," said Clara.

"Nice to meet you," said Gwen, showing that she had nice straight teeth and a pleasant personality.

"Glad to meet you too," replied Lizzie, reflecting a small slightly intimidated smile back at her. The girls waited in the kitchen for dinner to be served and then, once the signal was given, they sat down, exchanged words with Mr. Culmer and Clara's two younger brothers, and then ate the chicken-and-rice meal with all the trimmings.

After dinner, the girls went upstairs, sat at the open window, and just waited and watched for the boys to return to the barn. They knew that the dinner bell was about to ring, and just like clockwork, it sounded as the boys seemed to come from everywhere and were quickly huddled around the barn door, like vultures waiting for their prey to arrive.

Gwen carried the white covered tray to the barn, placed it on the ground, and left without a word.

"She's new," said Thomas. He quickly grabbed a roll and a piece of chicken.

"Cute, too," said Billy, watching her walk into the main house. This was the first kitchen lady who even remotely looked nice and not like the old wrinkled kind of woman who usually carried the food.

Billy waved toward the upper window in the main house, and, yes, the girls caught it. Clara waved back immediately. Lizzie noted that Billy had grown not taller but thicker, and his upper body looked more powerful. Also, the other boys were getting taller and stronger looking. She thought about Tawny. Would he have changed, or, even if he changed just a little, would Lizzie notice? Nevertheless, she liked the transformation she saw in Billy. The girls continued giggling, gesturing, and just being silly, with the focus clearly on the meeting tomorrow night.

Lizzie had bought a small silver ring at the square, last winter, and she really wanted to give it to Tawny tomorrow night and asked for Clara's thoughts. "It's fine," Clara told Lizzie. "Just don't make it out like you're throwing yourself at him."

Lizzie paused, looked at Clara in admiration, and then said, "Maybe you're right. I'll hang on to it for a while."

Realizing for the first time that her best friend now seemed to have a lot of answers, Lizzie pressed, "Where did you get all this information?"

"Here," she said as she pulled two brown thick books from under her bed. The two inquisitive young girls spent the entire night giggling and reading every word in these two books. They often reread sections that at first made no sense, and even after reading it the second time, it usually still made no sense. Lizzie could not explain the internal heat she was experiencing from reading these two books about relationship sex. Clara agreed she was experiencing the same feelings only for Clara this was her third time. Perhaps it was the subject matter itself that caused Lizzie to the sweat, or maybe it was simply her curiosity on a topic that no one ever talked about, ever. In any event, by morning, they were two well- but not necessarily accurately-informed girls on the subject of human sexuality. Martha had given these books to Clara, hoping that it would keep her younger sister away from boys. A year ago, Martha's idea might have worked....

The rooster squealed a bit, and the girls found themselves downstairs in the kitchen grabbing their breakfast as Clara asked Lizzie, "Do you want a cup of coffee."

"What?" replied Lizzie, startled. "You don't drink coffee!"

"I do now," said Clara, bobbing her head back and forth like she just won first place in a contest. "Try it, you might like it."

"Ok," said Lizzie.

They went to the front porch and sipped their coffee and ate crumb cake, which tasted perfect, thought Lizzie, now being somewhat of a judge with baked goods.

Clara noticed that Gwen was coming out of a room usually reserved for guests and quietly asked her mother about it because she didn't want to call attention to it, especially in front of Gwen.

"She's staying here for the time being, paying room and board to Dad, of course," said Mrs. Culmer. "Remember your Aunt Velma?"

Clara thought hard. "Your dad's brother Robert, the one who lives in Cornwall?" Clara still couldn't recall him. "The one who sent us a box of plants two years ago?" Mrs. Culmer was now running out of relationship references. "Anyway, Gwen is his daughter, and we've agreed to keep her working here for a year or two."

That explains the smile, thought Lizzie; she is family and therefore is going to act differently than the hired help.

Clara's Uncle Todd and Aunt Grace arrived from Simcoe with their two small children. The two families had a small get-together; the young Culmer children played at the side of the house on the swing, the men walked around the barns, and the women enjoyed sitting on the porch watching the children play while sipping lemonade. Clara and Lizzie kept to themselves, as they usually did, but did make an occasional appearance, but only to keep away possible suspicion about their plans later tonight.

After dinner, the girls went upstairs to Clara's room and started to read the books again, especially the sections that describe things in great detail. After a while, the newness of this subject had worn off, and the giggles started. It was only a few hours until they were all going to be together talking about what happened last winter, the planting season, and the other things. They waited until they saw the boys leave the barn. Then the girls slipped out of the house and followed. This was the existing plan.

Chapter 32

The Saturday Night

The night air was a little chilly for this time of year, but it didn't matter—the girls were sneaking out of the house and meeting the boys at the big elm tree, and nobody was going to stop them, not tonight. Lizzie and Clara crept through the kitchen, slid past the half door, and then before long were running around the barn and approaching the newly planted fields, when suddenly, Clara stopped in her tracks and Lizzie jerked, following suit.

"We have to walk in straight lines. We can't leave foot prints on the ground or Dad will catch us. So be careful where you walk." Clara looked for a row that would lead to the end of the property line. "There," she said quietly as they ran in a straight line to the edge of the field. It really didn't take long to get there and, yes, the tree bridge was still there, connecting the two properties. At first glance, it looked like winter hadn't changed the special place, and everything seemed to be the same, except for the tree leaves, which now were light green with baby leaves.

"Who's there?" came a voice from the darkness.

"It's me," whispered Clara, as she slowly approached the big elm tree.

"Oh, Billy, it's you." She relaxed a bit as they smiled at each other.

"Hi, Lizzie," said Billy.

"Hi. Where's Tawny?" Lizzie looked everywhere for him.

"Not here yet," answered Thomas, approaching from the cre ek bed.

The ones who were already there didn't wait for the others to arrive as they started talking about basically anything, with each one taking a turn relaying what was on his or her mind or telling something that he or she had done during the past six months.

"Let's see what happened to your hand." The crooked, ugly white scars marked the flesh of Billy's hand.

"I know—Clara told me. How did he know it was you?"

"Lizzie, I was dumb. I left my jacket in the horse stall." Billy now seemed ashamed.

Thomas stood and bent over into Lizzie's face. "You should have seen it. It was the most hideous thing." He began to describe details.

"Stop that, Thomas!" Lizzie felt sick to her stomach, waving him away.

Crack, crack! They all heard the sound. It came from down the path. Totally still, the children sat, watched, and waited.

"Boo!" Tawny stepped out of the dark, threw his arms out to his side, and just stood there grinning. Lizzie ran to him and they hugged for a long time, as she did not want to let go. Six months is a long time!

"You scared me!" said Billy. He and Tawny shook hands and hugged as old friends do, slapping each other on the back. Both were getting taller, wider, thicker, and stronger, but what they didn't know was that everyone else was noticing as well.

"Hello," Jimmy's cracked voice came from behind Tawny. Before long the six of them were just being teenagers, sitting around saying anything that came to their minds. Tawny learned about the hand-burning incident, which made him angry toward Clara's dad, but he kept quiet only because Clara was right there. He didn't want to spoil the get-together.

On the subject of winter, they all agreed that it was a cruel, hard, and a tedious six months. Lizzie and Clara also agreed that winter was a terrible thing to endure and that it depressed everybody, except the farmers, because they had money from last year's crop and couldn't spend it even if they tried.

They all laughed at Jimmy, who was developing into quite the joker, as he mimicked Lathrope almost to the letter, doing one of his speeches on plowing. Tawny had noticed that Lizzie and Clara were both growing up much faster than he anticipated or even thought about during the past six months, and he liked what he saw.

The air was growing cooler, but the atmosphere around the big tree was splendid and joyous as the next hour flew by.

"Swoosh, swoosh" was heard by all of them around a hundred yards away, in the opposite direction from the tree bridge.

"Quiet," whispered Tawny.

Swoosh, swoosh. The sound came again, only this time it was closer. Billy and Tawny rose and walked slowly toward the sound, but now they could see a person coming toward them, swinging a stick at the ground.

"Who's there?" Tawny knew he was taking a chance, but as he figured it, he didn't have a choice.

"It's George."

"Hey, it's George!" yelled Tawny, as he ran up and hugged him tightly.

"Hi, George," added Billy, remembering him from the boat and train trip.

Tawny sat next to George and introduced him to the girls. They were amazed to learn that George was on the second farm down the road past Clara's farm, and only three farms away from where the wagon was ditched last year. George loved that story.

"I can't believe you found us!"

"Easy, Tawny. I just followed the creek for a while. Saw the water last year and wondered where it led, I did," said George, now enjoying being the center of attention. "Can only stay a little while, you know. Mr. Fraser is a hard man to work for."

The topic of the farmers started. Billy explained the burning of his hand as he showed George the scars. Tawny explained being locked up in the cure barn, and George explained the whipping he received for not working fast enough and then showed them his scarred back. They all had worked themselves into a state of anger, and Clara was upset by what she was hearing, but she knew it was true. After she apologized to all of them more than a few times, Tawny realized that they were scaring her, which made him quickly turn the conversation in another direction.

"Have you seen any of the others?" asked Tawny. George hesitated, as though puzzled at the question, and then grinned. "No, can't say that I have. No, I don't think so; you were the only one."

"How often do you all come here?" asked George. "It is really nice here, but also a bit far for me to come all the time."

"We have no schedule, we just meet when the skies are nice and usually on Sunday, when the farmers are at church or in town," explained Tawny.

"That sounds good." George was preparing to leave. As he stood up and grabbed his walking stick, he said, "See you—maybe next Sunday."

George started to walk away, following the creek bed and making that swooshing sound. Soon he was out of sight. Tawny and the boys were glad to see George but had realized that George had changed into a different person. The George who was just there with them wasn't the George from the boat or the even the George from the train. This bothered Tawny, and he wondered if the whipping that George received had changed his friend—or was it something else, something that George didn't want to tell everybody? Tawny decided to himself that he would ask him next time they met, if there was a next time.

"It's getting late," said Jimmy.

"Yes, I know," said Thomas. Tawny sat next to Lizzie. She told him that she thought George was a nice boy, maybe a little reserved, but nevertheless still a good guy. This helped Tawny feel a little happier.

Lizzie and Tawny watched as her best friend and Billy held each other's hand and strolled toward the creek bank. Lizzie smiled at Tawny and couldn't stop wondering about the two books they read last night.

"Tawny, are you ready to go?" asked Jimmy.

"In a minute," replied Tawny.

Lizzie grabbed Tawny's hand and held it tightly as she knew that he wouldn't leave until Clara had returned. Lizzie looked hard into the night and couldn't see her best friend anywhere, nor could she hear anything, which made her feel anxious. Lizzie's mind circulated images of what they had learned last night and there was one thing that she knew for sure: Clara would tell her everything in great detail, later that night, when the coast was clear.

Clara and Billy returned to the big tree, still holding hands. Lizzie looked at her best friend in an inquisitive way, and Clara awkwardly grinned. Lizzie knew something was different about her best friend. She would get the details later.

Chapter 33

The Accident

The walk home on that Saturday night was awkward for Lizzie. She knew something was up with Clara, and Clara was not telling. And the more Lizzie begged her, the more Clara refused. This made Lizzie even angrier.

"Wait until we get home," was all that Clara would say.

They had to get to Clara's bedroom and they also knew it was very late or possibly very early the next morning. Once in bed, Clara started to tell her story of what happened earlier. Lizzie was amazed at what her best friend just told her and a bit more taken with how easy Clara was able to tell her about it. They both started to giggle and just lie in bed, knowing that they both were not going to get any sleep for what was left of the night.

The rooster crowed, and it was clear now that morning was taking over. The darkness was being swiftly replaced by light, and they knew that they wouldn't get any sleep.

They changed their clothes and went downstairs to find Gwen in the kitchen firing up the stoves and getting the trays out for the day's meals.

"Good morning," said Gwen. She was making the coffee.

"Morning," the girls answered. Then they sat at the big kitchen table after pouring glasses of milk.

"Good night was it, last night?" asked Gwen. The girls looked at each other, wondering if Gwen knew something.

"What do you mean?" asked Clara.

"Don't worry, I won't tell anyone." Gwen smiled at the young girls, who now sat at the table, trying to act as though they were not tired and had done nothing wrong.

"Where did you go?" asked Gwen quietly. Lizzie nodded at Clara as if to say, I guess we can tell her. Besides, she's family.

"We have a place, on the farm, where we meet our friends," said Clara. "A place to get away and be by ourselves."

"I think that it's great idea to have a place like that." Gwen smiled again. "I used to do those kind of things several years ago, back on my dad's farm."

With that, the other two kitchen ladies entered the back door and said, "Good morning."

Gwen and the girls answered politely. Lizzie and Clara went back upstairs to change into their clothes for the day.

"I like her," said Lizzie, as she stuffed clothes into her bag. "And she is pretty."

After washing, the girls made their entrance for the benefit of the rest of the household. Now, however, Mrs. Culmer was also there, and the girls made this time look like it was their first, as they entered the kitchen and said good morning to everyone.

"Did you girls sleep well?" asked Mrs. Culmer. She poured a cup of coffee and adjusted her apron.

"Yes, Mom," answered Clara, shooting a look in Lizzie's direction.

"Oh, yes, Mrs. Culmer," echoed Lizzie, holding back her laughter. The girls retreated to the front porch, where they giggled quietly about last night, and Lizzie continued to hound Clara about what had happened.

Mr. Culmer came outside and scanned the skies to see what the weather would bring. "Good morning, girls."

They answered and, for the first time in her short life, Clara felt strange around her father. She now saw him in a different light; not as a kind and loving parent, but rather as a man who did bad things to the boys.

If he knew what she'd done last night, he would be angry. Clara shivered. She felt both uncomfortable and afraid. She knew that, sooner or later, she would have to deal with it; the situation wouldn't get easier.

Mr. Nate brought the buggy around from behind the main house, and the family left the farm for the trip into town as the girls just smiled at each other for the entire ride. After church, they dropped Lizzie at the entrance to the town square. She waved good-bye and made her way to the bakery. Clouds filled the sky, but rain held off as the Culmer family returned home.

Life was the same on the Lathrope farm as Tawny and Jimmy were just hanging around the special place as the family went to town for church. The walk to the special place was a little different since the boys had to reroute their trail to avoid stepping on plant beds and getting caught. They knew Lathrope paid attention to every detail in his fields. They didn't want to give him the opportunity to show his angry side.

"Time to go," said Jimmy.

"Yes; let's get back," Tawny replied. The two boys gingerly walked back to the big barn, only to find the other three boys playing a game of tossing the rock at the cans. To play the game, they stood three cans around thirty feet away and threw rocks and tried to knock a can over. It wasn't a complex game, but it did pass the time and sometimes provided a laugh or two. The boys were happy that the crop planting was finished and for the next few weeks, they had a lull in the workload. However, they also knew Lathrope would find things for them to do, and he always did.

"I think we're going to move the horse dung behind the big barn," said Mark. "I heard him saying something about it last week."

"Thank God he didn't make us move it two weeks ago," said Tawny, and then thought to himself, "When the bloody pile was thirty feet tall."

Just as Mark said, Mark and Peter spent next week moving a small pile about fifty feet further away from the barn because the kitchen staff could smell it in the house. The other boys continued to bring water from the creek to fill the big water tanks. It was hard, tedious work because the ride to and from the creek took about thirty minutes, which was added to the time it took to fill the twenty buckets and carry them to the wagon.

On Friday, on their third trip of the day to the creek, the boys could not believe how much water those tanks could actually hold. They parked the wagon next to the creek, as close as possible without having it roll into the creek or into the horse. Jack used a rock as a wedge between the ground and the wheel, which usually worked well to keep the wagon from shifting on its wheels. Tawny loaded his last bucket onto the wagon, and Jimmy and Tom carried their final buckets up the steep bank.

Jack was already on the bed of the wagon, moving buckets around so they could fit all twenty-three. Two boys had to sit on the back of the wagon while the other two drove it. That was the only way all four could ride back.

It was just before the morning meal bell. Tawny and Jimmy sat on the back of the wagon waiting to leave, while Tom had the reins and Jack removed the rock. After kicking aside the rock, he then would jump onto the seat next to Tom. This procedure had worked well all week.

Jack grabbed and yanked the rock free, but this time, as he jumped onto the wagon, he put his hand on a piece of wood, which acted as a holding rail. Just before he leaped, his hand slipped off and he fell feet-first into the wheel spokes. Tom couldn't stop the horse as the wagon jerked forward.

Back at the main house, Mark and Peter heard Jack's scream. He lay there, pinned, and blood gushed from his leg. His eyes seemed to go dark with pain as he grimaced, screaming again. The boys were frozen in terror.

Jimmy, get Lathrope!" Tawny helped the younger boy down. "Quick! As fast as you can run!" Jimmy raced running back to the main house.

"Do something!" begged Jack.

His leg was wedged into the wagon in an upside-down, hanging position. His back was on the ground, and his leg was upright but mangled where it protruded through the wheel spokes. The blood now flowed down his leg and onto his lap.

"Back the horse...one step," yelled Tawny. "Go on do it now! Tom...one step back," said Tawny, "One step back."

Tom grabbed the reins and quickly jumped in the wagon but was so nervous, he froze and couldn't remember one step forward or one step back or two steps forward or two back.

"Stop," said Tawny. "Don't move."

Tawny raced around the wagon, grabbed the reins from Tom, and walked up to the horse as he took the horse's head strap and actually walked him back one step and then yelled to Tom to wedge the rock against the wheel.

"Bloody hell! Awww!" screamed Jack. His leg now lay on the ground, looking like a crooked stick, bleeding.

"Tom, give me your shirt—quick," commanded Tawny. Tom did so. Tawny tied the sleeves around Jack's upper thigh. Then he pulled the ends as tight as he could. He remembered this from a class about first aid in the orphanage. Heddon would have been impressed. Tawny grabbed Jack's shoulders and had Tom grab the bent broken leg.

"Now as I pull, don't let the leg hit the spoke, all right?" said Tawny. He began pulling on Jack's shoulders, and the leg slowly started to come free of the spokes, but just as Tawny stopped and thought, they would have to move Jack's upper body to work the rest of Jack's leg out. This maneuver would require some work because Jack just wanted to lie still.

"Just cut it off! The leg..." pleaded Jack. Tawny and Tom knew Jack was delirious, but they didn't know that this often happened when you lost a lot of blood.

"What is going on?" Lathrope walked to the wagon. Jimmy walked behind him and stood, watching his friend on the ground.

"Move over, boy," said Lathrope. He bent over and grabbed Jack's shoulders and gave the final pull without regard for the boy's pain.

Jack's final scream for the day was even louder than the first one as Lathrope dragged the now-limp Jack, picked him up, and laid him in the wagon behind the water buckets. Jack had gone motionless. This frightened the other three, but Lathrope just told the boys to bring the wagon back to the barn. Tawny drove the wagon back to the barn, while Tom and Jimmy watched Jack.

"He's still breathing," said Jimmy as he bent over and could feel warm air coming out of Jack's open mouth but just faintly.

Once they got back to the barn, Lathrope carried Jack into the barn and put him down on the floor. He then went back to the house. Soon, one of the kitchen ladies came with a bucket of water and some rags. She worked on Jack by removing his trousers, putting a warm wet rag on his forehead, and then removing Tom's bloody shirt and replacing it with a cleaner one.

"He sure lost a lot of blood," the old lady said softly. Tawny saw the broken leg with the bone sticking out just below the knee. It looked bad.

The lady poured water over the wound and the blood rushed away, revealing a pink and light red flesh-colored opening, with a creamy white-colored bone, jagged at one end, slightly protruding.

"Move him over here," she said, as she motioned for the boys to carry Jack closer to the barn door. After Tawny and Tom carried Jack over and put him back down, the lady slid a rag under his leg, wrapped the wound with rags, and then tied them together. She then instructed Tawny to keep the cool rag on his forehead, change it every hour, and hope for the best. Tawny just looked at his friend Jack, He seemed to be sleeping with the same small grin he wore when he knocked down a couple of cans.

Tawny and the others huddled in a semicircle, watching Jack and wondering if he would live. Tawny's mind flashed back to his friend Colin, who died during that awful night on the boat.

Chapter 34

The Dark Day

The entire evening was quiet as Jack drifted in and out of consciousness. The boys could do nothing for him. They milled stood around and wished he would get better or even just stay awake longer than five minutes. Tawny and Peter changed the rag on Jack's forehead every hour religiously. The pain must have been terrible when Jack was awake. Maybe, thought Tawny, that's why he couldn't stay awake for long: too much pain.

Lathrope came in once during the evening to see how Jack was doing and, after looking at him once and just shaking his head, he quickly left again for the main house.

"He's a monster," said Tom.

"Yes," said Peter. "I hope he rots in hell."

"Hell is too good for him," whispered Tawny.

One by one, the boys made their way up to the barn loft and tried to get some sleep; there wasn't anything they could do for their friend but play the waiting game. Tawny and Peter would take turns tending to Jack.

It was on bad and scary nights like these that Jimmy reached inside and started to feel sorry for himself, only to start mumbling about somebody coming for him. "Me mum will come. I know me mum will come."

"Stop that," said Mark.

It usually took Jimmy around fifteen minutes to calm down, but for those fifteen minutes Jimmy felt abandoned and alone. This emotion controlled his thoughts and actions.

It happened very early in the morning, just before the sun rose, when Peter climbed down the ladder to change Jack's head rag. As he approached, Peter saw that Jack's head was slightly turned and open. His eyes were also slightly open, as if he were squinting. Jack's mouth showed his clenched teeth firmly pressing down on each other, and his nostrils were fully open. He wasn't breathing, however, and he wasn't moving.

"Tawny! Tawny, come here!" said Peter as he started to cry.

178

"What is it?" Tawny scrambled down the ladder and then quickly stopped in front of the body. He had seen this kind of face before.

"Peter, Jack's dead." Tawny hugged Peter as the others came down. Mark had never seen a dead person before and was more intrigued than bothered. He looked carefully at the lifeless body.

"What do we do now?" asked Jimmy.

"Wait for Lathrope," answered Peter.

Mark probed the lifeless body with his eyes, taking it in. Jack's face seemed almost white. He touched Jack's cheek. The cooling temperature of the body also seemed to interest Mark.

"I can't take this anymore," Mark said, as he abruptly stopped investigating the body. "I have to leave this godforsaken place."

Lathrope finally came around to the front of the barn, walked in slowly, glanced at the dead boy, and then sighed heavily. "Damn it. Ok, boys, we have to dig a grave. Come on."

The looks of hatred on the boys' faces would have enraged Lathrope if he had bothered to notice. None of that mattered to them now. The boys had already killed this farmer a hundred times or more in their collective dreams.

Lathrope pulled the big wagon around in front, and Tawny and Peter put the body in the back of the wagon. Lathrope covered it with a small burlap bag and then finally told the boys to get in. They rode through the trails, moving away from the barn.

Jimmy couldn't blame Lathrope for Jack's death; Lathrope was absent when it had happened. This was just plain bad luck; Jack was dead and this made, according to Tawny, the number of dead two—three, if you count the skeleton—and this started his young mind working: There could be more deaths.

Tawny worried that Lathrope was taking them to their special place. So far, they were headed in that direction, almost as if the farmer was following the footsteps the boys had made to and from the special place. As the wagon rounded the last bend, Tawny could see the big elm tree in the distance, and the wagon wasn't stopping or slowing. As they neared the big tree, Tawny's stomach turned. The wagon stopped, and Lathrope climbed out, walked around a bit, and finally pointed to the ground and said, "Dig here. Come on, you lazy bastards, start digging!"

The boys climbed off the wagon, took shovels, and began to make their friend's grave. They were near the creek bank and even closer to the big dead tree bridge. Tawny and the others were trying not to look at it.

The ground was hard on top but, as they cut through it, the darker soil was easier, except for an occasional root, which they chopped through by hitting several times with the side of the shovel. The hole deepened as Lathrope just stood there, with his arms folded, watching them. The farmer told them how long and how wide the grave had to be. Eventually, he said, "That's deep enough."

Tawny climbed out of the hole, around five feet deep now. Peter whispered that he was amazed how much dirt they had removed, which was now piled around the rectangular hole. Lathrope ordered Tawny and Peter to carry Jack's body and to place it into the hole. As they approached the grave, both boys stood rigid, holding their friend's body, and perhaps for the same reason, neither one wanted to drop the body in. They would have preferred to gently place the body deep into the grave.

While they stood there, staring into the empty dirt, they heard, "Throw it in. We have work to do today. Come on, throw him in!" Lathrope urged. "He can't feel anything. He's dead."

Tawny started to throw his end in first, and Peter had no choice but to do the same. The body lay at the bottom of the hole, curled and on its side, at one end of the hole.

Lathrope nodded and then muttered, "Start shoveling."

Mark threw the first shovel of dirt, and the next three, before the others started. The grave filled quickly. Finally, only a small mound of dirt over Jack's grave remained. It looked strange to Tawny, but stranger still was Mark's face, stony and pale. Tawny felt that something happened to Mark, but he didn't know what. The boys were taken back to the big barn to eat breakfast, which the kitchen lady brought. They sat near the open door, as always, but today, no one ate much. They talked about Jack.

"I'm leaving," said Mark a little later. "For sure."

"Going barefoot?" asked Jimmy, just before he took a drink of milk.

"I don't care. I'll wrap rags around my feet."

The boys spent the rest of the day filling water tanks. Mark kept saying he was leaving the farm later that night. The others listened and soon gave up trying to convince him that it would be better to stay than to leave. Mark didn't really know where he would go. However, after almost a year with Mark, the boys knew he was stubborn and that you couldn't tell him anything. So, the boys accepted the idea that he would leave after dark.

The evening meal arrived and the boys ate a good meal of pork chops and fresh rolls. They sat near the open door, with the sun slowly setting, a smear of yellow, gold, and ruddy colors. Only the huge bonfire, usually reserved for the winter months, more fully captured their attention.

Mark finished his pork chop, a roll, and then a glass of milk. Then he stood and said, "Good-bye."

With no hesitation, he picked up a bag of rags and walked through the barn door. They all watched Mark as he quickly strolled away.

"I wonder if he is going to the special place?" asked Jimmy, as he gave a final desperate wave to his departing friend.

"No," said Tawny "He'll follow the creek bed to the train. Maybe he hopes he'll find a train."

The rest of the evening, they just looked at each other and wondered what Lathrope would do when he learned Mark was gone. They had to work out a plan, and it was Peter who had the best idea. "We'll tell him Mark left in the middle of the night, and that we don't know anything about it. It'll also give Mark more time to get away."

Tawny agreed that this plan was best. They all prayed that Lathrope wouldn't return before they went to bed. Tawny then decided that they should just go up to the loft and stay there on this night. They all knew that any punishment Lathrope could bring upon them would most certainly come in the morning.

The four boys huddled in the loft and started to tell stories about their friends, Mark and Jack. They laughed quietly, at least for the next two hours, at which time they drifted off one at a time. The morning would be different, as soon as Lathrope got there.

"Wake up boys!"

"Here we go," said Tawny, as the four boys climbed down and walked slowly toward the farmer, who waited in front of the same wagon that they had used yesterday to transport Jack.

"Get in."

As they made their way down the trail, Jimmy whispered, "He didn't notice." All the boys smiled.

They returned to the grave to throw more dirt into the hole; it had settled a foot or so. Suddenly, Lathrope stared at the boys and then looked quickly around. "Where's Mark? If he is still in bed, I'll whip him."

"Don't know where he is," replied Peter, as he kept throwing dirt onto the curved pile that was formed over the grave. The boys made a small mound above the grave. At Lathrope's prodding, they quickly climbed onto the wagon and lurched along the ruts back to the big barn.

Lathrope stormed into the barn and flew up the ladder. He came thundering back down, grunting, only to leave the boys standing dumbfounded. He stopped after five feet or so and quickly turned back to face the boys. With hat in his hand, he growled, "Do any of you know about this?"

"No, sir," said Tawny. "He was gone when we woke. Mu st've left during the night. We were sleeping."

"Tawny's right," said Peter. Jimmy and Tom also supported Tawny.

Lathrope made his way to the house. The boys waited for their morning meal in front of the big barn door. Jimmy moved closer to the edge of the barn, listening for any noise from the main house. It was silent for the moment, until he heard a lady's voice. "No! Don't do it!"

A door slammed. Lathrope returned to the barn, with an anger in his eyes the boys had never seen. He grabbed Tawny by the shoulders, threw him onto bed of the wagon, and drove off. He returned ten minutes later and repeated his actions until all but Jimmy were gone. Then he came for Jimmy. As the little boy sat in the wagon, he started again about his mum coming. They reached the cure barn. Jimmy started crying uncontrollably. Lathrope just picked him up, threw him into the cure barn, and then yelled, "Grow up."

Tawny looked around. He was again locked in a cure barn. So, he did what he had done before and made a small pile of sludge next to the door—the driest part—and just sat. He thought about this better life in Canada. He held tightly onto the silver chain and medal.

Chapter 35

The Summer of 1908

The four boys had been isolated from each other for two days. Lathrope finally brought them back to the big barn, only to scold them that this was his farm and he had to know what was going on. They huddled around the barn door and ate the morning meal. The buns and milk tasted sweet on this morning, as they had not eaten since being locked in the cure barns.

By now, the plants had grown a bit, with tiny green sprouts everywhere and for the most part in straight lines. Lathrope had instructed the boys to walk the fields, pulling out the smaller plants. This was a time-consuming exercise and fairly easy work. They spent the next three days trimming the fields.

"The goal is to make the crop secure and allow the plants room to grow." Lathrope made sure that the boys were well trained in pulling plants that were not wanted or would hinder the growth of the healthier ones. This would yield the biggest profit.

It was hard not to think of Jack and Mark, who just vanished into thin air, quietly and quickly. Tawny thought occasionally about Billy and wondered how his friend's life was going ahead. He couldn't wait until they met again at the special place—probably this weekend if the weather held. He also wondered about George, who miraculously found the special place and shared his comments about his life. Tawny couldn't believe the change in George; those marks on George's back were frightening.

The summer was hot, humid, and long, with only a few bright spots. The temperature continuously rose and yielded good weather, with the occasional rain that Tawny knew helped the farmers. One major thunderstorm rolled through the community in mid-July, but caused no damage to Lathrope's plants or fields.

Lizzie spent the summer doing only three things: working at Owen's bakery four days a week, going to church on Sundays with her family to meet Clara, and quickly growing into a young woman. She and Clara had managed to arrange a couple of sleepovers. This gave her time to see the boys, especially Tawny.

She looked forward to these outings and enjoyed the closeness of her friends and the fun-filled nights at the special place, talking about growing up and generally anything on their minds. She was also amazed that Mark had just left, and she also wondered if he was all right, if he was doing ok wherever he ended up. She grew more than fond of Tawny, yet her other inner voice, the stronger one, told her to wait.

Lizzie had her thirteenth birthday party, a small affair attended only by her family—Clara was busy. She enjoyed herself for half a day because she had to work later at the bakery, and her Uncle John had teased her about turning thirteen and that she was about to enter womanhood. But what he didn't know was that Lizzie had already entered this state (emotionally, at least). One Saturday evening, in the middle of the summer, they all met at the big elm, and the closeness between Lizzie and Tawny went a bit further than she had intended. Clara had told her that it was no big deal and that was fun. Clara had also told her that twice, in the middle of the night, she had crept out of the house to meet Billy in the barn.

Lizzie was stunned at her best friend's actions and felt that Clara was miles ahead of her. She asked herself if this is what she wanted. She was confused and a little fearful of it all.

Clara had told her that Tawny wouldn't object and would be willing because he liked Lizzie, which was obvious to anybody who was around them. Lizzie told Clara that she would have to think about it and that it was harder and harder because her emotions were running wild.

The other bright spot of the summer was her sister Mary's wedding. Mary and Hubrey had their wedding in late summer (instead of early spring), on a perfect Saturday afternoon. Lizzie was maid of honor. They went to the church and had a small ceremony, followed by a party at Lizzie's parent's house. There, she saw all her cousins, uncles, aunts, and other older friends of her parents. Uncle John got drunk and sat on a chair the entire afternoon, just smiling and occasionally spitting food as he chatted with anyone who started a conversation with him.

Fred and Arthur kept to themselves for the most part, and Lizzie's father made sure that everyone had a good time, except for one instance; father told Fred to shut up because Fred was complaining that he would have to clean out the outhouses tomorrow because of today's heavy traffic. The cake was beautiful; Mr. Owen and Lizzie created it. The cake resembled a small white tower and was topped with two little bride-and-groom figurines, which were ordered and shipped in a tiny box all the way from New York City.

Lizzie's mother, Nellie, handled things well, considering that her oldest daughter was now married and would soon start her own family providing Nellie with grandchildren. Lizzie talked to her Uncle Jim, who worked for the railroad, and discovered that he was nice, but he kept teasing her about becoming an aunt. He also told Lizzie about Mary and that every time he came into the bakery, she would hound him to find out when the passenger trains were arriving. Lizzie finally realized that her Uncle Jim was responsible for her meeting Tawny.

She thought about telling him about Tawny, but decided against it—maybe another day. The neighbors were also invited, and they brought trays of food. Everyone enjoyed a collective feast, especially Hubrey, who for the first time met the entire family. With his humor and charm, he was an instant hit.

Mary and Hubrey opened their gifts, which consisted of a few small boxes and several envelopes. Lizzie couldn't wait until they opened her gift, which she bought at the general store two weeks earlier. Mary opened the box, pulled out a small book, and then started crying as she thanked Lizzie by hugging her. Hubrey rounded up everyone, arranged them in lines, and then took several photographs, which the family thought was a nice thing to do.

Lizzie pulled Mary aside and told her about Tawny and that they had met, they kissed, and that she really liked him. Mary's only advice was to be careful and patient, and she repeated it at least three times during their conversation.

Lizzie also asked Mary about Hubrey's family and why they didn't attend. Mary said that his family agreed on a small party, after the honeymoon, with his mother and his brother in Toronto; they were all the family he had.

As afternoon melted into night, everyone drifted off. Lizzie asked Mary about their honeymoon plans. They were going to spend the following weekend in Hamilton at the Royal Windsor Hotel. The way Mary described it sounded great to Lizzie and made her think about Tawny and how she wished he could have been there to enjoy this wonderful day. They all hugged and said their good-byes as Hubrey waved and drove the buggy off, carrying a few gift boxes and a lot of wrapped-up food.

The boys spent the entire summer walking for miles, picking weeds. For the girls, it was trying to see the boys as often as possible.

Life was routine at the farms, with the days melting into nights, and the boys grew bigger and stronger. The girls grew wiser and rounder. The plants grew at a fast pace, and soon it was a year that the boys had been in Canada. Their anniversary passed without them giving it a second thought.

In mid-August, on a Saturday afternoon, Lathrope went into town with his wagon, only to return later with a new boy. Greg was a small eleven-year-old who had bright red hair and a round, freckled face. Tawny and Jimmy, along with the others, tried to make him feel welcome and actually enjoyed talking to this red-haired boy, who came from another orphanage in London. Greg talked about life back in England, the long trip, and the promised new life here in Canada. Tawny and Jimmy warned Greg about promises that were made and also enlightened him about the hardships he was about to encounter in this "better life."

Little Greg fit right in with the others as he had a personality that at first made him enjoyable to be around. He never seemed to be at a loss for words.

Lathrope woke the boys on one Monday in early September and soon had them snapping the purple flower tops of the protected plants in the field closest to the main house. Tawny knew that Lathrope used these plants for the next year's seeds and liked this job only because it was easy on his back and required no special talent.

Greg worked hard and kept a humor about him that the others welcomed as somewhat of a temporary relief from the grueling daily tasks. However, Tawny knew that the harvest approached and soon the boys would be working hard, filling up the cure barns with bundles of tied leaves.

Lizzie and Clara were back at school. This year, they were the two oldest students in Miss Kemp's class, since the oldest student, Ruth, had just disappeared. Clara had heard a rumor that she was very sick and that her parents sent her away to get better. Clara and Lizzie also knew that when something like this happened, it usually involved a baby. Lizzie really didn't mind being one of the oldest students; besides, she loved being around Miss Kemp.

This year, however, Lizzie had to take Cecil every day and get him used to school, which he did quite well and never complained. Clara invited Lizzie to the house on the next weekend for a sleepover, and this made Lizzie excited about seeing her friends again. She couldn't wait to see Tawny. Within the past year, the girls had grown so much, both physically and emotionally.

Lizzie hadn't seen Tawny for five weeks, and she was ready to catch up on everything. She still wasn't sure about doing anything physical, but she didn't rule it out. Often, she thought that it would be nice. Lizzie was just glad to be going to Clara's for the weekend so she could see her Tawny again.

Friday came quickly. Mr. Nate was taking the girls back to the Culmer farm for their sleepover.

"Hello, Lizzie." Mrs. Culmer had waited on the porch for the girls to arrive, as always.

"Hello," replied Lizzie. "How are you feeling?"

"I'm fine," she smiled. "My back is sore from tomato canning, but I'll survive. How are your parents?"

"Fine, Mrs. Culmer. Just fine."

Clara and Lizzie retreated to the bedroom upstairs and discussed the plan for tonight, the usual stuff: hiding clothes outside, unlocking the Dutch half-door, and the slipper rags, which were used to wipe off the excess mud and dirt.

"Hello," said Gwen, as she carried a tray of baked chicken to the oven and placed it inside.

"Hi," said Lizzie, smiling. She noticed that Gwen wore her hair down today; it was quite long and shiny.

Lizzie and Clara grabbed some cookies and went to the front porch. They gazed at the fields, but couldn't see any boys.

"Where are they?" asked Lizzie, nibbling on her cookie.

"Don't know," answered Clara. They scanned the horizon for activity.

"Here girls, I brought you lemonade." Mrs. Culmer set the glasses on the wood table and returned to the kitchen. Clara had informed Lizzie about the telephony, which was being delivered Monday by the general store people, and that she should ask her dad to get one too. Lizzie thought about it and told Clara that her dad didn't like those things. It would hurt the family because discussions would be isolated to one person and not the entire family. Clara quickly changed the subject; she didn't seem to want to have a lengthy discussion about it.

Evening came, and after dinner the girls were in Clara's room talking about the upcoming meeting at the special place. All they had to do was wait for Clara's mother and father to fall asleep. Gwen was also waiting, but for her own reasons.

Chapter 36

The Night of Desire

A week earlier, Gwen had been in the kitchen, helping prepare the evening's meal when she overheard Clara asking her mother about having Lizzie over for a sleepover. For Gwen, life on her uncle's farm bored her. She was used to a more exciting life with her friends; she didn't care what her parents thought. She believed that that was why she had been sent here—according to her dad, two years here would straighten her out. Being cooped up in this house, even though it was a beautiful place, took its toll on Gwen. She had to do something quick, or else she would just simply run away.

On Tuesday, the day after Clara received permission for Lizzie to come over, one of the older women didn't make it to work. Gwen rang the dinner bell, which was actually a large steel triangle that hung on the front porch.

She then carried food to the open barn door. The boys quickly gathered to devour the contents. Her eyes focused on her newest interest, Billy. He was clearly the tallest and cutest. She returned to the main house and cleaned up after dinner. Mr. Culmer asked Gwen to carry the water bucket to the barn so the boys could clean themselves, and she made a little comment that it had been several days since they had bathed.

In the dark, Gwen filled a bucket and took it to the barn. She placed the water in the center on the floor, just as she had done all the other times, and then returned to the house carrying the tray of bones and empty glasses back to the kitchen.

After cleaning the tray, she wiped off the kitchen table, filled another water bucket, and then carried it back to the barn.

As she approached the open barn door, she noticed that Billy was standing, shirtless, in the center of the barn, bathing. She stood silent, looked over her left shoulder back at the house, put the water bucket down, and then watched. She couldn't believe the transformation that had taken place over the past few months. Billy had wide shoulders and a flat, muscled stomach. Gwen's mind raced. Occasionally, she glanced back at the house.

Watching Billy made her tingle with anticipation. She looked back at the house one last time. Then she picked up the bucket and entered the barn, acting as if she had seen nothing.

"Hello," said Billy, as if it were an everyday experience to be nearly naked in front of a woman.

"Hi," said Gwen, her voice, cracking a little. "Here is another bucket...to rinse."

"Thanks," said Billy as he stood two feet from her. He stretched his arms in the air, holding the water bucket high and pouring the bucket over his head.

As Gwen watched him, she decided then and there what she wanted and, by God, she would get it. Billy had no idea what was on this young woman's mind.

Gwen retreated to the main house, where she gathered a bundle of towels, and returned to the barn. Billy was gone. Probably up in the loft, she thought. The others stood waiting in line to clean up, but as far as Gwen was concerned, they weren't even there.

Gwen returned to the house, quickly finished cleaning the kitchen, and then placed the empty buckets outside near the water pump.

She said goodnight to Mrs. Culmer and entered her room, where she took a sponge bath using the big porcelain bowl and fresh white towels. She slipped into a long off-white dress. This kind of thing had happened only once before, with a man who had worked on her father's farm. She smiled.

The night moved along slowly as Gwen stared out her window at the dark fields. The little horse barn stood to her left, as her mind played out what would happen this night. She left her room and went into the kitchen, not for a drink but to check on the Culmers, to see if they were in bed.

They were. The lamp in the living room was dark, and the entire house was quiet, even upstairs, where Clara slept. She rose, fluffed her hair, opened the half door, and then walked to the open barn door, feeling the cool night air. She entered the barn, climbed the ladder. "Billy?"

"What?" he quickly answered and then rolled over and saw Gwen.

Gwen held onto the ladder rung with her hair completely let out and flowing in a gentle cross breeze.

"What do you want?"

"Come with me," she said softly, firmly, and convincingly. Billy followed Gwen out of the barn.

Billy knew something was up. He decided to keep his mouth shut. She walked toward the back door of the main house, and Billy stopped. "Where are you taking me?"

"Just come and be quiet," she reached out and took his hand.

She led him into the house and, for the first time, Billy saw the huge kitchen where their food was prepared, the dining room, and the living room. Furniture and glass coal lamps were everywhere.

"Shhhhh," she whispered; his bare feet made little noise as he took in as much of the house as he could. She opened the bedroom door and dragged him in. Gwen whispered, "If you ever tell anybody about this, I'll deny it, or I'll just tell the others that you made me do this."

He lay next to Gwen, smiling faintly and not knowing if he should say something or simply leave. Regardless, Billy, now feeling relaxed, said nothing and closed his eyes enjoying the moment. "You better go now. Remember, this didn't happen."

Billy nodded and still didn't know what to say. He slowly dressed, kissed Gwen on the cheek, and then left through the open window. Gwen fell back on the bed, smiled, and her thoughts were selfish. She had no idea how what she'd done would later affect everyone.

Chapter 37

The Birthday Party

On Sunday, it rained. Tawny had to go to the special place for only one reason, to see if Billy was there. He had been gone about thirty minutes when he returned to find Jimmy and the boys huddled around the fire barrel, talking a little about Greg's recent life back in England.

"We are meeting this coming Saturday. Billy told me," said Tawny.

"Great," replied Jimmy, "We can bring Greg along."

Greg and Jimmy discussed how the harvest was terrible and how it didn't allow them time for themselves. Tawny knew that Greg was too small to tie plants this year, let alone hang them in the cure barns. This year's harvest would take a greater toll on Tawny, Peter, and Tom.

"You'll have to come next week and put your initials in the big tree," said Jimmy.

"What big tree?" asked Greg.

"You'll see," said Peter. "I know you will like it."

The boys retreated to the loft and fell asleep, only to be rousted early in the Monday morning by the farmer.

"Get up, you lazy English."

The tired boys collected themselves, as they always did, and climbed onto the wagon, knowing that the harvest would end soon. Tawny couldn't wait to see the expression on Greg's face when the sun came up and he saw for the first time the endless plants on Lathrope's farm. He was right, as Greg talked and talked, and couldn't stop talking, about harvest time.

The boys repeated last year's harvest routine and, for the most part, they did a good job. Lathrope handed out no severe punishment, but Greg's talking became a punishment of its own.

"Do you think that's why his parents put him in the orphanage?" asked Peter, now snickering in Tawny's direction.

"Probably. The kid won't shut up," said Tawny.

Saturday was a few days away, and Tawny grew excited about meeting at the special place. By now, Greg had known about the meeting for three days, and he hounded the others about going. If the weather held, Tawny thought, the boys would be at the big elm tree, spending time with the others…and Lizzie.

The predictable work schedule continued. They plucked leaves, tied them together, and then hung them in cure barns. Tawny noticed a newspaper lying on the wagon front seat, rolled up and wrinkled. It had been read once, possibly twice. Tawny leaned over at tried to read the headline, but it was mostly hidden, and if Tawny wanted to know what it said, he would have to pick up the paper. He would risk a beating from Lathrope, which, at this point, wasn't going to happen.

Lathrope stopped the wagon, and for the first time this harvest season, Tawny realized that Lathrope was not just supervising, he was actually helping in the harvest. He also figured out why; there were only five boys now, and not six. Why then didn't he buy another boy? Maybe he thought that this way, he could keep tabs on the others. Besides, the boys were happy now that Greg worked with Lathrope. Once in a while, they heard Lathrope yell, "Shut up!"

Tawny grabbed the newspaper, as Lathrope prepared another wagon for him, and quickly noticed that the date read "September 24, 1908," and the headline told of tension mounting in Europe and that war was imminent. He decided to ignore the words, but the date interested him— Saturday night was his birthday. He quickly folded and returned the newspaper to the wagon seat, and he waited for Lathrope to return with the other wagon.

He thought about Billy again and how he was doing on his farm. Again, Tawny calculated his age. The answer didn't come easily or quickly. So, he did the math. I was twelve when I got here. Last year I turned thirteen. Finally, the answer came: He would be fourteen. Suddenly, he thought about Lizzie and hoped she was doing well with her bakery job. He also hoped she would remember to bring the newspaper to the meeting this Saturday night, the one he had requested. For some strange reason, Tawny now wanted to learn more about Waterford and its surroundings. He couldn't explain the interest he had for this part of Canada. Perhaps it was just a way to pass the time.

Lizzie walked to school on Friday, toting Cecil with one hand and carrying an overstuffed bag in the other. She always took a bag on Fridays, when she would go to Clara's for the sleepover, but today, a lot more than usual was in that bag.

"Hi, Clara," said Lizzie. She had sat Cecil down earlier and had returned outside to wait for her best friend. "Hello, Mr. Nate," she added. He answered, as always, by tipping his hat.

"Did you remember the cake?" whispered Clara.

"Yes. It's wrapped up in here." Lizzie glanced down at the bag, which bulged at the seams. "I hope it doesn't break."

Just then, the school bell rang. They went inside and listened to Miss Kemp teach mathematics, English, science, and history. Lizzie enjoyed the history lessons about the United States and their war about slavery, the North and the South, and the Union and the Confederates. She enjoyed learning about this period and loved to listen to Miss Kemp read the stories and then retell them in her own words. Around ten, Lizzie and the other classmates noticed a man in the hallway staring into the classroom. He wrote on a clipboard as he looked at each student. There had been no explanation of who he was and why he was there. Suddenly, Lizzie figured it out. "I know what's going on. I'll tell you at lunch."

During lunch, Lizzie remembered what Uncle John had told her dad just about a week earlier. "You see, the boys...you know, the farm boys, are supposed to go to school. The farmers are supposed to send them as part of owning these boys."

Clara blinked and said, "Billy and the others are supposed to be here at school with us, right now?"

"Yes, I think so," replied Lizzie. "That man must work for the government. The town brought him here to check on the farm boys, to see if they were being sent to school."

It was a little warmer when Mr. Nate came to pick up the girls, and although it didn't look like rain, clouds now blanketed most of the sky. On their way to the Culmer farm, Lizzie thought about the oversized bag. If Clara's mother took it from her as she always did, she might see what was inside. She decided to just wait it out and see what would happen. Besides, everything in the bag could be explained if she really had to.

"Hello, Lizzie," said Mrs. Culmer.

"Hello, Mrs. Culmer; I hope you are feeling ok," answered Lizzie, pausing for a moment before picking up the big bag and hoping Mrs. Culmer would turn away. She didn't.

"Let me get somebody to carry that bag for you," said Mrs. Culmer. "Gwen, could you please come here?" Gwen took the bag from Lizzie to Clara's room. It worked; not a word was said about the big heavy bag and what it contained.

The girls sat on the front porch and talked about everything, including a rumor that the Cott family was having a huge wedding in Simcoe tomorrow at which six direct cousins were going to marry each other.

Lizzie thought that this was wrong; you don't marry your cousin. Mrs. Culmer thought it was despicable that Mrs. Cott would let this happen, and as for Mr. Culmer, he didn't care about it one way or another and was actually glad that he and Mrs. Culmer weren't invited because now he didn't have to buy gifts.

Night came, and the girls found themselves in their usual place, sitting under the covers of Clara's big four-poster bed, talking. Just as they were falling asleep, it started to rain. It was the kind of rain, thought Lizzie, that supplied the land with much-needed moisture. It surely would be over in a few hours.

When she woke, Lizzie noticed that the rooster's call was absent. She nudged Clara. "What happen to the old rooster?"

"He died two weeks ago," said Clara, yawning and stretching. "Dad wanted to cook him, but Mom said no." Lizzie smiled.

The two girls spent most of the day in the house, waiting for evening. Soon it was dark, and the kitchen help was gone. They still had to wait for Mr. Culmer to go to bed. Like clockwork, the lamp in Mr. Culmer's bedroom went out.

As soon as the light went out, the boys took off; the girls would follow. The girls knew when the lamp went out because all they had to do was watch the boys and when they scurried, it was time.

"There, over there," whispered Lizzie, as she watched Billy and Thomas and one more leave the barn. "Let's go."

Soon, they were there at the special place, hugging and talking. Lizzie and Clara met Greg and were completely taken with this little redheaded mouthpiece. The others met Evan, a reserved twelve-year-old who Billy brought along because he thought he could use something like this to make his life more interesting.

Lizzie had everyone sit in a circle, and then she pulled the package from her pack. She unwrapped a small chocolate cake, a candle, and a match. As she removed the cake, she asked Clara to light the candle.

"Wow," said Greg, "A cake. I like this place already."

Lizzie insisted that everyone congratulate Tawny on his birthday. Tawny sat there, feeling warm and loved and just a bit weepy.

"Thank you all for this." He stood and kissed Lizzie. To his recollection, this was the first birthday party he had ever had. Lizzie reached in the bag, pulled out a small wrapped box, and handed it to Tawny. He quickly opened the box when they all heard, "Crack!" They stopped and all turned, like frightened deer, toward the Culmer side of the creek and stared for a while. They saw or heard nothing else, so after a few minutes, they resumed the festivities.

Tawny finished opening his gift from Lizzie. She had fixed the St. Christopher's medal for him and reattached it to the chain. His mouth dropped, and he looked at her intently and then said, "How did you get this? I thought I had lost it."

Lizzie smiled. "Small hands and big pockets. I had it fixed for you."

"Thanks," he said quietly, as he kissed her again. "I love it."

Billy and Clara were walking around the big tree, holding hands and taking the occasional kiss, with Billy trying to encourage Clara to leave with him for a few minutes. "I don't think so, Billy. We have guests tonight." Clara pulled Billy back to the tree and gave him a piece of cake. After only three minutes, the cake was completely gone, and only the piece of cardboard remained. Greg picked it up and licked it clean, making everyone laugh. Jimmy watched this new boy named Greg carefully; he didn't care much for him, probably because it was usually Jimmy—being the smallest—who made his friends laugh and received the most attention. Now the attention was directed at Greg.

From the darkness, they were watched closely by Gwen, who sat in the far grass on Culmer's side of the creek. She felt relieved that she was not spotted when that branch broke as she repositioned herself for a better look at the special place.

The boys started to say their good-byes. Gwen knew she had to leave; she had to get back to the house before the others did.

"Don't forget your bag," said Clara, as Lizzie gave Tawny a last kiss, which seemed to last forever.

Jimmy seemed a little reserved this evening, and now that Tawny had thought about it, he realized that Jimmy had been quiet during the entire harvest. Could it be that Jimmy was jealous of Greg?

Chapter 38

The Visitor from England

It was late September on a Saturday when the passenger train arrived from Toronto. On this trip, the cars brought a handful of regular passengers, no boys, and a tall gentleman who wore a black suit, dark glasses, and carried a hand case that was stamped with the imprint of the British government. The tall man entered the general store and asked to find accommodations. Mr. Small, the proprietor, indicated that Miss Brown's boarding house up the street would surely take him. He gave the Englishman directions.

"Thank you, good sir," said the man as he picked up his brown bag, adjusted his hat, and left the store. The walk past the shops was short, and when he got to the top of Main Street, he turned right, as he was instructed to do. Then he walked a few blocks until he reached the boarding house.

The Englishman looked at the big red brick house, put his bag on the ground, and then looked around at the trimmed street, which resembled England in some ways, but was more spread out. He strolled up the walkway and knocked on the front door.

"Hello," said Miss Brown as she opened the front door. She was a healthy-looking older woman with pulled-back brown hair and a warm smile.

"Hello. My name is Edwin Wallace. I've been told you have accommodations. I shall be here for several days."

"No trouble, sir. Please come this way." She led him to the table in the front hallway, where she asked him to fill out the registry. While he was doing so, Miss Brown chatted.

"So, you're here on business then? A tobacco buyer, perhaps?"

Edwin Wallace glanced up and smiled tiredly. "I'm afraid not. I am here on official government business."

He followed her up the stairs to the second floor, where she opened the third door on the left, the side that faced Main Street. They entered a spacious bedroom.

"It's two dollars a day. You have a private bath two doors down."

"This will be fine," Mr. Wallace said.

"If you need anything, please let me know."

"Perhaps you can tell me the way to the Lathrope Farm," Wallace said, but then quickly added, "No, not today. I haven't rested in two days. Please wake me in the morning early, will you, good lady?"

Miss Brown slightly bowed. "I will. Have a pleasant rest."

She closed the door, not before she noticed the black attaché case with the bright red, blue, and white emblem. Mr. Edwin Wallace, thought Miss Brown, was surely going to cause a little commotion on the Lathrope farm.

Miss Brown tapped on the door a few times, with Mr. Wallace acknowledging the early wake-up call on this Sunday morning. After he washed and smoothed out his clothes, he went downstairs to the living room.

He rang the desk bell in the front room of the Brown house.

"Yes, can I help you?" said Miss Brown. Her voice entered the room seconds before she did.

"Oh, good morning, Mr. Wallace. I hope you rested well last night."

"Yes, Miss Brown. I did indeed." Wallace smiled brightly. "Now, the directions to the Lathrope Farm?"

"Yes; go to your right, down Main Street until you come to the Culmer Farm. You'll know it by the green-and-white house on the left side of the road. Go left from there, for five miles or so, or maybe six, until you come to a big blue-and-white house," she said.

"Wait a minute," Mr. Wallace said, as he wrote the directions on a piece of paper he pulled from his jacket pocket.

"The Lathrope farm is right there," she said, now interested in why this man was looking for that particular farm.

"The one with the blue-and-white house?" he asked.

"Yes, sir. You can't miss it. By the way, do you mind telling me what this is all about"?

"Sorry, madam. You see, I'm under orders from the Crown. You understand." He folded the paper and slipped it back into his pocket. Miss Brown knew that this business from England had to somehow involve the farm boys. "Is transportation to this farm available?"

"I'm not sure," she said, "Let me see; please wait here."

Mr. Wallace sat in the living room, glanced out the window, and then noticed that this morning in Waterford was very cloudy. It seemed as though rain would come soon. He heard the back door slam shut and saw a small boy running away from the house toward town.

"Would you like a cup of tea while you wait?" asked Miss Brown.

"Yes, I would. Thank you," He felt a little bothered by not knowing how he was going to get to his destination.

"We'll know whether you can get a ride in a minute. I've sent Robert to see if a wagon is going that way."

"Thank you very much." He stood, looked around the room, taking in all the pictures, pondered the wall hangings, and then stared outside, as if anxious to get on with his business.

"Here you are, then." Miss Brown handed Mr. Wallace a cup and saucer.

"Not too much longer," Miss Brown called from the kitchen as Mr. Wallace could hear the dishes being washed. Finally, the little boy ran into the house and said something to Miss Brown that Mr. Wallace couldn't understand or hear.

"In about fifteen minutes," said Miss Brown, as she entered the living room with a plate of cookies, "a wagon is going that way in fifteen minutes."

"That will be fine," said Mr. Wallace. "Where do I get this ride?"

"Just go to the general store and ask for Mr. Fraser."

"Thank you." He put the tea down and then left the house. He walked toward the town square holding his hat in the light autumn breeze and carrying the black case under his arm.

Mr. Wallace entered the general store and asked if the Fraser ride was there yet.

The young boy pointed through the window at the horse and wagon. "Yes, sir; see that wagon outside, the one red trim and the white horse? That's the one you need."

"Thank you, lad." Mr. Wallace left the store and waited next to the wagon for someone to arrive.

"You the man looking for a ride?" The question came from a short, fat man dressed in work clothes.

"I am," answered the Englishman, holding the black case under his arm.

"Hop aboard, then," said man as he squirmed in his seat. Mr. Wallace climbed onto the bench seat, still clutching his case. "Shouldn't be to town today, bein' it's Sunday and all, but the missus needed flour and yeast. The name's Fraser." The farmer snapped the reins, and the wagon jerked forward. "Where you going?"

"The Lathrope Farm."

"We'll pass by it in about twenty minutes."

The wagon left at a slow pace, revealing all that Waterford had to offer on this cloudy autumn day. "Our new town hall," said Fraser, pointing to his left.

"Very nice," answered Mr. Wallace.

The ride became monotonous as they passed farms, one after another, in an unending brown landscape of post harvest fields. Fraser was a naturally nosey man. "What do you want at the Lathrope Farm, then?"

"It's personal business," replied Wallace. "You understand."

"Are you from the British government?" pressed Fraser.

"I work for the Department of External Affairs, under the director, Miles Burke. I'm here on official business, and I'm not at liberty to discuss more than this. I am really sorry, sir."

Fraser sat back on the wagon seat, and they continued down the main road, approaching the turnoff. Tossing this arrogant Englishman off the wagon might be fun, but Fraser decided that it wasn't worth it and that it probably would just cause him grief.

"There's the Lathrope Farm," said Fraser, as they slowly approached the open gate.

"Thank you, good sir," said Mr. Wallace. After the wagon drew to a stop, he hopped down, brushed off his clothes, repositioned the case under his arm, and began the walk up the drive to the house.

After a loud knock, Mrs. Lathrope opened the front door "Hello?"

"Good morning, madam. My name is Edwin Wallace. I am here on official business from the British High Commission."

Mrs. Lathrope paled. It took a great deal of effort to compose herself, as she quietly said, "Please come in and have a seat. I'll get my husband right away."

Mr. Wallace sat in a huge winged chair and studied the enormous living room. Most of its contents were middle class. Perhaps this was all they had in Waterford.

Lathrope entered the back door to find his wife in a turmoil. "There's an Englishman in the living room!"

"Calm down, woman." Lathrope figured that it was probably a random check to see how the boys were doing and she was not to worry.

Lathrope entered the room, removed his hat in a friendly gesture, and then firmly shook the man's hand. "I'm Lathrope."

"My name is Edwin Wallace, senior attaché to the Director of External Affairs in Great Britain. I'm here on a matter concerning, I believe, one of your boys." Wallace held out the piece of paper. "One James Burke. You see, Mr. Lathrope, his father is the director, Miles Burke. I have been sent here to bring James back to England, by orders from his father."

"I see," said Lathrope now feeling relieved. He was also impressed with this man and his ability to use the English language properly and forcefully.

"We are almost done with harvest," said Lathrope. "Can you wait for another couple of days? I really do need Jimmy to finish. Besides, our arrangement—"

"I need to catch the train this Thursday afternoon, which gives me three days," said Wallace, making a note in his little black book. "If you take me back to the town center, I will return on Wednesday. Please make the necessary arrangements for James to leave."

"What arrangements?" asked Lathrope, who now felt cheated and taken advantage of.

"There are papers to sign; all procedure, no problem," answered Wallace.

Lathrope was still angry, but just said, "Just stay put, we'll leave in a few minutes." Lathrope changed his clothes, thought a little about Jimmy, and then wrestled with the fact that the boy was leaving and not being replaced. Lathrope was being cheated because he had already paid for this boy! How was he going to get his money back?

He huffily entered the living room and sat in a chair next to the window, all the while staring at the Englishman. "Mr. Wallace, you know that I paid for Jimmy, and I really could use him, so my question to you—"

"Yes, sir," replied Wallace, quickly cutting off the farmer in mid sentence, "You need compensation. I understand." Lathrope did not know what that word meant, but he liked the way it sounded. He nodded and grinned.

Soon, everyone was on the Lathrope buggy, including the Englishman, and they were headed to the town center. The ride back seemed shorter for Mr. Wallace and after twenty minutes, he said good-bye to Mrs. Lathrope. Mr. Wallace, case under arm, turned to Mr. Lathrope, looked him directly in the eyes, and said, "You will make sure that the boy is ready to travel, my good man."

Lathrope, at a loss for words, nodded. The reins snapped, the buggy left, and Mr. Wallace retreated to his room at Miss Brown's boarding house. Lathrope, although rattled by the sudden visit, realized that this was just a father looking for his son.

On Wednesday, Mr. Wallace promptly returned to the Lathrope farm, and after saying hello to everyone at the main house, he made his way to the barn to confront little James. After hearing the news, Jimmy broke down and cried. "I told you so!" he said over and over.

"Me mum sent you?" whimpered Jimmy now wiping dripping teardrops from his cheeks.

"No, not your mum, master James. Your father," replied the kind-looking man. "Get your things; we have to walk back to town now. We're leaving tomorrow on the afternoon train."

The other boys now stood around, feeling warm for Jimmy, but a little jealous. Jimmy stood rigid and looked puzzled for a moment and actually considered staying on the farm with his friends. Then, he decided. He was going home to be with his father and, perhaps, even his mother. Home!

Jimmy, now wearing winter boots that Lathrope had tossed to him earlier, hugged Tawny. "Thanks, for being a big brother to me."

Both of them were crying now. Tawny took a deep breath, wiped his eyes on his jacket sleeve, and then made himself stop. "Good-bye, my friend."

"Are you ready?" asked the tall man, and just like that, Jimmy was gone. The boys watched them—one tall and well-dressed, the other short and wearing rubber boots and little more than rags—stroll down the driveway toward the main road and, soon, out of sight forever.

Lathrope was now short two boys for the next year. Tawny knew he would request replacements in the spring. And he knew they would be delivered on the first shipping run, next year, from England.

Chapter 39

The New Arrival

By the way Lathrope grinned, smoked cigars, talked, and even smiled as he sat on the porch or walked around drinking whiskey, the boys knew the harvest was a complete success.

Tawny, Peter, Tom, and little Greg huddled in the barn loft, passing time as Greg got an earful of what winter was like. After ten minutes of this, the little boy was thoroughly frightened. Soon, the cold air, ice, snow, and freezing rain would take more bites out of the boys.

Lizzie was hard at work, attending school, still thinking about Tawny, and trying to get Clara to invite her over again for a sleepover. Winter approached and, soon, they would be cooped up for months.

Billy and his group also huddled in their barn, talking about how life stunk here and how they wished for something to do during the winter months beyond fetching cordwood and shoveling manure.

Mr. Culmer made an appearance to give the boys their rubber boots. It was late October as the boys watched the last tobacco wagon roll off the property, carrying the last load of leaves. The farm now was stripped bare, and the land would again be blasted by Mother Nature's icy fury.

Clara came to the barn one night and asked Billy if the boys wanted to go to the Pumpkin Festival again this year. Billy reared back. "No!"

He wanted to save his other hand from Culmer. Lizzie and Clara had already assumed that Billy wouldn't want to go, so they devised a plan to meet at the special place for that evening, only a week away. Almost every day, it seemed that Lizzie would remind Clara to tell Billy to tell Tawny about the upcoming meeting.

All Billy had to do was execute Gwen's prearranged plan, just like he had been secretly instructed earlier that day. He had to wash up and wait until Mr. Culmer's lamp went out. Finally, Billy was on his way to the side of the main house, where Gwen's bedroom window would be open. As he approached the window on this night, he heard noises. He listened as he walked toward the window.

Billy moved his head slowly up and then peered through the window. Billy quickly sat on the ground under the window and took a deep breath. Could it be Culmer? It looked like him a little. He looked again. Billy sat back down.

He still didn't know who was with Gwen. He heard a muffled grunt and then everything went silent. Billy tried hard to hear something—a voice, anything—but he was rewarded with total silence. Sitting still on the grass beneath Gwen's window, he suddenly realized that this man might just leave through the window! He quickly crawled to the side of the house. From there, around the corner, he waited and watched.

After about thirty minutes of stillness, Billy rose and started back to the barn, keeping one eye on Gwen's open window. She never appeared. Back at the barn, Billy wondered: Mr. Culmer? Mr. Nate? They were the only two men who Billy knew were in the house. Then, he realized that Gwen might have been forced. Was it possible? Or was he making excuses for the woman?

The weekend came, and the boys made their way to the special place immediately after the families left for the festival in Simcoe. Clara and Lizzie arrived, carrying bags of food and drink. It was a cold but extremely clear night; dim stars flickered dimly behind the glare of a nearly full moon.

"How did you manage to stay behind? Tawny asked Clara.

"We told them we didn't feel good and just wanted to read for the night. It worked, and here we are."

Lizzie hugged Tawny a few times. She knew this was probably the last time they would be together until spring. Billy and Clara wondered away, lost in conversation, to sit next to the creek bank. Lizzie heard that Clara was telling Billy about her dad and Mr. Lathrope making a deal about a motorized wagon they would share. She also told him they both got really drunk a couple of nights ago, and Mr. Lathrope had to spend the night.

"Wednesday night?" asked Billy.

"Yes, I think so. Why?"

Billy stammered a little and then said, "I thought I heard them, you know...being loud."

That Billy seemed lost in thought bothered Clara. "What's wrong?"

"Nothing." Billy leaned over and kissed her over and over again. About ten minutes later, Clara and Billy returned to the others and joined the conversation.

Greg was busy being noisy, trying to get involved with the others. Lizzie, however, had had enough; she threw him a bag of peanut brittle. "Eat this and shut up."

"Tawny, come here, will you?" Lizzie stood, grabbed his hand, and then led him down by the creek bed.

"What's wrong?" asked Tawny as he sat down on the grass.

She smiled. "I just want us to be alone. After tonight, we won't see each other for a long time." They gave each other a long kiss. After a while, they hugged and returned to the group.

The rest of the evening was a sobering one; they all knew that winter was cruel, hard, and long and it was coming fast. They would have to wait several months before they could visit this place again. Soon, they all said their good-byes and were off on their separate paths home.

Billy and Thomas returned to their barn and drifted off soon after they wrapped themselves with their blankets. Tawny and the others retreated to their loft and went to sleep as well. It had been another great night, and Tawny was feeling good about Lizzie and the world in general. He often thought about the good things, which were so few in number, and, once in a while, the hardship of living on this farm. Nevertheless, he was glad to have the bright spot named Lizzie in his life.

Late in November, the first snowstorm hit the Culmer farm. It was immediately followed by a fierce storm that coated the world with a thick layer of ice. The boys stayed in the loft until they were needed to shovel dung or go to town for wood. The ride to town was enjoyable, but the icy air wasn't. Christmas came and went. The snow piled up higher and higher, so they had to shovel pathways from the house to the barn, from the barn to the main road, and virtually anywhere Culmer wanted to walk. Billy had not seen Gwen in several months; besides, it was way too cold and there was too much snow to be sneaking out, and for some reason, she no longer brought the food trays.

In early March, two days after another severe ice storm crippled the area, Gwen slipped on an icy patch near the back door. She fell down the stairs, striking her back and head several times on her way to the bottom.

Billy, who was breaking a path through the ice-encrusted snow to the outhouses, saw Gwen fall. He dropped his shovel and ran to her, sliding and trying desperately to keep his balance. Even before he reached her, he began shouting.

"Help! Somebody, help!" Gwen didn't move.

Mrs. Culmer stuck her head out of the back door and shouted for Mr. Culmer to come quick. "Oh, God!"

"She's hurt." Billy picked her up; she was limp and heavy, much heavier than he remembered, but he attributed it to winter clothes. As he scooped her into his arms, he felt something wet and warm seep through his raggedy coat as he carried her into the house and to her bedroom.

In the background, he thought he heard Mrs. Culmer say, "How do you know this is her room?"

Billy put Gwen down, confused about what was happening. Mr. Culmer entered, tossed Billy aside, and started taking off Gwen's clothing. Gwen was pregnant. Her belly was large and round, and her belly button was stretched to its limit.

"Her water broke," said Mrs. Culmer. "I think the baby is coming."

Mr. Culmer left the room, dragging Billy with him. He motioned for the older kitchen lady to help. She hurried to Gwen's room carrying a water bucket and several white towels. The farmer glared at Billy. "How did you know where Gwen's room was?"

Billy didn't know what to do; he was confused and didn't feel like playing games, so he simply said, "You think I'm the only one who was with her. You're wrong. I've seen someone else in here."

Billy flinched, expecting a punch or a cuff from Culmer. But the blow didn't come. Mr. Culmer walked around the kitchen and then again stood before Billy, his voice unusually calm. "Gwen would never say who did this to her. Did you see who?"

"No, sir. I don't think it was Nate. So, according to my best guess, it's mine, yours, or Lathrope's."

"Lathrope?" Mr. Culmer nodded slowly, turned, and looked out the icy window. "He did spend the night around seven months ago. Got all liquored up talking about his wagon deal."

Suddenly, Culmer seemed confused. "How did you know about Lathrope?"

"Clara had told me one day when we were talking, just talking." Billy now felt like he'd let the cat out of the bag.

At that moment, Mrs. Culmer, with tears in her eyes, came out of Gwen's room carrying a brown burlap bundle.

"She's dead. Gwen's ok, but the baby is dead."

Chapter 40

The Confrontation

Clara ran downstairs after hearing the commotion in the kitchen and was told by her dad, "Go upstairs. This doesn't concern you."

Clara glanced at Billy and then realized that this was a serious matter. She reluctantly went back upstairs.

"Is Gwen all right?" Billy asked Mrs. Culmer.

"She'll be fine." Mrs. Culmer handed the bundle to Mr. Culmer.

Billy ran into Gwen's room where the other older lady was gathering up towels and making Gwen comfortable in her bed. He bent over, kissed her forehead, and then said in a gentle soothing voice, "I'm sorry." Gwen lay still, as if in a deep sleep. Billy returned to the kitchen. Mr. Culmer was leaning on the table, shaking his head. It was the first time in almost two years that Billy noticed that Culmer didn't seem to know what to do.

Billy stood still and remembered the passion-filled nights with Gwen and that this baby could be his. He looked at Mr. Culmer. "We need to do something."

Culmer just stared at the burlap bundle on the table and shook his head.

"I don't care if it's yours or Lathrope's. We have to take care of it."

Culmer turned pale and said quietly, "It's not mine! My God, she's my niece!"

Billy somehow knew by the pain in Culmer's voice, his sadness, that the farmer told the truth. Now, only two possibilities remained.

Culmer picked up the bundle and went outside to the horse barn. He laid the bundle into the box of one of the wagons. Billy followed and watched; Culmer seemed to unravel before the boy. With this incident the farmer showed a side that Billy had never witnessed before.

During the next few days, the weather had grown unseasonably warm, melting the ice at a rapid pace. The baby still lay in the wagon in the horse barn. Billy wrestled with the idea that this baby could have been his, and he had to do something about it. Culmer doesn't care one way or the other, thought Billy.

Tuesday, late in the afternoon, Billy dressed in warm clothes and rubber boots. He would make it right. He made his way through the slush to the horse barn and found himself staring at the small burlap bundle, at the baby who might have been his. But "might" really didn't matter any more. In his mind, it clearly was his daughter. He couldn't stop thinking about the baby girl. He picked her up, cradled her in his arms, and then started walking toward the special place.

Thomas and the others knew about the incident and felt bad for Billy, but decided to stay in the loft and wait for whatever happened. No one saw Billy leave the farm, not even Culmer or Clara, who was now beside herself; her friend Billy was now involved with her cousin.

Billy trekked through the slushy fields. He rested a bit at the special place and then continued until he stood in front of Lathrope's barn. Billy, distraught, screamed, "Tawny, are you in there?"

Tawny and the others were sitting around, just passing time until the evening meal arrived. He answered, "Is that you, Billy?"

"Yes. Can you come down?" Tawny, climbed down the wooden ladder from the loft and walked to where Billy now stood, at the open main doors of the Lathrope barn.

Billy, holding a burlap bundle in his arms, walked into the barn. Tawny saw his friend's face and the cloth wrappings around his rubber boots, held together by leather straps. "What's wrong?"

Behind Billy, Lathrope entered. He stopped and said, "What's going on here? Who in blazes are you?"

Billy slowly turned to face the farmer, who stood so close he could smell his breath. Billy had a look of pure determination. "We have a problem."

"What are you talking about, boy?" growled Lathrope. Tawny and Billy hadn't backed down; both were now standing, face to face, with the farmer.

Billy didn't really seem to care what happened. He stared coldly into Lathrope's eyes. "This baby is mine, or she's yours. We have to do something about it. She's dead."

Lathrope stepped back two steps, as though frightened by the anger he saw in Billy's eyes. For the first time, the farmer realized that these two boys were now slightly taller and far stronger than he was. For the first time, Lathrope seemed intimidated. For the first time, he noticed that Tawny wore the silver Saint Christopher's medal, and he surely knew something about that medal.

"What are you talking about?" said Lathrope, his voice slightly cracking.

Billy allowed his anger to rise, but he fought back the urge to hit this useless piece of human garbage. "I seen you with Gwen last fall, when you got drunk and slept over at the Culmer's farm."

"Calm down," said Lathrope. The farmer removed his hat only to wipe his forehead from the sweat that now formed.

"What are you doing with that?" asked Lathrope.

"I don't know if it's you or me that's the father," said Billy. "I saw you!"

"Calm down," said Lathrope, going pale. For the first time, thought Tawny, Lathrope was frightened.

The farmer moved from side to side, kind of swaying, and then in a quiet voice said, "Come with me."

They left the barn and went outside where they stood close together and beyond the hearing of the other boys, who had been glued to this confrontation and were gazing over the loft, probably hoping one of the boys would hit Lathrope.

"Tawny," said Lathrope, "get the small wagon ready. You two stay here until it's dark, then go to the train station and get rid of it. Put it in an empty rail car."

Tawny made his way to the horse barn and hitched up a small wagon and horse as the sun set. Billy carried the bundle to the horse barn and put in the back of the wagon. Lathrope entered the barn. After making sure that the wagon was ready to roll, the farmer looked at Billy, and said, "I am sorry about this, but if I ever see you on my farm again, I will kill you."

Billy now felt more rage than he'd ever felt before. "Don't worry, you won't, you useless pile of crap."

Tawny snapped the thick leather reins, and the wagon moved down the main road toward town, sliding from side to side on the slushy ice-covered road. It was hard to keep the wagon steady.

"Go to the train station," said Billy.

"Ok. Whatever you want," answered Tawny.

They approached the town square. It was very quiet in the dark and totally deserted—it felt strange to Tawny. He stopped the wagon in the empty lot behind the stores and tied the horse to one of the poles. The boys walked toward the train station and sat on the platform bench, waiting for a train to arrive. Through a window, Tawny noticed one man inside. He looked busy reading something. It was over two years ago that Tawny, Jimmy, Billy, and all the others stood on this same platform, waiting to be sold to Lathrope and the other farmers.

The memory made Tawny's blood run cold for a moment, until he suppressed those terrible feelings with thoughts of Lizzie and Clara lying behind the grassy hill watching him and the others. He thought about those big brown eyes staring at him when he fell and cut his face over his eye.

The night melted away as they waited on the platform, not talking and completely out of sight from the window. On this night, they wanted no questions of what they were doing.

Then they heard the whistle from an approaching train. They stood and walked away from the station, toward the tracks, still trying to keep out of sight. The train slowly rolled to a stop.

Billy pointed up the tracks. "Up there. Boxcar with an open door." He motioned for Tawny to follow him. Billy climbed inside with his bundle, and Tawny stood at the slightly open door, peering into the darkened interior. Billy didn't reappear.

"Billy, Billy! What are you doing?" asked Tawny.

Billy didn't answer.

"Billy, are you all right?" said Tawny, thinking he was possibly saying a couple of last minute words over the baby. The whistle blew again, and the cars lurched and then moved slowly forward, picking up speed with each second.

"Billy! Billy—get off," Tawny began to run through the slush to stay even with the open door. It became harder and harder to keep up. Still no sign or answer from his friend.

"Billy! Billy! Billy!" Tawny yelled as the train moved faster. Tawny finally had to stop because the train was now moving faster than he could run. At that moment, Billy's head poked through the opening and he waved. With a huge grin, Billy shouted, "See ya, governor," Billy suddenly disappeared leaving Tawny with that last image of his friend engraved in his mind.

Tawny slowly waved, feeling empty and alone, as he watched the train until it was out of sight, carrying Billy and the baby's body to some other place in Canada. Tawny stood with his feet wet from the snow and ice, his heart hurting, almost breaking. After the train had gone, he composed himself, threw his shoulders back, and headed back to the wagon.

He untied the horse and drove toward the farm, still battling his feelings. He should have just jumped on that train with Billy and left this hell on earth, this so-called better place, Canada. He didn't understand why he was taking the wagon back to Lathrope, but he did know that he was no longer afraid of the farmer. This knowledge made him feel stronger and more confident. Tawny thought about everything in his life, especially his lost friends: Colin, Jimmy, Mark, Jack, and now Billy. Then he realized why he hadn't just gone with Billy: Lizzie.

The ride back was slow. As he pulled into the drive, Lathrope waited for him. The farmer helped pull the wagon to the horse barn. "Where's Billy?"

"Gone! He's gone. He didn't get off the train," replied Tawny in an icy voice that could have stopped rain.

"Oh," said Lathrope, who seemed to look at Tawny in a new light. Respect or maybe fear, thought Tawny.

"I'm tired," said Tawny. He left Lathrope to tend to the horse and went back to the barn loft, feeling confident but slightly sad.

"Everything ok?" asked Peter.

"Billy's gone."

Tawny put his head down, wrapped his blanket around him a few times, and then closed his eyes. He thought of how crazy this all was, that they arrived by train and Billy left by train. He felt bad for Billy, but knew his friend would be all right. Besides, he left Tawny's life as fast as he had come into it. Life on the farm would be different from now on, and Tawny knew this. Still, Lizzie occupied his thoughts, which helped him deal with his new life and the hardships of Canada. Soon they would be together, perhaps when the weather let up—maybe even next week.

Chapter 41

The House on Green Street

Lizzie poured herself a cup of tea, sat at her kitchen table, nibbled on an oatmeal cookie, and gazed out the window to see the new spring flowers across the street. Then she thought about how she had come to this little house on Green Street in Waterford. She smelled the aroma of the chicken soup boiling on the wood stove and this usually comforted her because she knew it was Tawny's favorite soup, which contained two onions, carrots, and her family secret—celery tops. She was also grateful to her father and Uncle John for arranging the house deal with the bank. Mr. Jones had died and left unpaid bills; the arrangement that her dad made allowed her and Tawny, along with the baby, to move in. They had lived here for two weeks now.

She thought about her wedding last June and knew she had no choice but to change the marriage certificate back one year from 1915 to 1914, since the baby, Lillian, was also present at the wedding ceremony, in her belly. Besides, her mother had reminded her to think of her daughter's feelings as she grew up. The overpowering need to protect her family gave Lizzie the strength and courage to change the document.

The flowers always made Lizzie think about last Easter, when she and Tawny met at the special place on that warm Sunday afternoon and conceived Lillian Viola Dewberry, now sleeping upstairs. That special day under the big elm tree was beautiful and showed a side of Tawny that Lizzie rarely saw, the compassionate, caring, and gentle one that didn't surface often, probably because of the way he had been treated at the Lathrope farm.

Lizzie took another sip of tea and thought about how lucky she had been to get that job at the Lathrope farm. It had allowed her to be close to Tawny for two years! She also remembered the time Tawny asked her to ring the breakfast bell a little earlier than usual because he was going to be extra hungry and she'd done it—despite the scolding she had received from Lathrope. That monster, she thought. The farmer had nearly destroyed her husband.

She knew that Tawny had changed a lot over the past two years, and that growing up on the farm wasn't easy, especially working for someone as brutal as Lathrope. Tawny had hardened tremendously since the night Billy left.

Lizzie could only imagine what her husband had felt. Billy was the last real friend he'd had from his old world. Not being accepted or feeling loved by a family and not fitting in: She'd spent countless hours handling those feelings. They talked for hours about why he felt that way, or why he didn't feel another way. She knew in her heart that he was a good man and that he was worth the efforts she made.

Lizzie's thoughts drifted again to their wedding in Simcoe. She wondered if Mary was doing all right with her family—Lizzie now had a couple of nephews—and whether Hubrey's new photography business was going well. She was thankful that Mary and Hubrey took that day off and assisted them with the wedding, which was held at the Baptist church. Pastor Newcombe deserved kind thoughts, too, for his patience and kindness during the ceremony, including his instructions for registering the license with the county courthouse.

She remembered the day Uncle Jim had told her that Tawny had been accepted at the Michigan Central Railway Company, one of the most coveted jobs around, and that he could start immediately. She was so proud and happy to see Tawny leave the Lathrope farm two years earlier than scheduled, at sixteen, to take on his new job. Lizzie knew that her mother and father were also grateful for the assistance from Uncle Jim. She knew that it was Will who had awkwardly suggested that Tawny live with Uncle John and Aunt Mabel down the street, no doubt a prearranged event.

Lizzie nibbled at the cookie and washed it down with a sip of tea, which made her recall the day Tawny freed himself from the farm—in the middle of planting season—after telling off Lathrope to his face!

She remembered standing on the front porch, watching as Tawny stood toe to toe with Lathrope. She knew that, to Tawny, it felt great to have the last word just once before he left. Then, he just walked to the town to meet her Uncle John.

Lizzie laughed a little as she wondered why she stayed for another week before she left the farm to take her old job back at Owen's Bakery. She remembered how good her life was a couple of years ago. Tawny was living with her family, working at a great job, and saving money. She was back in town, close to her parents, and not dealing with the farm. She knew it was too late for Tawny to change back to the innocent boy that he was when he first tripped in front of Lizzie at the train station, but she really didn't care. She loved him.

She thought about her brother Fred and knew he was all right working in Hamilton, doing the stonework on several buildings. He turned out to be a fine mason, just like their dad. She didn't see him often now and knew he was involved with a girl, but she would just have to wait to meet her, probably this summer, maybe at a family picnic. Her other two brothers were still at home, helping around the house and attending school, which made her think about Clara.

This saddened her because she hadn't seen Clara for almost two years; Lizzie wondered what she was doing. Tawny had told Lizzie all about the trouble on the Culmer farm, the accident and the baby, the confrontation with Clara's dad, and then how Clara disappeared soon after that, never to be heard from again. Lizzie thought that she might be in Buffalo, possibly with her older sister Martha or the uncle that Martha once visited. This eased her worry and allowed her to accept the fact that she might never see Clara again. She would see Miss Kemp, her old schoolteacher, at the bakery, buying pastries and cakes. That tall man she'd first seen in the school halls, making notes, was now courting Miss Kemp. This made her smile because she always liked Miss Kemp.

Lizzie remembered her wedding again and how both her and Tawny agreed not to call each other by those names; she hated "Lizzie," and he no longer wanted to be called "Tawny." From now on, it was Henry and Elizabeth to family, friends, and would be to their children too. However, trying to get everyone to say Elizabeth was hopeless. She knew it would never happen, but for now, it was tolerable, and actually made for humorous conversation, but the two accepted nicknames only from them.

Lizzie thought about the past year and how close Uncle Jim and Tawny had become. She believed it was a teacher/student relationship. Uncle Jim was pleased with Tawny's performance and dedication to the railroad and knew that he was an asset. This pleased her twice: first to see it and second to hear about it.

Lizzie looked around her kitchen; this house was theirs, and everything in it was also theirs, including the baby upstairs who soon would start crying for her second feeding. Lizzie enjoyed these quiet moments and knew that they were few and eventually would be gone. Both she and Tawny wanted at least four children—two of each would be great—but they would settle for whatever they received and maybe, just maybe, she was pregnant right now.

The baby started crying. Lizzie rose from her kitchen chair, quickly went upstairs, took Lillian from the bed, cradled her in her arms, and then, to Lizzie's amazement, it happened—the crying stopped! This always fascinated Lizzie; how did this little creature know that it was time to stop crying? Maybe because of smell or maybe because of touch, but in any event, the crying usually stopped.

She returned to the living room holding the baby. There, she sat in the straight-backed blue-winged chair, her favorite for breast-feeding. She let Lillian nurse.

Another of God's miracles, thought Lizzie. Feeding time usually took a half-hour, with two burps in between, which, according to Lizzie's mother, was necessary before the feeding could start again and (also according to Lizzie's mother) made the baby sleep better.

During feeding, Lizzie's mind would wonder, and she would start thinking about things that happened years ago, things that happened yesterday, or even things that she just saw or remembered seeing. She thought about the time she and her parents took a buggy ride to Simcoe to shop and when they rode by a white horse standing in the field. Suddenly, her mom clenched a fist and then covered it with the other, open hand and chanted, "Lucky, lucky, white horse, lucky, lucky, lee; lucky, lucky, white horse, bring good luck to me." Why Lizzie remembered these things was beyond her, but she enjoyed the activity of her mind very much because it usually brought joy and fond memories.

Her mind returned to Tawny. She thought about his lunch: Was it enough? Was it what he wanted? Then she tried to stop her thoughts but to no avail; she returned to the transformation that she had witnessed in her husband, going from an innocent young boy to a hard young man, from a free to a controlled spirit. She again thought about the time Tawny faced down Lathrope and gave him a piece of his mind. He didn't back down or show fear. At that moment, Lizzie had realized that this was the man that she wanted to spend the rest of her life with.

Lizzie put the baby on her shoulder and patted her a few times, until Lillian's burp echoed through the living room. Was that the first or the second burp? She really didn't care; the baby would eat as much as she wanted and then, after a change, would fall back to sleep. Lizzie looked down and saw Lillian's eyes flutter a few times and then finally shut tight as her little lips released. Lizzie had a few more minutes before she would take the baby back upstairs to bed.

Lizzie laid Lillian down on the bed, wedged two pillows, one on each side, kissed the baby's forehead, and then returned downstairs to skim the chicken soup, pour herself another cup of tea, and wait for her mother to arrive. Nellie usually made an appearance around this time. Lizzie knew it was to check on her. The daily visit didn't bother Lizzie because her mother looked out for her and the baby. Lizzie tried to learn as much from her mother as she could about child rearing, often asking questions. Nellie enjoyed her new role of grandmother.

Lizzie and her mother sat the kitchen table and talked about many things, but one subject was off-limits—Tawny's life on the farm. Tawny and Lizzie had both agreed not to discuss those painful years with anyone, not even with their family.

Chapter 42

The Reflections

It was a Friday, in the middle of June 1958, a beautiful day with above-normal temperatures, that Henry slowly and painfully walked the half-mile from the railway station in Niagara Falls to his home. As he walked, he thought about his anniversary and how Lizzie enjoyed the flowers that he bought her. He knew that she loved flowers. The pain in his right hip was tolerable but continuous—probably arthritis, the product of his environment—and it caused him discomfort at every step. He realized that his life was almost over and that retirement would be painful, possibly boring, yet what was he to do? He had no hobbies like others he knew, nor did he have plans to start one. Henry knew that his mind of late had been disturbingly very active taking him places for short periods and then wandering his thoughts to somewhere else. Today Henry's mind was more active than normal. The time it took Henry to walk home allowed him look back on his life. He often wondered about all the farm boys, and specifically about Billy. He wondered if he was all right, wherever he went. Henry grinned and knew that Canada was huge. Billy could be anywhere.

He thought about Lathrope. The farmer was probably dead by now. For this, he felt better, but he also remembered that the last two years on the farm, when he was treated like a hired hand rather than like a slave, were far better than the first two. The afternoon sun shone down on him, and by now his ankles had swollen and his shoes were tight and uncomfortable.

He turned onto the walkway of the tall green-and-white trimmed house at 614 Eastwood Crest, walked past the old blue Chevrolet in the driveway, and then painfully climbed the steps to the back door. There, he dropped his lunch box to the floor, hung his summer jacket, and eased into his brown winged chair. For a moment, the discomfort in his hip and knees lessened. He gazed around at his living room, and he started thinking about his life.

He knew, for at least the past ten years maybe eleven that he'd become a miserable man to live with. He felt bad about this. He also believed that he was now too old to change. He thought about the orphanage (which was a blurred memory), the trip to Canada on that boat, and the train, and he knew, regardless of the ultimate outcome, that it remained a highlight in his life. His mind drifted again to farm life, but he quickly suppressed it because it caused him embarrassment and pain. He felt terrible about not telling his children what had happened back then, but he also knew that he and Lizzie agreed to keep secret that part of their lives.

He still wondered to this day how Lizzie had managed to get the job at the Lathrope farm, working in the kitchen for the year and a half, before he'd finally left in the middle of planting season. He occasionally thought about Lizzie's sister, Mary, and her husband Hubrey, and he was so thankful that they stood up for them on their wedding day in Simcoe. At the same time, he felt bad that a few years ago, Mary had left Hubrey and their four children and vanished to Hamilton. There were the two terrible days, when first Will and then Nellie died. Henry liked Lizzie's parents. This made him think of that devastating day when little Cecil died from a rare blood disease. He wondered about Lizzie's best friend, Clara, and how she disappeared the year that baby had died. He was saddened by the loss that Lizzie endured, not knowing what had happened to her best friend. Later, Lizzie had learned that Mr. Culmer had sent Clara to a boarding school to keep her from being involved with the home children. He thought about Lizzie's Uncle Jim and how he had arranged a job on the Michigan Central Railroad. For this, Henry was truly thankful. He appreciated that Uncle John allowed him to live at his house for the first two years while working on the railroad and getting his life together. Henry developed a close bond with Uncle John, enjoying him immensely. He had been grief-stricken the day that John died.

Henry loved his wife. Lizzie provided security and stability to their family, and even though he rarely showed it, he felt bad about not being able to show Lizzie the vast love he had for her. He often wondered if it was his upbringing that prevented him from showing the love that he'd bottled up inside.

He loved his children. They filled his days and nights with both joy and pain. He also enjoyed watching them grow up, even though it was only for a few hours each night. Lizzie always tended to their needs during the day, while Henry worked.

Lizzie entered, shuffling her feet on the wood floor (this was a symptom of the disease that she didn't yet know she had), and asked Henry if he wanted a cup of tea. Henry nodded, twitched in his chair to relieve his hip pain, and then continued remembering all he'd done for his family and whether he was a lucky man or just a plain provider. He was pained by certain events in his early life and wondered if those events caused his children to become the people they were. Lillian, the oldest, married a boy named Clifford and assumed the role of a farmer's wife in Dunnville, Ontario. Dunnville was close to Waterford, where he had met Lizzie. Henry was proud of Lillian, her family, her mildness, and her determination to make things better. He would often think about the others, Lena, Ken, Hank, Millie, Madeline, Lorene, Pauline, and the youngest, Shirley. He also thought of the several grandchildren and again wondered whether he gave all he could give to his family, whether he showed them enough affection. He knew he was weak, very weak, in that area.

He was proud of every one of his children and their families. They were self-supporting, some better than others, but all of them did all right and the clan expanded to a point where he couldn't remember grandchildren's names. His mind would usually shut down when thinking of how fast his family had grown and of the numerous children entering the world carrying his bloodline.

Several questions still haunted Henry and, for the most part, he put them out of his mind. He wondered about his brother, still in England, and it made him furious that he had not known he even had a brother until three weeks earlier. However, he would never know that he actually had three other brothers — Frank, George, and Jim—and even a sister, Emily, who all lived in England, with the youngest brother, Jim, a successful recorded musician.

He felt that his life neared an end and wondered if he was ready to call it quits and leave Lizzie by herself. He hated to think about this; so did what he always did at this point -- he refocused his thoughts.

He felt as though he had cheated the railroad by retiring two years early, but basically, he had no choice. The pain in his joints dictated his decision, and for this he blamed those years of going barefoot on the farm. His mind wandered all over, he thought about how life had transformed his young strong body into an old painful shell. A week into his retirement, he went to the hospital to get crutches. He would use them until he went to the rest home.

He knew that Lizzie wanted the stones in the front yard painted white, and he would stand with the crutches, painting those stones in quiet agony, trying not to fall on the grass, trying to make her happy. His thoughts drifted to the time the family was quarantined because of the scarlet fever that his daughter Madeline got after right after her birth. He laughed about that time, how he had to stay at a friend's house for two weeks until Madeline recovered. Lizzie had accused him of having an affair with his friend's wife. He chuckled again at the confusing two-week period away from his family, but he also knew he'd had no choice.

He thought about the amazing inventions that he'd witnessed over the years: radio, TV, cars, airplanes, and the many timesaving appliances that he purchased. He would never comprehend the impact that computers would have on society in the future. Henry loved it that he could make his own beer in the damp basement that had a five-foot ceiling and remembered how Lorene would help him siphon off the air before it was ready to drink.

He would know about the twin towers called the World Trade Center built in lower Manhattan in the Sixties. However, he would not know about their demise thirty-two years later. He still wondered about the child that he and his friends found in the hollow tree trunk. In his heart, he knew that Lathrope had murdered the boy, but he couldn't prove it. He thought about the silver medallion Lizzie had fixed for him and he was proud to wear it all the time, until one day, when he was working on the railroad, the chain broke, and he lost it.

Lizzie knew her husband was thinking about his life. He did this a lot, and recently, he began doing it more often. Her daughters warned her that retirement might do this. Still, she approached him and said, "Tawny, here's your tea." Tears welled up in his eyes. He had not heard his nickname for several years; it was he who had requested that Lizzie not call him that once they were married. She never had, until today.

Hearing his nickname returned him to those hard farm years and how he was treated so badly, just like a slave. It also made him think of the good times, few in number that always included that special place by the riverbank where he and his friends would often meet.

He wondered what his life would have been like if he had been able to stay in England. But no; Canada had eventually provided a better life, although it had been a hard and painful life during his younger years. No, he thought a little more, Canada was in fact his home, and Henry felt extremely proud to be a Canadian.

Henry would not know that he had thirteen years left, he didn't know that he would die exactly fifty-four days after Lizzie, and he didn't know that he would spend three years in a retirement home, not able to walk or care for himself.

He wouldn't feel the gut-wrenching pain of loosing a child. He would remember, however, the letter that Heddon gave him and knowing that, according to Mel, it was the only letter ever written and given to a child who made that ocean voyage to Canada. He never learned that Headmaster Heddon, who was supposed to be a doctor, was investigated in the late 1900s, and it was discovered that he wasn't a doctor after all, just a rich businessman who capitalized on selling children to Canada and Australia.

He would also remember that Heddon had taught him about integrity, commitment, and honesty, and Henry had tried to live his life based on these principles. For the most part, he knew that he had a good reputation in the work place and that he was respected at home.

Henry remembered the day he went to Toronto to play the euphonium on the Canadian radio station. His family in Waterford listened to the radio in their living room, filled with pride and joy over Henry's talented sounds.

Henry pushed himself up from his chair and then quickly sat back down only to reposition himself for comfort. His thoughts turned again to Lizzie and what she had gone through in the latter part of her life, particularly those shock therapy sessions at St. Catherine's. He hated that the most, and he silently cursed those religious groups for planting seeds of guilt and sin in her mind about church, God, and lying. He knew Lizzie had altered their marriage license because she had been pregnant with Lillian on their wedding day. Henry knew this bothered his wife a lot and was possibly the reason she agreed to the therapy. He also admired Lizzie for caring for the children during the lice outbreaks; she had combed their hair for hours and hours.

He would not know the name of the disease that would take his wife away, and he would not know that his daughter Millie would also succumb to the same terrible bone-loss disease.

He would know that his false teeth were a pain to take care of, the result of a young dentist yanking his teeth out. He also knew that clattering his false teeth in a child's face was the best way to scare off the child and to avoid showing love or compassion. Yes, it worked over and over, as the grandchildren stayed away from him.

Henry enjoyed playing the horn in the town bands in both Chippewa and Waterford. He also remembered fondly that the Canadian Army tracked him down and insisted that he play in the Canadian Army Band when World War I started. He remembered when Lizzie gave him an old horn, his first, on his seventeenth birthday.

He also was glad that Lizzie had, after numerous arguments, put her foot down and insisted that he not take part in the war effort.

He would often and sometimes without reason flashback and think again of Jimmy, Colin, Billy, and the others. Then just as quickly, he would force those thoughts and everything they stood for from his mind, only because he did not like remembering that time in which he and the others were treated like slaves.

He hated the tobacco industry for obvious reasons, but enjoyed the occasional cigarette or cigar. He also thought that he had never worn a mustache in his entire life and laughed a little to himself, thinking he might look really silly. It was little things that made Henry laugh.

He would know that they put a man on the moon but could not understand how they did it, nor could he ever fully understand how television worked.

Lizzie entered the room and slid the ottoman over. "Henry, raise your feet."

He did slowly and painfully. "It's hard, with a bad hip and knee joints."

Henry examined his hand; crooked, wrinkled fingers, now aching with arthritis. He wondered: If he had it all to do over again, would he? He made a fist and realized that his hand was still partially open. Henry knew then that he would never make a tight fist again. He also knew that how he had turned out was not the way he wanted to, and certainly he felt that they way he was, was not the way he was born into this world.

He knew his character was a product of his environment and the life he had to live and especially of the love he didn't receive as a child. The psychologists would have a field day, he thought.

He took another sip of tea. He liked the tea with lemon the most, but regular tea was fine for today. Besides, he liked the way Lizzie prepared it, steeping it for a good while.

The black-and-white picture on the TV had a lot of snow. The newscaster discussed a problem in one of the rural counties in Buffalo, and this made Henry think about Lathrope's farm again. He got angry, which he did every time he thought about that period. Henry forced himself to think about something positive.

He rose from the easy chair. Those first two steps were always the hardest. He walked to the front window. The local newspaper was coming any time, and that meant that dinner wasn't far behind.

He watched the young boy—Henry didn't know his name—come up to the front porch and place the newspaper in the holder mounted on the wall. Henry opened the door slightly, took the newspaper, returned to his chair, and turned on the lamp. The local newspaper provided entertainment, and it took time to read. I have lots of time now.

He then thought that maybe he should wait and read the paper in the morning. On the other hand, Henry knew that this would alter his routine. He didn't know that his routine would change dramatically after the second week of retirement.

Henry had read an article about a little boy who was bitten by a dog, and he knew that it happened only a couple of blocks away. This made Henry sit back and think about his own kids and that using the orphanage as a scare tactic to keep the kids in line was a good thing. Never talking about the humiliating five years of farm life was also a good thing. He remembered being locked in the cure barn and the beatings he and his friends had received, especially the time that Culmer burned Billy's hand for taking the wagon.

He thought about the day he and Lizzie had met. It was a stroke of fate or luck, but he was extremely glad that it turned out the way it did!

Henry enjoyed the Sunday visits from his family, but he also hoped that not all the kids would show up at the same time. He also hoped that they would leave early after dinner and then realized that it was Friday, and in two more days, they would come again. The thought made him feel anxious. Lizzie had fixed a pork roast with mashed potatoes and gravy for dinner. Soon they would be eating what Henry liked the most, the gravy and bread.

After dinner, he took a couple of congratulatory phone calls from his kids, poured a glass of Molson's, sat back down in his chair, and let the memories play all over again until he fell asleep. His nap lasted about thirty minutes, and he woke up to a game show on TV, the one he liked: three blindfolded people, asking questions to guess who a famous person was or what they did. His mind wandered again, and he thought about wrestling and how he liked watching it, but that he would never admit it to anyone.

Tomorrow was Saturday. He had a few chores around the house that Lizzie had reminded him of three or four times during dinner. He determined he did not have to call anybody to help with these tasks. Usually, he called Kenny, the son with the handy skills. Kenny never said no. Henry thought about the strangest thing; he realized that he liked Saturday nights with the "Hockey Night in Canada" program. He watched and each time was amazed at how many people could fit into Maple Leaf Gardens. He didn't like the team owner, Mr. Ballard, but he did like the players. He enjoyed the TV commercials by ESSO, his favorite brand of gasoline. He enjoyed listening to Foster Hewitt's voice, first several years ago on the radio and then later on TV. He really did not understand the finer points to hockey—the plays, the offense, and the defense—but really enjoyed the fights and goals.

He remembered the hockey games that were played in Waterford. Although he'd never seen one in person, he had seen the kids skating on the frozen ponds, and sometimes on the roads if there was enough ice and then only if they were fortunate enough to own a pair of skates.

Again, Henry started thinking about his life and knew it was time to stop! Why couldn't he just stop thinking about this? Why did these thoughts hound him? Was this normal? Then, he closed his eyes and nodded off to sleep in his easy chair, a very tired man who had only one remaining thought: Did I provide a better life for my children than the one I was given? Did I?

He would never know that the answer was obvious to all but him. It was a tragedy that he never learned that he and his childhood friends weren't alone in that horrible slave trade called home children and that he was only one of a hundred thousand who shared the same experience.

The Home Child

Acknowledgments

I want to express thanks to my newly discovered cousin, Nell, in Peterborough, England, for her information about my grandfather's immediate family. I would like to give special thanks to my Aunt Lorene, who provided me with countless stories. I'm so glad that her mind has the clarity of a thirty-year-old, and I hope our journey into the past wasn't too painful. I want to thank my Aunt Shirley, who took time to share her experiences about her parents. To my Mom, Pauline, who actually helped in two ways: She provided facts and she passed on her methods of child rearing, which were surely a carbon copy of her parents' methods. Thanks to Tom Collins of Waterford, Ontario (a distant relative, I discovered, for his knowledge of Henry and his young family. Thanks to the two boys (I can't remember their names; I never did ask them) who were so helpful at the Waterford Historical Building. The staffs of the historical libraries of Simcoe and Niagara Falls deserve thanks for their help and advice. I want to thank my Canadian daughter, Jocelyn, for her interest, advice, and patience in this project. I also want to thank my American daughter, Beth, for both her advice and her short love affair with Jimmy. To my Canadian son, Rich, who offered an ear and listened to my efforts with full support. My American son, Tony, and his family, provided me with the spirit and conviction to finish this project. A special, and heartfelt thanks to my lovely wife, Elaine, who has read this story numerous times and offered her criticism and ideas. For her dedication to my efforts, I truly thank her.

I would like to thank my proofreaders, Eileen and Anita, and the time they took to read the entire story and offer valuable criticism. Neal and Cindy also need a pat on the back for their early involvement steering me correctly. To Don, who craftily managed to take my debut novel and massage it into a beautiful, smooth flowing story. His talents, knowledge, experience, and meticulous concern for details deserve more than I am able to express. Thanks, Don, for your patience, support, and guidance in this surreal journey. You are a true professional.

Richard P. Tanos

I need to thank Cindy Tallman for her talents on the cover and Amy Young for her cover design, bringing The Home Child to completion.

I would like to thank J. K. Rowling and her Harry Potter series for providing me inspiration to take my story to a higher level.

Finally, thanks to David Suzuki and his inspirational story, which aired on the radio about these abused children, which I heard while driving between New Brunswick and Montreal, more years ago than I would like to remember. His story provided me with just enough information that I became inspired to piece together my grandparents' lives and times in this so-called better place -- Canada.

ISBN 141200544-2